Robert Muchamore worked as a private investigator before starting to write a story for his nephew, who couldn't find anything to read. Since then, over twelve million copies of his books have been sold worldwide, and he has won numerous awards for his writing, including the Red House Children's Book Award.

Robert lives in London, supports Arsenal football club and loves modern art and watching people fall down holes.

For more information on Robert and his work, visit **www. muchamore.com**, where you can sign up to receive updates on exclusive competitions, giveaways and news.

BY ROBERT MUCHAMORE

The Rock War series:
Rock War
Boot Camp
Gone Wild
Crash Landing

The CHERUB series:
Start reading with *The Recruit*

The Henderson's Boys series:
Start reading with *The Escape*

ROBERT MUCHAMORE
CRASH
LANDING

*Hodder
Children's
Books*

HODDER CHILDREN'S BOOKS

First published in Great Britain in 2017 by Hodder and Stoughton
This paperback edition published in 2017

1 3 5 7 9 10 8 6 4 2

Text copyright © Robert Muchamore, 2017

The moral right of the author has been asserted.

A CIP catalogue record for this book is available from the British Library.

ISBN 978 1 444 91463 4

Typeset in Goudy by Avon DataSet Ltd, Bidford-on-Avon, Warwickshire

Printed and bound in Great Britain by Clays Ltd, St Ives plc

The paper and board used in this book are made from wood
from responsible sources.

Hodder Children's Books
An imprint of Hachette Children's Group
Part of Hodder and Stoughton
Carmelite House
50 Victoria Embankment
London EC4Y 0DZ

An Hachette UK Company
www.hachette.co.uk

www.hachettechildrens.co.uk

1. The Sheriff

Edinburgh youth court was part of a drab precinct, sandwiched between a boarded-up children's library and Jobcentre Plus. Scottish law bans British media from reporting on the trial of anyone who is under sixteen at the time of their arrest, but international media faced no restrictions and the drizzled pavement was populated by correspondents from more than a dozen countries.

Lulu Chi was a petite, geeky Parisian. Her *Chi Rock* YouTube channel had over four million subscribers. She'd just turned twenty, but regularly popped up on French and US TV as an authority on fashion and rock music, and there were rumours that she'd already penned a deal to host the French version of Rock War.

Lulu's camera was manned by her best friend from high school. She'd arranged the shot with the graffitied library as a backdrop. She'd been recognised by a couple of girls bunking school, who'd posed for selfies, much to the irritation of presenters from more established media.

Lulu's voice was high, and her manner in front of camera was more like a gossipy pal than a regular TV stiff.

'So, I'm here in sunny Edinburgh,' Lulu began, folding her arms and fake shivering to show it was a joke. 'We stayed the night in this hotel that had the cutest soaps! We're not allowed inside the court, but I kinda had to be here to capture some of the excitement.

'A quick recap of the drama – in case you've been deep under the ocean in a nuclear submarine, or you've just come out of a six-month coma – Dylan Wilton! Dylan is the son of Jake Blade, legendary front man of Terraplane. But there's no way we'll see Jake here today, because he's playing Nissan Stadium in Yokohama.

'So, after Dylan's band the Pandas of Doom got voted off *Rock War*, he went on a super-duper major bender and started snorting his rock star daddy's supply of cocaine. But that supply got cut off when his daddy went on tour, so Dylan started buying on the street here in Edinburgh. He was caught snorting coke and expelled from the posh Yellowcote school. Daddy booked Dylan into drug rehab, but instead Dylan stole a bunch of stuff from his home and ran away.

'He spent a couple of weeks living in a squat with some drug dealer here in Edinburgh. Sort of like that old movie, *Trainspotting*! Then another dealer realised Dylan had money and tried to rip him off. But somehow the robbery went so-so wrong, and Dylan ended up stabbing the bad guy and stealing his gigantic stash of cocaine!

'Now comes the fluffy-hearts romantic part! Dylan skipped Edinburgh and arrives at the house of another *Rock War* contestant, Summer Smith. They spent a couple of weeks together, and recorded two super-awesome demos, which I totally recommend you watch on Summer's YouTube. But just when it seems like things are gonna get hot and jiggly between Dylan and Summer, the cops catch up with him. Smash the door down in the middle of the night and bust his ass for aggravated assault!'

Lulu took an LG smartphone out of her bomber jacket and looked at the screen. 'This is what Summer tweeted this morning. *Gotta go to school today, but all my thoughts with @DylanWilton. Hope the sheriff cuts you a break!*

Lulu held up the chunky black smartwatch on her tiny wrist.

'So now it's just before eleven. Dylan pleaded guilty to all charges and hopefully he'll be arriving here any second. Also, while I remember, you've gotta stay tuned to the end of today's video because I'll be doing amazing giveaways of a whole bunch of Aqueous T-shirts and signed DVDs of that amazing Live in New York gig!'

*

Sixteen-year-old Dylan Wilton rode in the back of a BMW. Top of the line 7 Series, trimmed with open sky roof, vented seats and seat back TVs. His ink-blue suit had been tailored for a swanky party during *Rock War*, but cocaine and stress had cost him a dozen kilos and it dropped off his shoulders.

There was a lot in his head. The car belonged to the best

lawyer in town, but neither of his parents had bothered to turn up. His mind flashed memories. Summer sitting in class. The hot blood when he'd plunged a butcher's knife into a skinny drug dealer, and the gruesome photo of the hundred-and-thirteen-stitch wound on page sixteen of his sentencing review.

Everything came back to the first snort of cocaine, ten months earlier. It was the dumbest thing Dylan had ever done, but he'd have given anything to snort a line right now and snuff out the shame and dread.

He checked his phone out of habit, and a song came into his head. The same song every time he went to court: Bob Marley's 'I Shot the Sheriff'. He wasn't expecting any messages, but he found Summer on Messenger. He typed, *I love you*, but didn't tap send.

'Looks like a fair few press,' Jen the lawyer warned, from her tan leather seat. 'No good speaking to them.'

He thought they were still a few minutes from the court and was startled as they stopped on double yellows in front of concrete steps. A homeless woman stood by a supermarket trolley filled with all her gear, baffled by the cameras and the TV folk with good teeth and coiffured hair. Dylan took a look at the unsent *I love you* as his phone went into power saving, then hated everything as Jen's legal clerk opened his door from outside.

It was about half the number who'd turned up at his first court appearance, seven weeks earlier. Cameras popped. Teen lads in school uniform made wanking gestures and one shouted, 'Going down ya druggie.'

A microphone wearing a *Metal TV* logo brushed the side of Dylan's head as his lawyer walked round to grab a box of documents from the trunk.

'Are you expecting a custodial sentence today?' someone asked.

'Have you stopped taking cocaine?'

'Did you speak to Summer?'

'Is it true that neither of your parents will be attending the hearing?'

Dylan noticed one of his shoes was untied as he edged through the reporters.

'My client has no comment and there will be no statement after sentencing,' Jen said firmly, as she handed her clerk the box of files, pressed the plipper to lock her car and nudged Dylan towards the youth court's revolving door.

At the top of the steps Lulu Chi stepped in front of Dylan, arms spread wide. He'd never watched any of her vlogs, but his ex, Eve, had been obsessed with Lulu's posts, and he knew she'd praised the demo track that he'd recorded with Summer.

'Are you scared?' Lulu asked gently.

Dylan wondered why this weird-looking French chick had flown all the way to Edinburgh. Maybe she was just seeking publicity at his expense, but something about her question touched him and he ignored his lawyer's guiding hand and took the hug she was offering.

'I'm really scared,' Dylan mouthed, as his body shuddered.

Lulu had to go up on her toes to make the hug work. Her

camera operator was right in his face and all the other cameras swung around to capture the tiny blogger hugging the frightened teen in his too-big suit.

'Come on,' Jen said impatiently, as Dylan broke loose.

'Summer loves you!' Lulu shouted. 'You'll be OK.'

Dylan smudged out a tear as he pushed the revolving door. There was threadbare carpet, metal detectors and a dozen warning notices: *Mobile phones must be switched off*, *No Photography*, *No Eating*, *Physical or verbal abuse of court staff WILL result in prosecution*.

He knew the routine, putting phone, keys and coins in a tray before going through the metal detector. His belt buckle set off the detector, so he got a pat down as well.

Sheriff Johnson's room was on the third floor. Dylan and Jen shared the elevator with a burly tattooed dad, and a muscled skinhead son who looked like the scary cell mate Dylan imagined in nightmares.

The youth court seemed to get hotter the higher you went and the hallway outside Sheriff Johnson's room combined the heat with air freshener that failed to snuff aromas from badly plumbed toilets at the far end. They were due in at eleven, but Sheriff Johnson kept Dylan in suspense until twenty past.

She was a small woman, dressed in a pleated black skirt and cream cardigan. There was none of the high ceilings and wood panelling Dylan had seen in every TV courtroom ever, just a regular office with pictures of cats on the desk and two rows of four plastic chairs. He brought up a little bit of sick as he sat in the chair nearest the desk. The only other people in the room were a uniformed court officer and a legal clerk representing the prosecution in Dylan's case.

Dylan felt like he'd been shot as the sheriff tapped her papers on his desk. It had been seven weeks since he'd pleaded guilty and now it was a matter of minutes before he knew if he was going into custody.

'Now then, young man,' the sheriff began, as she put on the reading glasses hung around her neck. 'Are you still taking drugs?'

'No, ma'am,' Dylan said firmly.

The sheriff cracked a slight smile. 'Glad to hear it. This is quite an unusual case. It's a first offence and I note that you have an unusual, but relatively stable, family background. I see your father has offered to pay to send you to a drug rehabilitation facility if you are not put into custody.'

'If I may,' Jen the solicitor interrupted, as she pulled a document out of a file. 'My client has already been seeing an addiction counsellor, and I have this up-to-date record of urine tests to show that he's no longer using any kind of intoxicants.'

The sheriff held up a hand and firmly refused the sheet of paper. 'I'm not taking additional submissions. The sentencing decision will be made based on your previous submissions and the pre-sentencing report prepared by social services.'

'Of course,' Jen said, nodding politely. She'd known the sheriff would refuse the document, but still hoped that mentioning it might hold sway.

'But while there are many positive aspects,' the sheriff

resumed, 'I *must* also take into consideration the seriousness of Mr Wilton's actions. The nature of the stabbing was such that Dylan is lucky not to be sitting in a higher court, facing charges of murder or manslaughter. Although Dylan pleaded guilty to all charges and claims to have acted in self-defence, self-defence doesn't explain why he subsequently stole two kilos of cocaine and tried to sell them on to a dealer in Birmingham.

'Finally, I must take into consideration the fact that Dylan was booked into a rehabilitation programme by his father immediately after his expulsion from Yellowcote boarding school. But Dylan refused this opportunity, and chose to run away. This, along with the fact that he has a girlfriend living in the Midlands, make me question how serious Dylan's commitment to stay in a drug rehabilitation programme would be.'

Dylan glowered at the sheriff. 'You think I'd run away again, after everything that happened? And Summer's the biggest reason why I do want to behave and sort my life out.'

The sheriff stiffened slightly in her seat. 'Have you finished?' she asked firmly, as Jen put a hand on Dylan's shoulder, urging him to calm down.

The sheriff resumed her speech. 'This was not an easy decision, but ultimately I do not feel that this very serious assault, along with serious drug offences, can lead to anything other than a custodial sentence.'

Dylan shuddered and clutched his stomach.

'Therefore, I am sentencing you to eight months of youth

custody, followed by an additional twenty-four-month supervision period.'

'No,' Dylan yelled, as he shot to his feet and kicked the back of the sheriff's desk. 'It's my first offence. The guy I stabbed was a sleazy piece of—'

Before Dylan could finish the burly court official stepped across from the back of the office and put himself between Dylan and the sheriff.

'It won't end well,' he warned, as he put his chest up to Dylan's face.

Sheriff Johnson had stood up and opened a door directly behind her desk. 'Give him a few minutes to talk with his lawyer,' she said irritably. 'Then take him down to the cells for processing.'

2. Final Approach

Lynn and Becky were seventeen, identical twins wheeling overnight bags through arrivals at Los Angeles International Terminal. Becky didn't recognise the guy at first, she just found her eyes drawn to muscles under a grey tank top, beefy legs and tatty black All Stars. He stared down at an iPhone so you could barely make out his face.

'Is that who I think it is?' Lynn whispered, even though he was twenty metres across the noisy concourse.

'Who?'

'Check the tattoo,' Lynn said. 'On his neck.'

'It is!' Becky gasped, as she stopped walking.

'Even finer in the flesh,' Lynn purred. 'Look at the thighs on him.'

'We should ask for a selfie.'

Twelve minutes older, Becky always charged in, while Lynn cringed. Their target noticed the twins' nervous approach and peered over the top of his Ray-Bans.

'Theo?' Becky asked, though his neck tattoo left no room for doubt.

Theo Richardson cracked a slight smile and liked what he saw. 'Two for the price of one,' the eighteen-year-old said, as his subconscious stripped the twins naked.

'We love your show,' Lynn said, stepping into line with her sister.

Becky nodded. 'We watch *Rock War* every week, plus all the online extras.'

'She cried when Analog Stranger got voted off!'

'And your London accent is so cool! Can we get a selfie?'

'Anything for two beauties,' Theo said, as he stood up. 'So what brings you to LA?'

'This is home,' Becky explained. 'We flew to Toronto to check out McGill University. They have a great lit programme.'

'I read a book once,' Theo said, grinning as the twins set up their cameras. 'Each page had a cardboard flap and you had to find a puppy.'

Theo put an arm around each girl. A couple of tweens had also recognised Theo and were pointing him out to their parents. If he wasn't careful, it could become a scene.

'You need a ride or anything?' Theo asked, as one of the cameras in his face flashed.

'Our dad's in traffic on the four-o-five,' Lynn said.

'So I let you have a selfie, does that mean I can get your numbers?'

Becky's tone stiffened. 'I have a boyfriend. So, you know . . .'

'Good to meet you though,' Lynn said, giggling as she tugged her sister's wrist.

'Imagine Dad's reaction if we brought him home,' Becky whispered, as the pair hurried off, tailed by their rattling suitcase wheels.

The younger kids snapped a picture, too shy to come up for a selfie. Theo wondered if he should find somewhere more out of the way, but his phone gave a harmonica blast before his bum hit the plastic seat: *Jay Calling*

'We can't see you,' Theo's fifteen-year-old brother Jay said, slightly anxious. 'I thought you were waiting.'

'You're through customs?' Theo said, standing up and starting a jog towards the crowd at an arrivals door fifty metres away.

'Yeah.'

'With you in twenty seconds, bruv.'

Theo had spent most of his wild teenage years trying to escape a house filled with mum, stepdad and seven siblings. But he'd not seen his family in nine months and choked up when he sighted his mum, looking lost with a trolley stacked with baggage.

'Ma!' Theo said fondly, as he pulled her into a hug. 'You look great.'

'Pilates and not working all hours in that bloody fish and chip shop,' she explained. 'Plus I don't have to worry what you're up to.'

Jay hugged Theo as a couple of people in the crowd snapped pictures of the young host of the fifth highest rated show on American TV.

'Nice tan, Theo,' Jay noted.

Nine-year-old Patsy grabbed Theo around the waist, as he scooped each of his youngest siblings – Hank and June – into a muscular arm.

'Getting so big I won't be able to lift you soon,' Theo said, grinning. 'So where's the rest of the brood?'

'Adam's too loved up to leave the country,' Jay explained. 'Kai has a court date for mugging an OAP and Len's running a ballroom dance at Camden town hall.'

'Can we go to Disneyland now?' seven-year-old June asked, as Theo put her down.

'Why would you want to go there?' Theo teased. 'We're gonna go see my house. And I've got someone I want you to meet.'

'His girlfriend,' eight-year-old Hank said, screwing his face disapprovingly.

Theo was still only eighteen, but way more mature than the yob who'd narrowly escaped jail a year earlier.

Theo found the chauffeur-driven Cadillac Escalade he'd pre-booked and helped load it with the luggage, plus his mum and the girls.

'If you get there before us, the gate code is six-one-eight,' Theo said. 'Boys ride with me.'

Theo got told that *Rock War* was a great show, signed a girl's back and shook a couple of hands as they queued to pay for parking. There was another selfie and a kiss as they crossed a parking lot, warmed by April sun.

Hank practically peed himself when they set eyes on Theo's neon-orange Dodge Challenger.

'Wow! I get to ride in this?' Hank shouted.

'Subtle,' Jay said, envious, but suspecting he'd have gone for something more understated if he'd landed a multi-million-dollar TV deal.

'It's the Hellcat model,' Theo boasted, as they climbed in. 'Six point two litre supercharged, seven hundred and seven horsepower. Top speed, two hundred and four miles per hour. Even you'd get some babes if you had one of these.'

'I do all right,' Jay said defensively, as he let Hank clamber through to the rear seats, then helped his little brother find the right hole for his seat belt buckle.

'Still seeing that Bailey chick?' Theo asked.

'She's great,' Jay said, cracking a smile at the thought.

'Does Summer still hate you?' Theo asked.

'Haven't spoken to her since *Rock War* ended.'

'Get ready to rumble!' Theo said, as his finger hovered over a start button.

Hank whooped as the big V8 clattered to life. It got seriously loud as Theo revved the engine.

'Let's see if we can beat the girls to my house,' Theo said.

'Yeah,' Hank shouted.

Jay was more cautious. 'Try not to kill us,' he suggested, as Theo backed out of the parking spot.

But Theo's driving was another sign of his apparent change. He didn't seem too fussed about speed limits, but his driving was smooth, with no crazy overtakes or jumping red lights. Jay had never been to America and he got a buzz, taking in stuff he'd only ever seen on TV: palm trees, Dunkin Donuts, road signs pointing to San Francisco and Las Vegas, American cop cars and sixteen lanes of traffic.

'So this is my hood,' Theo said, as they rolled off the freeway. 'Santa Monica. You'll see the pier if you look left. Heaps of cool restaurants, bars, clubs. And it's one block from the ocean so the heat's less intense than downtown.'

After a run of stop signs, they arrived at a detached two-storey villa at the end of a short palm-lined driveway. Hank tutted, because the electronic gate was open and the chauffeur was unloading luggage.

'The girls won,' Hank moaned, as Theo cut the engine.

Patsy and June were running towards the car. 'Mum said we have to ask you before we jump in the pool,' Patsy gasped.

'As long as you don't pee in my water,' Theo grinned.

Jay grabbed a couple of bags while Theo tipped the chauffeur. There was a single step up to the house and the girl standing in the doorway was so beautiful she looked like she'd been Photoshopped. It was a nice place. Not huge, but fancy modern furniture, white walls and lots of sunlight.

'I'm Nessa,' the goddess said, as Jay felt acutely aware of how he was grungy from a twelve-hour flight and the luggage was making his skinny arms shudder. 'You must be Jay.'

Jay wasn't sure if he'd seen her somewhere before, or if she just looked like she ought to be famous. 'Were you on Disney Channel, or something?'

'Junior Admiral Becky Lou Beauregard at your service,

sir,' Nessa said, before stamping her bare foot and giving a salute.

'I was totally a fan!' Jay said, as Theo came in. 'Junior Space Corps!'

Outside there was a splash, followed by Patsy shouting. 'Hank jumped in with his socks on!'

'Gasping for a cup of tea,' Jay's mum said, as she wheeled in the last couple of bags. Then a warning to the kids splashing outside, 'Don't make me come out there.'

'So are you in a new show now?' Jay asked Nessa.

'I model full time,' Nessa said. 'I met Theo on a fashion shoot.'

Theo gave Nessa a kiss, then squeezed her bum gently and maxed his London accent. 'Put the bleedin' kettle on then, luv.'

Nessa smiled and Jay tried not to check her out too blatantly as she padded towards the kitchen. 'Theo's been teaching me how to make a proper cup of tea,' Nessa explained. 'I've actually got quite addicted to Yorkshire Gold.'

Theo looked at Jay as their mum stepped out through sliding glass doors to check on the little ones in the pool.

'So, what do you think about my crib?' Theo asked

Jay smiled wryly. 'You earn millions hosting a hit TV show. You've got a wicked house by the beach, your car does two hundred miles per hour and your girlfriend is a model. I officially bloody hate you.'

3. Fresh Meat

The prison transport was bottle green with a corporate logo: *Sentry Security – Protecting Scotland since 1889*. Dylan had to give up belt and shoes as he stood by the back door. Watch, phone, gum and keys dropped into a Ziploc bag. He eyed the prisoner next to him, a ginger dude with huge arms and underpants showing through the ripped back pocket of his cargo shorts.

''Cha looking at?' he grunted.

'Shut your mouth, Cargill,' a uniformed transit officer snapped, before moving in to pat Dylan down.

Cargill went into the van first. The shoulder-width hallway had five micro-cells off either side, like toilet cubicles with stronger locks. Dylan's socks stuck to the grungy floor and the air had the same mix of bodies and disinfectant as the locker rooms at his boarding school.

The cell had a moulded metal bench. There was a little window up near the roof and so little legroom that Dylan had to splay his feet.

'Mind your elbow,' the transit officer said, before shutting the door.

Dylan shuddered as the bolt went on. Every surface was scratched and discoloured from thousands of cleanings, but the light from above showed a dry crust on the wall in front where someone had puked. An urge to cry was disrupted by a palm smashing on the partition behind Dylan's head.

'I need to piss,' a kid in the cubicle behind shouted.

'You just went,' the guard moaned. 'You'll have to hold it.'

'I – need – to – go,' the guy screamed, pounding between every word.

Dylan wanted to tell the dude to stop hitting the wall behind his head, but didn't fancy making an enemy.

'I'll bang *you* if you don't cut that out,' another transit officer warned.

But the wall thumper got his way and by the time he'd returned from his escorted visit to the toilet they were ready to ship out. Dylan had never been car sick, but the stale air and not being able to see out made him queasy.

It was a forty-minute ride out of Edinburgh. Two lads with Newcastle accents who'd been sentenced together yammered random rubbish between cubicles, until a guard told them they were getting on his tits.

Dylan kept thinking about how dumb it was that someone with all his advantages had wound up here. He felt like knocking himself out by head-butting the wall, but he fought the urge by thinking about Summer. The fact that she'd stuck by him seemed like the only good thing in his life.

Six of the eight detainees were taken out at the first stop. A one-minute drive brought them to the second, and Dylan squinted, as he stumbled out, adjusting to daylight. He was behind a scrawny fourteen-year-old, who wore novelty Batman socks and had to use one hand to hold up beltless jeans.

'Last stop, unit B.'

Dylan was pleased to realise that Cargill and the rest of the scary dudes had been dropped off at a separate wing for seventeen- to nineteen-year-olds. But he'd done a lot of anxious Googling in the weeks before sentencing, and read plenty of stuff indicating that units for the youngest offenders are often the worst in terms of fights and bullying.

Dylan glanced around, beyond the car park, at all-weather football pitches, and shabby public housing beyond walls topped with razor wire. The tarmac was wet enough to soak his socked feet as two transit guards escorted the pair of teens to the entrance.

The single-storey building had white plastic glazing, rather than the bars Dylan expected. The sign on the door read *Whitburn Youth Training Centre*. The tiles inside had a high sheen and he skidded as he came to stop at a yellow line. There was a long counter, beyond which was a storage space lined with mesh shelving.

An ancient Grundig radio was tuned to a rock station, and Dylan recognised Led Zeppelin as a prison officer came up to the counter, took charge of the boys' shoes and belongings, before getting the reception officer to accept delivery of the inmates with a signature on a handheld computer.

'Wilton?' a stocky officer asked, as she leaned out of a door to the side labelled *Reception III*. 'This way.'

The room had a slim, wall-mounted desk and a pair of tatty green office chairs. The paint was curling and had purple smears from some half-assed graffiti removal.

'Take a seat,' the officer said warmly. 'I'm Katie.'

Unlike the transit officers, Katie wore jeans and a bright yellow polo shirt that reminded Dylan of his primary school uniform.

'Take a seat, Dylan. Thirsty after the ride?'

He nodded and sat, before being handed a small bottle of water.

'So this is your first time in custody?'

'Sure,' Dylan said, between downing half of the water.

'Frightened?'

'I guess.'

Katie locked her fingers together, and leaned back with one boot off the floor and her bum propped against the desk.

'Your feelings are understandable,' she said brightly. 'I'm not going to pretend that this unit or all of the young men inside it are particularly pleasant. But us staff are here to help make your adjustment easier. I'm going to start by asking you a lot of questions, about yourself and why you're here. First, I'd like you to try and read this.'

Katie handed Dylan a laminated card. Dylan smirked because the paper inside was photocopied from a reading book aimed at little kids.

'The captain stood on the deck in his stripy trousers and told his crew that they faced a dangerous voyage around Pirate's Cove . . .'

'It may seem silly to you, but I'm going to give you some leaflets to read, and over half of the young men here have some form of learning disability.'

Katie gave Dylan a wodge of paperwork, covering the rules, daily schedule, education programmes, visiting and what to do if you have a complaint about a member of staff.

'Now I need you to sign a form, saying that you've received the information and will take the time to read it later.'

Katie reached for a clipboard, but there was a knock at the door before she could hand it to Dylan. A man in medical scrubs asked Katie to step outside.

'Back in a flash,' Katie told Dylan. 'Sorry, pet.'

She left the reception room door open and the radio was loud enough for Dylan to catch most of what a waffling DJ was saying.

'*So they won the first season of* Rock War, *and since then Half Term Haircut have had three number one singles and a chart-topping album. This new single is the first material released from their second long player, and I've only heard it once, but I wouldn't bet against this topping the charts next week . . .*'

*

After more questions, Dylan got a full body search from a male officer, followed by a shower with evil-smelling lice-prevention shampoo and a trip back to the reception area to collect standard issue underwear, a tracksuit that crackled

23

with static, black canvas plimsolls and a set of personal items including deodorant, toothbrush, a small combination lock, a note-pad and a biro.

The final stop was the nurse's office, where Dylan gave blood and urine samples and had to fill in a questionnaire about his mood and whether he'd ever had thoughts about killing himself.

Dylan said no, but Katie took him to a cell opposite the guards' office, in which all inmates stay for their first five nights and where an officer would check every fifteen minutes through the night. After showing Dylan to the cell and warning him to keep everything in the metal locker, Katie asked an inmate called Archie to give Dylan a tour.

Archie was taller than Dylan, but very thin. Flat nose, looming posture and straight hair with a fringe drooped over his eyes. Dylan's suicide-watch cell was in a hallway, but the regular cells were built around an indoor courtyard with benches and ping-pong tables in the middle.

'How'd you get cash for the vending machines?' Dylan asked, as he noticed that the inmates hanging around wore brand name tracksuits and trainers.

'My mum puts credit on my card,' Archie explained. 'But it's best to leave your card with the guards' office and just buy what you need because you'll get ripped off.'

'And you can get your own clothes?'

Archie nodded. 'Visitors can bring trainers, tracksuits, underwear. No bright colours or football shirts. No hi-tops, because you can hide stuff in them.'

They'd crossed the indoor courtyard and Dylan expected them to go on down a short hallway that led to a second identical arrangement of twenty cells around a courtyard.

'Better not to cross into B2,' Archie explained. 'Unless you're going to see a pal when you get there.'

Dylan looked wary. 'Would you get stabbed or something?'

Archie shrugged. 'More likely a slap, or some unwashed prick putting you in a headlock . . . Education is down the other way. The double doors lead out on to the all-weather pitches, which are open until sunset. But I wouldn't venture out there until you've made a few friends.'

'Do you ever go outside?' Dylan asked.

Archie shook his head. 'Not exactly an alpha male, am I? A lot of nasty bastards wind up in here. So I keep to myself and try to stay out of trouble.'

'And how does that work out?'

'Not as much as I'd like,' Archie said, as he pulled up the front of his T-shirt.

The left side of his ribcage was a mass of bruises and there was a deep purple welt shaped like the tread of a training shoe.

Dylan gawped. 'Did the guards find out?'

'Scotland has two units for under-seventeens,' Archie explained. 'Snitches get two weeks in isolation, then they're shipped up to Dingwall. And everyone up there will know you're a snitch and give you shite. And if I'd wound up that far north, there's no way my ma or big sister could come visit.'

'So we're screwed,' Dylan said.

Crash Landing

Archie pointed at a big wall clock and smiled. 'Ten days, sixteen hours and eleven minutes, of sticking where the staff can see me. Then I'm the hell out of here.'

4. Sunset Beloved

Jay's first experience of jet-lag was a restless night, listening to crickets outside one of Theo's spare bedrooms. He felt like he'd only just got to sleep when his mum stole the duvet and told him she'd made eggs. An hour later, Jay, Theo, Hank, Patsy, June and their mum piled into a chauffeur-driven Cadillac Escalade so that they could go see where Theo worked.

'Take us along Sunset,' Theo told the driver.

The driver grumbled about morning traffic, but Sunset Boulevard was famed for giant billboards advertising blockbuster movies and hit TV shows.

'Your buddy DeAngelo Hunt,' Jay pointed out, as they rolled past the poster for the *Babylon 5* movie.

Two blocks along, a giant hoarding covered the entire frontage of a twelve-storey block. *Rock War ANT, 8:30et Fridays.* And a quote from USA Today, '*A smash hit! Reality TV reinvented!*' Theo and co-presenter Q-Bott's grinning faces stretched from just above the Mexican restaurant at street level to the air-conditioning units on the roof.

'Ain't that the most beautiful thing you ever saw?' Theo beamed. 'And I'm on another one two blocks down.'

Jay was squished in the third row of seats, with a sister on either side. He was half asleep until Patsy squealed. Theo's second appearance on the boulevard was a regular billboard. A moody black-and-white shot, advertising for Joe Mac brand undershorts, with Nessa alongside in a Joe Mac sports bra.

'I can see your rude bits bulging!' Patsy protested. 'Gross!'

'Don't scream in my ear,' Jay complained, cupping the side of his head. 'Jesus.'

'How much did they pay you for that?' Hank asked.

'Not sure,' Theo said. 'Couple of hundred grand maybe. Plus a lifetime supply of overpriced briefs . . .'

'You've got at least one sock stuffed down those designer cacks,' Jay said. 'You're not that well-endowed.'

'Never had any complaints,' Theo said, full of himself. 'You wanna get out and have your picture taken in front of my giant crotch?'

'Not in the slightest!' Patsy said.

Their destination was the sprawling American Network Television Studios complex, a couple of blocks off Sunset. Tourists were gathered on the street outside, looking through plate glass at the live broadcast of ANT's *Good Morning with Hattie Omagh*.

After a security barrier, the Escalade rolled between the

tatty exteriors of studio stages, where smokers outside doorways were the only sign of life.

While the first UK season of *Rock War* had toured the country, ANT had decided to host *Rock War USA* at the 4,500-seat McRose Theatre at the heart of their studio complex. Name badges were waiting at reception and Jay was offended that he got handed a goodie bag containing a baseball cap, crayons and a furry toy version of the ANT mascot, the same as his three much younger siblings.

An impossibly wholesome studio employee named Jackie offered to give everyone a tour of the theatre, while Theo got made up, to record some trailers for the *Rock War* episode being aired that weekend.

'You stick with me,' Theo told Jay, dragging him back as he was about to set off with his mum.

Jay glimpsed through a doorway into the theatre, while Theo chatted to his producer. The venue was far grander than the UK version of *Rock War*, with a semicircle of plush green seats stretching back fifty rows, a huge main stage filled with elaborate computer-controlled lighting, and two smaller side stages so that bands didn't have to hurry on or off stage.

'Remember Manchester?' Jay asked, as Theo led him down a thickly carpeted hallway, lined with photos of all the stars who'd recorded their shows here. 'With the electrics fusing and the rain coming through the roof of our dressing room?'

'That's not all I remember,' Theo said, as he swiped a card to unlock his dressing room and flipped the lights inside.

The leather sofas and glass table were freshly cleaned and

there was a thermos of coffee and bakery under cling wrap, but Jay detected marijuana smoke beneath the smell of furniture polish.

'Wouldn't be here but for you,' Theo said, as he squeezed Jay's shoulder. 'Especially that swim you took in the canal at Rock the Lock to save my ass.'

Theo reached behind one of his dressing room sofas and pulled out a black leather guitar case, embossed with the Gibson logo.

'Don't know much about guitars, but our music director watched some videos of you playing, and reckoned you'd like this one.'

Jay opened the guitar case, and gasped as he saw a jet-black Gibson B.B. King special edition.

'Nice,' Jay purred. 'These are like four grand . . . Is this really for me?'

'If you don't like it the shop will switch it for something else.'

'Screw that, it's perfect,' Jay said, as he pulled the black beast out of her case. 'You didn't have to do this.'

'Wouldn't be here but for your scrawny ass,' Theo admitted. 'Forming Jet. Nagging me to rehearse. Covering for me.'

'You seem like a different person out here,' Jay said.

Theo shrugged. 'I'm not thick, you know?' he said. 'I just really hated school. Got bored off my ass and started messing around. And where we come from, if you're thirteen and you've nicked a couple of cars and your dad's in prison, everyone's basically written you off already.

Out here I've got money, a girl, a job. What's my incentive to create havoc?'

'Mum'll smell the weed if she comes in here,' Jay warned.

'Q-Bott and some people were in here after Saturday's show,' Theo explained. 'Never been into drugs. I'm an athlete! Did I tell you I'm training for a charity thing? Celebrity boxing.'

Jay smirked. 'Don't get that pretty face damaged.'

Tears welled as the brothers hugged.

Ten minutes later there was a knock at the door. Jay was on a couch plinking his new guitar, while Theo was in front of a mirror with a make-up artist touching him up for his promo pieces.

Sean Cox was a chunky fellow with curly hair. Touching sixty, he'd spent years working with Terraplane and Harry Napier. He was an executive producer on the American version of *Rock War* and the US head of Jake Blade and Harry Napier's record label, which had recording contracts with all the *Rock War* bands in the USA and UK.

'What I do wrong now, boss?' Theo asked, as Sean ambled in, aiming a thumb at Jay.

'Came to see baby bro, matter of fact,' Sean said. Then to Jay, 'So how's your first taste of Yankeeland?'

'Good,' Jay said. 'But I'm still pretty jet-lagged. It's early evening back in London.'

'Is the rest of your band here?'

Jay shook his head. 'Flew out early with my ma and my siblings so we could catch up with Theo for a few days. Alfie,

Salman, Erin and Babatunde are flying in Thursday for our appearance on *Jennifer Moon*.'

Sean nodded. 'Shame they can't stay longer, but I get that parents don't like taking kids out of school.'

'You can get fined and stuff in the UK,' Jay explained.

'I hear Jet's London gigs have been going down well?'

Jay nodded enthusiastically. 'Jet has a different line-up from the one that played in *Rock War*. We started playing a regular gig at an under-sixteen night last October. We built a following there and we've been playing other local gigs, and even supported a couple of bands at O2 Brixton. We've got over sixteen thousand new fans on Facebook. My stepdad, Big Len, is hoping to get us more London gigs, and maybe some festival bookings during our summer holidays.'

'Sounds good,' Sean nodded. 'I actually met Big Len, back when he ran Lovegroove recording studios.'

Jay nodded. 'Len told me he was at Lovegroove when Terraplane recorded their first album. Reckons he helped come up with the intro for their first big hit, "Grace".'

Sean scoffed. 'If I had a dollar for every session musician who claimed to have written some hit song, I'd be sunning myself by the pool in some Bel Air mansion right now.'

'It can happen,' Jay said, remembering how his *Rock War* rivals Half Term Haircut had used one of his riffs on their first song.

'Anyhow,' Sean said, keen to change the subject, 'I got my assistant to pull up some numbers on how Jet are doing on this side of the pond. The first season of *Tenured* has had great reviews, decent viewing figures, and is tipped for Emmy nominations. Your theme tune for the show has over thirty thousand paid downloads and five million plays on streaming sites like Spotify.'

'Is that enough to call it a hit?' Jay asked.

'It's just outside of the top thirty tracks,' Sean said. 'So it's not a monster hit, but "Strip" getting picked as the theme tune for a major network show has given Jet a toehold in the US marketplace. Hopefully your appearance on Jennifer Moon's show will be another stepping stone and my publicity team are trying to set up some radio interviews. We also need to start working on follow-up tracks in the studio.'

'Sounds good to me,' Theo yelled, from the make-up chair. 'Jay might be as famous as me some day, but he'll never be as beautiful.'

But Jay was less cocky. 'The way Jet sounds now, with keyboards from Alfie and Erin doing vocals instead of Theo . . . it's *very* different to how we sound on "Strip".'

'Been in this business more than thirty years, kid,' Sean told Jay patronisingly. 'If something works, you gotta stick with it.'

Jay straightened his posture and sounded prickly. 'Well, Big Len is Jet's manager, so I guess you'll have to talk strategy with him after we get home.'

5. The Old Firm

Dylan spent two hours on his bed. He skimmed the papers Katie had given him when he arrived but was too anxious take anything in. He made up his bed, took a piss, then sat staring at graffiti scratched into the custard-coloured walls, wary of the occasional outbreaks of noise.

He'd memorised three numbers to put on his telephone contact list. His dad's mobile, his dad's office and Summer's mobile.

'Wha' 'bout your ma?' a strongly accented guard named Nash asked, next time he checked in.

'Not in the picture,' Dylan explained.

'Summer Smith, you were on the telly with her, right?'

'Sure.'

'Girlfriend?'

'Not exactly,' Dylan said, having often wondered what the answer to that question was himself.

'If it's no' family, it has to be approved by the governor's office,' Nash explained. 'Best get in touch with your pa, soon as. Get some clothes and maximum twenty-five pounds credit. Reckon he can afford that, yeah?'

Dylan smiled slightly. 'I reckon so.'

'Terraplane are the bollocks, man,' Nash opined. 'Saw 'em at Ibrox in 1990. So you wanna call your dad?'

The guards' office was across the hall. The phone on the desk was old-skool with a dial. His dad's mobile seemed dead, which was no surprise because he was on the other side of the world. Dylan had more hope of catching his dad's assistant, Mairi, at Wilton Music's Edinburgh office, but he only got an answerphone.

'Can I call Summer?' Dylan begged, checking the clock on the wall. He was sure she'd be home from school and loved the idea of hearing her voice.

'Immediate family only, until you get approval.'

Dylan sighed. 'These clothes suck. And I could buy a Snickers or something.'

'Go join the line to get fed. Archie showed you where to go, didn't he?'

'I'll just stick in my cell.'

'Meals aren't optional,' Nash said, his tone firming up. 'Now scoot.'

'Can I try calling again later?'

'Night staff come on after dinner,' Nash explained. 'You'll have to wait till morning.'

Dylan felt eyeballs watching as he crossed the courtyard. The dining room was above the cells and the queue snaked down a staircase with CCTV cameras top and bottom. The inmate on the next step was heavily built and trailed the smell of his sweat-soaked vest. The guy who joined behind started talking over Dylan's head and when the queue moved he shoved Dylan into the wall and took his place.

'Any problem?' he yelled in Dylan's face.

Both guys could snap Dylan, and he thought about Archie's bruises. 'Got nowhere to be,' Dylan said, trying to be casual but his voice gave away nerves.

The youngest inmates were fourteen, but luckily for Dylan the next pair to join the queue looked about twelve. Once he reached the landing, the kitchen staff had clear sight. Dylan copied the guys in front, grabbing a metal tray and a juice box. There was sausage and mash, fish fingers, fusilli and peas. Dylan spooned a bit of everything, along with orange jelly with cubes of tinned fruit floating in it.

'What have you been told?' a woman in a hairnet barked, as Dylan grabbed a fork and a super-blunt knife like you get inside airports.

'Are you deaf as well?'

'He just arrived, miss,' one of the little guys behind explained.

'Potato *or* pasta,' the woman snapped. 'Sausage *or* fish fingers. Remember that next time.'

'Sorry,' Dylan said weakly, as he looked at a dozen four-seat picnic benches and went for the nearest one.

'Not there,' the little guy warned, as Dylan straddled a bench.

'Can I sit with you?'

'If you give us a fiver,' the little kid said, cracking a cheeky grin.

Rather than follow him, Dylan sat at the next nearest table. He wasn't sure if he'd taken someone's spot, so he tried eating fast. But he was too nervous to eat, so he wound up forcing down two sausages and hurrying off to scrape the rest into recycling.

He hurried back down a different staircase, and when he searched for his cell it took him a few seconds to realise that he'd crossed into the near-identical B2 courtyard that Archie had warned him to avoid. The only people around were two guys playing cards at the far end, so Dylan decided to cut across rather than go back upstairs.

He crossed back to area B1 and had just eyed the hallway where his suicide-watch cell was when a body shot out from between two vending machines. He was a big freckly dude, dressed in black trackies and Nike Air Max.

Before Dylan knew it, the guy was muscling him across the courtyard, six steps and into a cell. Three more guys were in there, though the rules said you weren't allowed guests in your cell.

All Dylan saw were legs and trainers, moving clear as he got driven face first into a bed. The sheet was filthy and he breathed piss and crotch funk as his attacker twisted his left arm behind his back.

'Rangers or Celtic?' the freckled guy shouted. 'Wrong answer and I'll break your arm.'

'Look at him shaking!' someone else shouted.

'Rangers or Celtic?' Dylan's attacker demanded.

With his face buried in the bed, the only things Dylan could see were a grimy sock and a family photo on the wall. It showed Freckles with his mum and three similarly chunky siblings in front of a crummy old Volkswagen. The number of kids made Dylan guess he was Catholic.

'Celtic,' he gasped, and the grip on his arm released.

'Lucky boy,' the yob shouted.

But the luck didn't extend to any kind of relief to the pressure driving his face into the bed springs. Another dude knelt across the bed, flipped open a Zippo lighter and teased Dylan's face with the flame.

'Burn the queer's eyebrow off!' someone shouted, before howling with laughter.

Dylan moaned into the bed as the flame singed a couple of facial hairs. The pain increased as someone stepped on his ankle, then he got rolled on to his back, enabling a proper breath and a sighting of his attackers.

'Move a muscle and we'll kick tha shite out of you,' his original attacker warned, as they all backed up.

They looked like clones. Broad-built, cropped hair, trackies and trainers. The guy who stepped up now was a couple of inches taller than the others, dressed in a Hollister polo.

'We know who you are, Blade,' the guy sneered. 'Thought Yellowcote was supposed to be all tough rugby players. But you don't look much.'

'Wilton,' Dylan said. 'Blade is my dad's stage name.'

'Like I give a shit,' the leader said. He aimed a kick, but Dylan slammed his legs closed so the foot got trapped between thighs before reaching his balls. 'Either way, Daddy's practically a billionaire.'

The leader pulled out his trapped foot, placed a knee on Dylan's legs to stop him balling up and slugged him twice in the gut. Dylan groaned as chewed sausage and stomach acid surged into his throat.

'Name's Stuart,' the leader said, as he backed off, then spat on Dylan's T-shirt. 'Two ways I see your little holiday here panning out, Dyl-bo. The first one involves a lot more of this. Four of us, one of you. Punches and slaps. Burning off your pubes, gob in your food and give our toilet bowls a nice regular tongue cleaning.

'The other way is, I give you a set of bank details and we sort it so you pay five hundred up front, then two hundred a week for us to look out for you.'

'That's chicken shit to you,' Freckles added. 'Millionaire boy.'

'My dad's rich, but I don't have access,' Dylan stuttered.

'Liar,' Stuart said.

'I ran away,' Dylan gasped. 'I got into trouble for stealing drugs. If I could get my hands on my dad's money, I'd never have ended up here.'

Stuart didn't know exactly what Dylan had done, but he could see the logic in what Dylan had said and seemed confused. The fattest of the quartet shoved Dylan into the cell wall and stepped up, wagging a finger with chewed nails.

'In that case, you're well in the shit, boy.'

Stuart cottoned on to this logic. 'Better *find* a way to get your hands on some money, Dyl-bo.'

Rather than discuss further, Stuart grabbed the waistband of Dylan's trackies, tugged him off the bed then kicked him in the back.

'This ain't nothing,' someone warned, as Stuart kicked again.

Dylan wrapped his arms over his head as the rest of Stuart's crew waded in with more kicks. After twenty seconds getting stomped, Dylan got picked off the cell floor. His hands trembled and his bottom lip dripped blood.

'Guards hear one word 'bout this and I'll slit your throat,' Stuart warned. 'And next time you visit, you'd better have something for us.'

6. Disconnected

Summer Smith had never been into acting, but her school tried to get every kid involved in at least one extra-curricular. Her form tutor taught drama, so she'd wound up being badgered into joining the Thursday afternoon drama club.

Summer came out of the drama studio in leggings, hoodie and blue Nike Free trainers, with her maroon school blazer sticking out the top of her backpack. Mobiles were supposed to stay off on school premises, but Summer always left hers on vibrate in case there was an emergency with her nan, and it was almost five, so the school corridors were deserted.

She had three messages. The first was her nan, saying that she was staying with Mira across the street for dinner. The second was from her fellow *Rock War* contestant, Sadie, in Belfast:

Sorry bout Dylan. Here if u want to talk. Noah sends hugs.

The most recent message was a voicemail notification. She hoped to hear Dylan's voice, but it was his solicitor.

'Dylan asked me to call. We were hoping he'd avoid custody as a first offender. But you've probably seen that he got eight months. He'll only do half if he behaves himself. They're taking him to Whitburn Training Centre. He said he'll add you to his contacts list, but you're not immediate family, so don't be surprised if it's a few days before you hear from him. I'll be in court this afternoon, but email, or call me tomorrow if you have any questions.'

Summer had found out when she checked her phone at lunch-time. In theory, Dylan's sentence was confidential, but someone in court had leaked info to the foreign press. All the big American entertainment sites had Dylan's plight on their home pages and it was all over social media.

Son of Terraplane Front Man Jailed . . . Mother says her boy was close to death after being robbed and stabbed by 15yo 'terror'. The headline failed to mention that the boy who'd been stabbed was a twenty-two-year-old drug dealer who'd tried to rip Dylan off.

But although Summer had known for four hours, the solicitor's voice had stirred an intense mental image of Dylan, alone and scared. She'd imagined this outcome, but also the happy version where she bunked drama club and rushed out of school to speak to Dylan, grinning her head off as they finalised plans for a half-term visit.

'Everything OK, Summer?'

Deep in thought, Summer almost bumped into Mrs Stanton. She was a sweet-but-disorganised geography teacher, who'd taught her in years eight and nine.

'More or less,' Summer said.

'Put the phone away,' Mrs Stanton said, but not in an *I'm a teacher and you must obey all rules* way but an *I know it's not doing any harm, but I have to enforce this mind-numbing rubbish from senior management* kind of way.

Summer had chosen not to go through the hassle of changing schools when she'd moved to a bungalow on the edge of Dudley, but it did mean two bus rides or a forty-minute walk each way. There were a bunch of older lads from Dudley Further Education College at the back of her second double-decker. She wound up sharing their bus once or twice a week. They usually just blatantly checked her out and said hello, but today a guy called Ed with a triangular face came forward and plonked down, dressed in work boots and jeans caked in sawdust.

'Looking for a man, now your boy's in the slammer?' he said, as he offered a pack of Airwaves gum.

'Do you know any *men*?' Summer asked acidly.

All of Ed's mates laughed at the burn. Summer was pleased with herself, but also upset because everyone saw Dylan as this spoiled brat who had everything, but missed out on how Dylan was deeply lonely, with no family, apart from a dad who'd play a gig in Japan rather than go to his sentencing and a mum he'd not spoken to in years.

'Us lads are going bowling Friday night,' Ed continued. 'There'll be plenty of lasses around for company.'

Summer glowered out of the window. 'I'm not in the mood.'

Ed was determined. 'Yer too pretty to sit home alone.'

'Listen to Mr Smooth!' one of the lads up back shouted.

Summer kept staring at condensation on the window until Ed tapped her shoulder and sounded irritated.

'You all stuck up, just cos you went on TV.'

'And your album was a bag o' shite,' another lad added, getting the biggest laugh yet.

Summer didn't want to yell, because the college boys would have a ball if she lost her composure. Luckily there was a bearlike man with a bag of plastering gear sat a couple of rows in front. He'd been on the phone, but now he turned round and hissed through missing teeth.

'Why don't you show the young lady some respect and sling your hook?'

'Or what, slaphead?'

The bear swung out over the edge of his seat, raising a ham fist. Ed shot down the aisle like a firework as his mates jeered.

'I'm not afraid of you, old-timer,' Ed blurted.

'I can see that,' the guy said, laughing.

Summer gave the bear a nod of thanks, but knew she'd encounter the lads again.

'My little girl, Maddie, always voted for you on *Rock War*,' the bear said, looking backwards at Summer. 'She was watching your new one on YouTube. Has it been released yet?'

'It's just a demo I recorded last summer,' Summer explained, then tailed off mouthing, 'with Dylan.'

'Would it annoy you if I asked for an autograph? I haven't got a paper or nothing.'

Summer realised it had been months since she'd signed an autograph. She pulled the centre page from her English lit workbook and signed it *Fly High Maddie*, with a little kite flying off the end of the E.

The bear nodded thanks, because he'd taken another call. 'I told that Ricky to leave the key under the mat. Now he's moaning that I've not done the skim . . .'

Summer felt stares from the lads up back. She'd have loved to get off the bus, but it was a twenty-minute service and as you got close to six the buses packed out with people who commuted into Birmingham. Sometimes they were too full to even let passengers on at the stop.

So Summer suffered ten minutes of awkwardness and Ed flipped her off through the back window as the double-decker pulled away from her stop. The dustmen had been, so she wheeled two empty bins up the drive and stepped into the empty bungalow.

Summer was pleased that her nan had found a few pals around the sheltered community where they now lived, but there were times when she missed their old high-rise and the sense that it was just the two of them versus the world.

She tidied the kitchen while the oven heated up, then put a Morrisons lasagne in. The seven messages on the answerphone were all journalists asking for comments about Dylan, but she had to go through them all because her nan's surgery was due to call and confirm a doctor's appointment.

Part of her just wanted to crash, but she was grungy from morning PE and drama club so she showered, snuggled in a super-thick robe and wound up on her bed with lasagne, baked beans and a David Bowie album that Dylan had recommended when she'd called to wish him luck the night before.

Her laundry basket was spewing over, there was maths and tech homework to do and she'd promised Dylan that she'd keep practising her guitar and try to write some songs. But she didn't feel up to any of it because Dylan's plight was dominating her thoughts.

She had no intention of returning the journalists' calls. If *Rock War* had taught Summer anything, it was that journalists will keep you talking for hours, then they'll pluck one or two sentences out of context, which happen to suit whatever agenda they're trying to push.

But while she didn't want to speak to journalists, she wanted to do something about the way Dylan was being portrayed as some knife-wielding, rich-kid maniac. Was there a way she could put out a more sympathetic viewpoint?

Summer yelped as lasagne and peas dropped off her spoon, slid inside the robe and burned her chest. It was an undignified sight, but nobody witnessed as she frantically scrambled off the bed, threw her robe open and wiped hot mince and béchamel sauce on to her sleeve. She managed to laugh at herself, and decided to write a Facebook post about Dylan as she returned to her bed.

She spooned the last peas off her plate and considered going to the kitchen for cheesecake as opening lines rattled around. *Dylan Wilton is a decent person who fell into a trap when he started taking cocaine . . .* Or maybe, *Dylan Wilton may be a rich kid, but that doesn't mean he doesn't have the same problems and vulnerabilities as every other teenager . . . If I thought Dylan Wilton was a bad person, he would not be my friend. But . . .*

Summer succumbed to the slice of toffee honeycomb cheesecake and was back from the fridge when she opened her laptop and considered simply posting *I love Dylan Wilton*. It was bold and it would probably cause a whole bunch of press attention that Summer didn't need, but she loved the romantic notion that Dylan would find out what she'd written when he was trapped alone in his cell.

There was a serious practical issue of how Dylan would see her Facebook, when he was behind bars and had no internet. But before Summer could think this through, she was surprised to find a pop-up on her laptop screen.

This fan page has been suspended at the request of the owner.

The password was auto-saved, but Summer typed it in twice manually and got the same message.

'*I'm* the owner, you stupid machine,' Summer growled.

She tried Facebook's help pages. Then decided that if Facebook was being awkward she could make a video blog instead. But all her videos were gone and YouTube said that her account was deleted. As a last resort, Summer tried logging into her profile on the *Rock War* website, which she'd used to post vlogs while the show was on air.

This contestant is no longer active.

Summer realised that while she had personal social media accounts that she used to chat to close friends, the accounts that were followed by thousands of fans and which she wanted to use to post her pro-Dylan statement had been set up by *Rock War*'s production company, Venus TV.

Summer opened her personal Snapchat and checked to see if any of her *Rock War* friends were online. Noah showed as active, so she tapped him a message.

> SUMMER: Thanks for the hugs earlier! Much needed today! Have u tried using your Rock War login, or Facebook fan page lately?

Noah's reply took a couple of minutes to come through.

> NOAH: Sorry, just getting ready for archery practice. I think Venus TV shut down the accounts for all the series one contestants a few days ago. Except Half Term Haircut, obviously!

Summer gasped, and tapped her phone frantically.

> SUMMER: I posted all my demos with Dylan on YouTube. The only backup copies are on his phone!!!!
>> NOAH: Sucks big time. They deleted all the funny blogs that me and Sadie recorded as well ☹. Didn't even get a chance to back any of them up.
> SUMMER: Scheisse! Not my day today.
>> NOAH: REALLY sorry, but I'm at the archery centre and Dad is threatening to cancel my data plan if I don't stop messaging!

SUMMER: Hit a bullseye for me!!! TTYL.

Summer felt a bit tearful and was tempted to leap off the bed and do a big dramatic wall-punching scene like you see in movies. But she knew she'd just hurt her hand. She probably would have sobbed for a bit if she hadn't heard her nan's key in the door.

'You home, pet?' Eileen yelled, as her powered wheelchair came inside, followed by the familiar thump of the front door.

Summer checked her eyes for signs of crying, before sliding her feet into furry polar bear slippers and putting on a smile for her nan.

'You look ready for bed,' Eileen said cheerfully, as Summer followed her into the living room. 'I had to let Mira win at Scrabble. She shows off terrible if she loses.'

'Cuppa?' Summer asked.

Eileen was about to nod, but she could tell when her granddaughter's mood was off. 'How'd it go down with the boy?'

Dylan and Eileen had got along fine during the two weeks he'd lived in the bungalow. But Eileen had been less than impressed when the cops busted Dylan in the middle of the night, and found a big stash of cocaine he'd hidden under her kitchen sink. She'd not uttered his name since.

'Eight months,' Summer said, sadly.

Eileen's voice was firm. 'Hopefully it'll straighten the boy out before it's too late.'

'I'll make the tea,' Summer said, as tears welled.

'Get here,' Eileen said firmly. 'Give your old nan a hug.'

Summer had to go down on one knee to be level with the wheelchair. Her nan smelled like cake and extra strong mints and stroked Summer's back in a way that made her feel like she was five years old.

'Dylan's a good guy,' Summer said.

Eileen made a slight tutting sound. 'I saw the mess drugs made of your mother. And years of blood tests, till we were sure *you* didn't have HIV.'

'You know I'd never do drugs,' Summer said, as she kissed her nan's cheek before standing up. 'Now this tea won't make itself, will it?'

7. Nutritious Breakfast

Dylan kept having nightmares and waking up to find that they'd all come true. His busted lip bled on his pillow and there didn't seem to be any position he could keep without one of his bruises hurting. The night staff did things by the book, and every fifteen minutes the viewing port in his door clanked and a torch shone through.

He'd told Officer Katie that he wasn't suicidal. It had been the truth, because the one thing Dylan found worse than eight months in this shithole was the thought of never seeing Summer again. But then again, what did he really have to offer her? Summer was hot and she went to school every day, surrounded by guys. Guys who were tall and funny. Guys with muscles, facial hair and charm. Guys who sweated confidence and knew every move in the book.

The viewing slot in the door clanked and torchlight hit the wall. 'Dylan, you alive in there?'

'Yeah.'

'Don't pull the covers up over your head. I have to be able to see you're breathing.'

The cell got unlocked at seven. Nash was back on duty and told Dylan he could go for a shower if he wanted, but Dylan had heard bad stuff about prison showers, so he just took a crap in his cell and washed the dried blood off his chin.

'Hey,' Dylan said, when he came out of the cell and saw Archie heading upstairs. 'Breakfast?'

'No offence,' Archie said, holding up his hands and bolting off as if Dylan was radioactive.

'What's your problem?'

He got no answer, just Archie bounding stairs two at a time until he hit the back of the queue. There were big tubs with cereal, sliced apple, or porridge with golden syrup. Dylan ladled porridge as he sighted Stuart, Freckles and the other two guys who'd stomped him. He tried to sit at an empty bench, but Freckles was waving him over.

Dylan thought about ignoring him, but there were two kitchen staff and a guard in the room, so he figured they couldn't do anything too blatant and that it was better not to piss the bad guys off. He had to squeeze between Stuart and Fat Man on a bench meant for two.

'Food's bland in here,' Stuart said, as he leaned across and spat in Dylan's bowl. 'Get some flavour!'

Freckles glanced around, making sure the guard wasn't looking before dragging Dylan's bowl across and adding more spit. His neighbour chimed in with a string of chewed-up Cheerios and apple.

'I hate seeing food wasted,' Freckles said, as he stirred the bowl and pushed it back in front of Dylan. 'Kiddies starving in the world and all that . . .'

Dylan flashed the idea of grabbing the plastic bowl and throwing it in Stuart's face. But he was squeezed in and probably wouldn't even get the bowl off the table. The delay earned him two fingers in the ribs from the fat guy.

'Get it down,' he warned.

Smiles broke out as Dylan dipped his spoon and raised it to his mouth. There was only a slight taste of apple and Cheerios, but knowing he was eating four guys' spit made swallowing hard.

'You planning to snitch on us?' Stuart growled, close enough for Dylan to feel his breath. 'There's no cameras in cells or classrooms. Stab you six times in ten seconds, make sure there's no fingerprints and ditch the shank at the scene. Wouldn't be the first time that's happened here.'

Dylan shuddered as he swallowed another mouthful.

'Put the call in to rich Daddy yet?'

'He's in Japan,' Dylan said. 'We're not close.'

'I'll give you forty-eight hours to come up with my five hundred,' Stuart said. 'If I don't hear good news by rec' time on Sunday morning, that busted lip will be the least of your problems, got that?'

'Sure,' Dylan said.

He had to lick the bowl clean before Stuart let him up. This time he knew which staircase exited into his part of the cell block and his mind spun the whole way. Archie made it clear that snitching didn't help much. The trouble was, communicating with his dad or his dad's office was tricky. And even if he got through, he had no idea if they'd pay the five hundred, or report what had happened to the prison and make matters worse.

The only person he trusted to listen to what he'd say and actually come through with the money was Summer. She had money from her big recording contract and he could pay her back when he got out. But since she wasn't immediate family, he'd have to wait for the approval before he was allowed to contact her.

'How long till I can call Summer?' Dylan asked Nash, as he leaned into the guards' office.

'Nothing gets reviewed over the weekend,' Nash explained. 'Monday at the earliest, but Tuesday or Wednesday most likely.'

'But my dad's not answering,' Dylan said. 'Can they push it forward, since I've got nobody to talk to?'

Nash shook his head. 'Forty per cent of the kids in here are in state care. A lot of 'em got nobody to call at all.'

Dylan looked at the phone on the desk. 'Can I try my dad again now?'

'I'll give you an emergency ten-pound credit so you can try him on the payphones,' Nash said. 'You've got your learning assessment in the education block at nine. Come back lunchtime and I'll have it ready for you.'

'Cheers, boss,' Dylan said half-heartedly, as he started backing out into the hallway.

'Hang on, get up here,' Nash said, squinting as he studied Dylan's face.

Dylan moved further into the office and Nash crouched.

'What's that?' he asked.

'My chin,' Dylan suggested.

'Your lip,' Nash said irritably. 'Someone punch you in the mouth?'

Dylan considered honesty for a second. 'I'm used to a double bed. I hit the wall in the night.'

'Really?' Nash said, clearly not believing it. 'Nobody hit you?'

'Nah,' Dylan said.

'Would you snitch if someone did hit you?'

Dylan hesitated. 'Would anyone?'

'Situations escalate quickly in here,' Nash warned. 'If you speak to a member of staff, we can often nip things in the bud.'

'I'm good,' Dylan said hesitantly. 'It's the single bed. I'll get used to it.'

'If you say so,' Nash sighed. 'Get outta my sight.'

8. Long Distance

Jay was beating the jet-lag and woke at a decent hour on Saturday morning. He was happier still when he grabbed his phone off the nightstand and saw his girl Bailey online. He flattened out his hair and pulled a clean T-shirt over his head before making a video call.

'How's it been?' Bailey asked.

'Better than school,' Jay teased. 'Thursday we just hung out, saw the studio where Theo works. Went for a nice meal and a stroll on the pier. Yesterday we did Disneyland.'

'Fun?' Bailey asked, as Jay noticed that she'd packed on the make-up.

Jay shrugged. 'Disney rides are pretty tame. But it's school time, so we barely had to queue and Hank and the girls had a blast.'

'There's a vomiting bug going around at school,' Bailey said. 'Four guys in our class are off. And your brother Kai battered some Asian kid in Chicken Shop outside the back gate.'

Jay nodded. 'Kai's an animal, and Ma's been stressed over it. So you look nice. What you up to?'

'Tasha's party,' Bailey said, making it sound like Jay was an idiot. 'We were supposed to go together.'

'Isn't it like four in the afternoon where you are?'

'I'm at Tab's place, trying on outfits.'

Bailey was mostly into cool stuff like comics and rock music, but she went all girly-girl when it came to dressing up for a night out. And if she wanted to go shopping on a Saturday you basically had to write off the whole day.

'Don't have too much fun without me,' Jay said.

'Says the guy in California! So when are you filming your TV thing?'

'This afternoon. The rest of the band arrived last night, but they're in a hotel across town.'

'Back at school, bright and early Tuesday,' Bailey said.

'Don't remind me,' Jay groaned, then with slight urgency, 'Be good to see you, of course.'

Bailey laughed. 'Such sincerity. If you're not careful, I'll put on my leather mini and flirt with Joe Winston at the party tonight.'

'Good luck with that,' Jay said. 'He's gay as.'

'Is he?'

'I'm guessing based on the amount of time he spends preening that hair in the school lavs . . .'

'Jayden, you are so full of it,' Bailey said, but she cracked the smirk that Jay always found cute and made him tingle by saying, 'I'm actually missing the shit out of you. It's boring when you're not around.'

Bailey's mate Tabitha appeared in the background, half undressed and holding a pair of white Uggs. 'Hey Jay!' she shouted, when she saw him on screen. Then to Bailey, 'You can borrow these, but *don't* walk in mud.'

'I'd better go get some breakfast,' Jay said. 'See you Tuesday. Enjoy the party.'

'I'll be thinking about you while I've got Joe Winston's tongue in my mouth,' Bailey said, as she flipped Jay off. 'Enjoy your day, superstar.'

'He's out of your league,' Jay laughed, before blowing Bailey a kiss and ending the call.

*

Summer had nothing on all weekend. She thought about the scene on the bus. Would it have been so terrible if she'd accepted the invite and gone bowling? Actually, those guys were assholes, but she'd turned down other opportunities.

Why did I say no when the girls at drama club asked me to their movie night? Shouldn't I be out having fun, instead of crushing on a boy locked up three hundred miles away?

But even though she'd had a Christmas number one and performed on stage and sung in front of thirty thousand people, Summer was tormented by the idea of turning up at a party in the wrong outfit, or saying something dumb in front of friends, or getting trapped in a corner with nobody to talk to.

It was one of the reasons why Dylan rocking up at the bungalow had felt so important. Apart from her nan, Dylan's stay was the only time she'd ever felt completely comfortable around another person and it was a feeling she craved.

Keeping busy was Summer's strategy to stop fretting about Dylan and her non-existent social life. She woke at half eight on Saturday, cooked bacon, mushroom and potato waffles for brekky, then sat at the dining table and worked through a history essay and a chemistry worksheet, before spending half an hour staring at chapter fifteen in her GCSE maths textbook. She could usually handle maths, but Friday's lesson had gone over her head and she was seriously worried about the B she needed to get automatic acceptance for A levels.

After abandoning maths, she vacuumed the whole bungalow and was about to hunt the fridge and ditch out-of-date food when her mobile rang with an unrecognised number. Part of her wanted to let it go to message, in case it was a journalist, but there was a chance it might be Dylan, so she answered excitedly.

'Is that Summer Smith?' a woman asked.

'Who's calling?' Summer asked stiffly, suspecting a journalist or a sales call.

'This is Mairi at Wilton Music. I'm sorry I didn't respond to your email yesterday.'

'Right,' Summer said, thrown off slightly as she sat at the dining table. 'I wasn't expecting you to call on a Saturday.'

Mairi sighed. 'Eighteen months ago, Wilton Music had a couple of greying metal bands, plus the Terraplane back catalogue. Now we've got Terraplane on a billion-dollar tour, Half Term Haircut, plus you, and all the bands from two seasons of *Rock War*. We've taken on staff, but we're still under strain.'

'Doesn't sound fun,' Summer said. 'I emailed because someone has shut down my Facebook fan page and taken all my YouTube and Instagram offline. And I've spoken to a couple of the other season one contestants and they've all been cut off, except for Jet and Half Term Haircut.'

'I spoke to Sean Cox and a couple of other people at Venus TV,' Mairi explained. 'The decision was taken to refocus *Rock War*'s social media presence upon bands who are still in the current series of the TV show, or who are still generating significant revenue for Wilton Music.'

Summer shuddered at the thought of Sean Cox. He was the guy who'd bullied her into rushing out an album of mediocre pop covers eight weeks after *Rock War* ended. After one-star reviews and two flop singles, the album and plans for a tour got buried as Wilton Music focused on Terraplane and Half Term Haircut.

'I know my album did poorly,' Summer said, through gritted teeth. 'But they took down demos I recorded with Dylan Wilton on my YouTube channel. One had over a hundred thousand views and people were saying nice things about them. And I wanted to log in and write something about Dylan, because he's a cool guy and it's out of order the way he's getting slated by people who've never even met him.'

Mairi gave a warm laugh. 'I'm glad you're a friend to him.'

Summer was surprised. 'You know Dylan?'

'I've been with Wilton Music since the beginning,' Mairi

explained. 'I used to sit building Lego with him while his father was in meetings with Mr Napier.'

Summer smiled at a cute mental image of a small Dylan with Lego bricks. 'Some of the other bands are upset too,' Summer said. 'They still play gigs, or upload new tracks, and they were using the channels to communicate with fans.'

'I'm a bit of a dinosaur when it comes to all this internet-y stuff,' Mairi confessed. 'But even if your album wasn't a big success, you are still a solo artist under contract to Wilton Music. In my book, that means you deserve attention and respect.'

Summer smiled. 'So is there any more you can do to fix it?'

'I'll make a few more calls and try to see if we can get your videos and things back online.'

'I just need the administrator passwords,' Summer explained. 'I'm happy to look after the accounts once they're reactivated.'

'And since you're under contract and nothing is going on with you career-wise, I'll try to set you up with a meeting.'

Summer seemed less sure about this. 'Sean Cox made it pretty clear he's got no intention of recording new tracks, or doing any promotion.'

'But you said your videos were popular,' Mairi said. 'Sean Cox is working out in LA now. His replacement will want to review everyone signed to the label.'

'*Will* review?' Summer asked curiously.

'Harry Napier is headhunting a new label head,' Mairi explained.

'Can't be any worse than Sean Cox,' Summer said unguardedly, then, 'Sorry, I mean . . . No disrespect.'

Mairi laughed. 'Between you and me, I shed very few tears when Mr Napier moved Sean across the Atlantic.'

Summer laughed with relief.

'So here's what I'll do, sweetheart,' Mairi said. 'I'll make some more calls, and try to fix it so you can access your social media wotsits again. And I'll make sure you're on the radar when our new head music honcho starts his job. The only thing is, with Harry Napier on tour with Terraplane, Half Term Haircut selling out arenas and *Rock War* running in seven countries, I'm working seven days a week and nothing is happening very quickly.'

Summer felt like she'd found an ally in Mairi and smiled broadly. 'That sounds great. I really appreciate your help.'

'No worries,' Mairi said. 'And if you speak to your boy, tell him Auntie Mairi sends her love.'

9. Shoot The Moon

Jay hadn't realised how big LA was. Theo was prepping for that night's live episode of *Rock War* and the little kids had persuaded their mum to visit Universal Studios theme park, so Jay was alone for the seventy-minute limo ride out to Orange County.

Jennifer Moon was a phenomenon. Born in Austin, Texas, she'd had a couple of country number ones in the noughties, copped a two hundred million dollar settlement after divorcing a hedge fund manager and now ran the USA's number one-rated chat show out of her own purpose-built studio in the affluent suburb of Irvine. It ran three nights a week on ANT, including the Saturday slot after the *Rock War* results show.

Jay's band mates were piling out of a swanky black bus as his limo rolled in. His cousin Erin, plus school-mates, Alfie, Salman and Babatunde.

'This is crazy shit!' thirteen-year-old Alfie grinned excitedly. 'Laws Angerleeees!'

Jay knew what he meant. Being with these people, halfway across the world, and wearing sunglasses in April seemed kinda crazy. Last off the bus were Alfie's mum, Mrs Jopling, and Jay's aunt Rachel, who was lead singer Erin's mum.

The studio lobby was gloomy, and after stepping out of the sun Jay was half blind as they got their security badges. Sean Cox from Wilton Music was waiting and shook everyone's hand, apart from Rachel and Mrs Jopling who got kissed on the cheek.

They were halfway to the dressing room when Jennifer Moon stepped out for a meet and greet. She wore a cowboy hat and acted like her presence was a big hoop-te-doo, but there was no buzz because *Jennifer Moon* didn't air in the UK, so nobody in Jet had even heard of her until the interview got booked two weeks earlier.

'Nice legs for her age,' Salman commented, as a runner unlocked Guest Dressing Room III.

'Those tits are *never* real,' Babatunde said, loud enough to earn a scowl from Mrs Jopling.

Jay was used to dressing room nibbles, but Moon Studios upped the ante by ordering in from a local restaurant and they got a full lunch before rehearsals. Jay was stuffed with angel hair pasta and tiramisu as he led the band out to rehearse on set.

'Tha hell's that?' Alfie said admiringly, as Jay took out his new Gibson.

'Spending your songwriting royalties, cuz?' Erin asked.

'You probably won't believe this, but Theo bought it for me.'

Alfie and Salman laughed. 'If you got it from Theo it's probably still got the security tag on it.'

'Handling stolen goods,' Babatunde teased. 'Jay'll be writing his next song from Folsom Prison.'

Jay was about to tell his band mates about Theo's newly spawned maturity, but the stage manager and her assistant wanted to get the rehearsal moving.

'Opening with "Strip",' the stage manager said, reading off an iPad. 'When you finish, you walk across to the sofa while Miss Moon tells a few gags. You chat for approximately two minutes, you buzz off when the second commercial comes on, then you're back up at the end to play the show out with "Blast Floor".'

'"Blast Door",' Erin corrected.

'Now I need to hear you play both tracks through, so we can adjust timings and to get the audio balance.'

Erin lacked the vocal power of a natural singer like Summer Smith. But she had a good set of lungs and a deep voice that was a surprise coming out of a relatively slender fifteen-year-old. Where Theo's snarl suited heavy rock with a high tempo, Erin's voice bloomed when she got a chance to sing, so Jay had arranged 'Strip' with a slower pace for his band's new line-up.

The stage manager seemed happy and Jennifer Moon's assistant came out to say that her boss had the rehearsal patched into her dressing room and loved what she'd heard.

'Blast Door' was a new track, that Jay and Babatunde had written, and the producer was all smiles as they headed off stage.

Back in Jet's dressing room, Sean Cox was growling and shaking his hands around his ears. 'What am I hearing?' he shouted. 'I've spent twenty grand flying you all out here to promote a hit song and you go on stage and play something that sounds totally different.'

Alfie was a little guy, but he didn't hold back. 'The TV version was recorded when Theo was in the band. Did you expect Erin to sound like a six-foot-tall bloke?'

'Where *is* Theo?' Sean asked. 'Is there any way we could get him here for the taping?'

'*Rock War*'s on air in an hour,' Jay said.

'And we wouldn't play with him if you did,' Salman added. 'He's *not* in this band anymore.'

Sean looked at Babatunde. 'How's your vocals, big fella?'

Babatunde burst out laughing. 'Erin's our singer. And I haven't rehearsed, so it ain't gonna happen, even if I sang like James Brown.'

Jay's Auntie Rachel, stepped up. 'And how dare you speak about my daughter that way. Hitting her confidence right before a big performance.'

'OK,' Sean said, giving ground as Rachel got up in his face. 'So she sings different. But you changed the tempo too. It's nothing like the version that plays on *Tenured*.'

Jay was totally exasperated. 'Adam and Theo left Jet,' he yelled. 'There's thirty-five videos of us playing online, plus two demos which we sent to Wilton Music. How could you not know that we now sound different?'

Sean didn't like getting backchat from a bunch of teenagers. 'I've been in this business since before you were born,' he roared. 'If you want to make a minor hit into a chart topper, you gotta promote that hit. I pulled a dozen favours to get you exposure on the biggest chat show on American television and this is the shit you pull?'

Mrs Jopling and Rachel stepped between Sean and the five members of Jet.

'I think it's best if you leave,' Mrs Jopling said firmly.

'Fine,' Sean roared, as he opened the exit door. 'Ignore my advice. Play it your way, but do not expect one iota of support from Wilton Music USA from here on in.'

'Follow your advice?' Jay sneered, as Sean headed out. 'The only way you could have blown Summer Smith's career any faster is if you'd shot her in the head.'

*

Jennifer Moon's show was taped in front of a small audience a few hours before broadcast.

'*Tenured* is one of the best TV shows of 2017,' Jennifer told them, as stage lights caught the diamonds round her neck. 'Y'all been humming that theme tune in the shower like I have?'

A few whoops came out of the audience.

'It's a brain worm, for sure,' Jennifer continued. 'But I was properly blown away when I heard that the song was written by a schoolboy from London named Jay Thomas. Maybe tonight's show will be remembered like the Beatles on Ed Sullivan some day! All I know for sure is that these kids are a major talent, and they're named Jet!'

The fight with Sean had set the five band mates on edge, but that all washed out as Jennifer gave them a nod and the audience roared with approval. 'Strip' may have sounded different to the version on the TV show, but Jennifer's intro had put the audience in their palms and they loved the whole three minutes fourteen seconds.

'Great stuff,' Jennifer said, as she beckoned the five members of Jet towards her cowhide couch. 'So how old are y'all?'

They all smiled and spoke their ages.

'And you were on very first season of *Rock War*, over in the UK?'

'Yeah,' Erin said, taking the lead like she'd been told to do. 'But me Alfie and Salman were in a different band, called Brontobyte.'

'And which band won?'

'We both got the boot,' Erin said sadly, as the audience laughed. 'These guys called Half Term Haircut scooped the prize.'

'Indie kids,' Babatunde said. 'Not even proper rock.'

'Now, Jay,' Jennifer said, showing off her expensive dental work as the stage manager gave a signal for Jay to look at camera two. '*Tenured* has been a big hit here in the USA and 'Strip', the song that you wrote, has been a big part of that success. But I understand you had no idea it had been picked for the show.'

'Nobody at my record label bothered to tell me.'

'And how did you find out?'

'I came home from school and there was a letter on my bed,' Jay said, bending the truth slightly to make the story more dramatic. 'I thought I was in trouble at school, so I hid it from my mom and opened it in my room.'

The audience laughed.

'Then I opened up and it was a cheque for over thirty grand.'

Jennifer laughed. 'Jay, you've gone all cockney on me. What's that in US dollars?'

'About forty-five thousand,' Jay said, as the audience whooped.

'Sure beats my pizza delivery job when I was your age,' Jennifer said, getting more laughs. 'And you get paid more every time the show airs?'

'Royalties, sure,' Jay grinned, feeling his face flush red.

'So if the show's a big hit and it goes into syndication, you could be set for life based on a song you wrote when you were how old?'

'Fourteen,' Jay admitted.

'Nice work if you can get it!' Jennifer said. 'What a great story! Now I've been *gripped* watching the American version of *Rock War*, which airs right before my show. Can you guys follow that from the UK?'

Alfie nodded. '*Rock War USA* airs on 6point2, which is a satellite-only channel.'

'*Nobody* watches 6point2,' Erin added, giggling.

'I've watched a couple of episodes,' Babatunde said. 'Mainly just to see how it's different to the version we were on. We got this draughty old pile out in the countryside, and the American version has the contestants rehearsing on the beach in Malibu!'

'So who's your tip to win *Rock War USA*?' Jennifer asked.

'I've only watched a couple of episodes,' Babatunde said. 'But there's a bunch of girl rappers called Boom Dog and they are just *so* talented.'

'Peel are a great band too,' Salman added. 'But the standard is super-high. I'm glad we don't have to square up to those guys every week.'

'Well, thanks for flying out to be on my show,' Jennifer said, as she stood up for a piece to camera. 'That's Jet. We'll be hearing another of their songs to play us out at the end of the show. Their single "Strip" is out now and I think we'll be hearing a lot more from Jay, Alfie, Salman, Babatunde and Erin in the future . . .'

10. 4G

Dylan's suicide watch finished and he carried his stuff across to a regular, single cell late Saturday afternoon, while a bunch of lads bickered over *Final Score* on the courtyard TV. When he came back from dinner there was a massive unflushed shit in his toilet and piss over his new bed.

Nash – the only guard Dylan knew – was off duty and Archie wasn't the only inmate who wouldn't speak to Dylan. Stuart had put out word that Dylan was his mark and that any inmate who spoke to him or helped him in any way would face his wrath. 1B had its own tough guys, but nobody would stand up to Stuart's crew on Dylan's side of the unit.

There'd been two fights out on the all-weather pitches earlier in the day, so lockdown was brought forward to six p.m. Dylan didn't mind, because nobody could get to him once he was locked in. He couldn't sleep on piss, so he started by rinsing his pillowcase, using a bar of soap, then wringing it out over the toilet because his sink was barely big enough to get a hand in.

The cell had no hooks, or anything else you might use to hang yourself, so he draped the pillowcase off the window ledge and weighted it with the SQA English textbook he'd been given by the education department.

The sheet was a much bigger problem and Dylan was just starting to wet the edge when the guy in the next cell thumped on the wall.

'Wilton?'

The walls were thick, but a distorted voice carried through vibrations in the plumbing, so that muffled words seemed to emerge behind the toilet. He was pretty sure it was Stuart's giant friend, who most people called Fat Man.

'Hey,' Dylan said warily.

'Did you like my welcome gift?' the guy asked. 'You're getting some hard beats tomorrow.'

Dylan hadn't given anyone lip to their face, but the wall gave him courage. 'How brave are you?' he shouted as he kicked the wall. 'Four against one.'

'Stuart cracked a guy's skull,' the neighbour teased. 'They only added thirty days to his sentence, and I think he prefers it here to the outside.'

'Screw you,' Dylan shouted, as he grabbed another textbook and hurled it against the wall.

'Quiet down,' a guard shouted, making Dylan jump as the guard whacked a big torch on the outside of his cell door.

The guard shone the torch through the viewing slot and saw Dylan's floor, wet from the dripping sheet and the pillowcase hanging by the window.

'What's going on, lad?'

Dylan froze in the torch beam.

'What happened?'

'I spilt water on my bed.'

The guard laughed. 'You wash off *water* with more water?'

Dylan's mouth opened but no words came out.

'You want some dry sheets?'

'I guess.'

'Right,' the guard said.

The guard went back to the office, unlocked Dylan's cell and put on his light. It didn't take a genius to work out that someone had sprayed piss over the sheets, rather than the damp patch you'd get in the middle if Dylan had wet himself, but the guard just stripped the bed without asking questions and used them as foot rags to dry the floor.

The guy in the neighbouring cell shouted out across the courtyard through his viewing hatch. 'Dylan shat in his bed!'

'Dirty bastard!' someone else shouted.

Dylan was just in his boxers and backed up to the wall, feeling pathetic as the heavily built guard wiped the rubberised mattress down with disinfectant before throwing down a fresh pillow and a set of clean bedding.

'Have you showered since you got here?' the guard asked, as he looked Dylan up and down.

Dylan shrugged. 'No.'

'Why not?'

'Dunno,' Dylan said, rather than admitting that he was

terrified of getting naked in an area where there were no cameras.

'You're in for eight months, you gotta wash, lad. Get your towel. Three minutes and wipe the floor when you're done.'

There were still shouts coming out of the cells.

'Shit's running down his legs!' someone shouted, as Dylan hopped across the courtyard to the showers.

'Next person shouts gets unlocked for a full contraband search,' the guard shouted. 'Now shut the hell up.'

The shower room was small, with black mould growing out of cracks between tiles. There was a changing bench along one wall, four shower heads built into the ceiling so nobody could try to hang themselves and no curtains or partitions for privacy.

Dylan pushed a button to work the soap dispenser and another button for the water running on a timer. The water was properly hot and Dylan tilted his head back and forgot where he was. Closing his eyes and imagining Summer stepping up behind and planting a kiss on his shoulder.

'My dad worked security for Terraplane back in the day,' the guard said, from just outside the shower door. 'Said it was a good set-up. Paid top whack and the boss bought everyone beers at the end of the tour.'

'Cool,' Dylan said, realising that he was having something like a conversation for the first time in two days.

'Fair few bruises there,' the guard noted. 'Stuart and his boys giving you a hard time?'

Dylan shrugged as he pressed the button to keep the water

flowing. You couldn't snitch, but the guards weren't stupid.

'Keep in sight of us guards, try not to rile 'em up. With a bit of luck they'll get bored and find a new target.'

'Sounds like good advice,' Dylan said half-heartedly. He figured he'd had his three minutes and grabbed his towel off the bench.

*

Dylan cried himself to sleep and woke up feeling condemned.

'Day of reckoning, Mr Shit Pants,' Freckles teased, as he walked to breakfast.

Dylan hadn't developed a taste for his enemies' saliva, so he didn't pick up any food and surprised Stuart by stepping up behind him.

'Can I sit here?'

Stuart didn't have his crew around for once and slid quickly across the bench. 'What you got for me, Dyl-bo?'

Dylan sat. There was a proper cooked breakfast on Sundays and Freckles rocked up with bacon, hash browns, scrambled and beans.

'Listen . . .' Dylan began, and got cut off straight away.

'Nothing good ever begins with *listen*,' Stuart noted.

'I arrived Thursday,' Dylan said. 'They didn't vet my callers Friday and the admin office is closed on weekends. When I talk to my girl, I can explain the situation and you'll get your money.'

'You got family,' Freckles stated.

'I told you already,' Dylan said. 'I ran away after rowing with my dad. He's not my biggest fan and he's playing in

Shanghai tonight. I have a number for his office, but I don't know those people and I have no idea what they'll do if I tell them you want money.'

Stuart flicked an eyebrow. 'Sounds like you're shit out of luck.'

Dylan faked confidence and went for an argument he'd rehearsed fifty times in his head. 'If you wanna beat the crap out of someone, there's plenty of guys to choose. But you want a few thousand in the bank when you get outta here, I'm the only show in town.'

Stuart looked across at Freckles, who had cheeks stuffed with hash brown and egg. 'Question is, what do I enjoy more, money in the bank or kicking his ass?'

Freckles swallowed. 'I guess it depends how much money.'

Stuart laughed loud enough to make a guard look his way. 'Five hundred's not much for the son of a zillionaire. How about seven fifty up front, then three hundred every week you're here.'

Dylan moved his head closer. 'I can do that, for a smooth ride. You make sure nobody lays a finger on me and end this shit where I'm ostracised.'

'Ostra what?' Stuart asked.

'Us not letting anyone talk to him,' Freckles explained.

Stuart reared up and glowered at Dylan. 'All your big words. Trying to show you're smarter than me?'

'Where does winding you up get me?' Dylan asked.

'All right,' Stuart said. 'You call her up, you get the money?'

'Exactly.'

Stuart pointed at the breakfast counter. 'Go get fed. But it's gonna come hard if you're messing with me.'

Dylan was too anxious for food, but he put some bacon between two slices of bread and tried his best. At the very least, he figured he'd bought himself a couple of days' peace and then he just had to hope that Summer didn't freak out and go snitching when he called her. He'd have to plan out how to explain the situation without alarming her.

But Dylan had less time than he'd assumed. Half an hour after breakfast, Stuart and his fat neighbour piled in. Fat Man grabbed a towel and held it over Dylan's mouth, as Stuart grabbed Dylan's wrist and set a lighter aflame at the tip of his thumb.

The pain built over ten seconds, before the flame and the towel got taken away.

'We had a deal,' Dylan shouted, sobbing in agony as Stuart put the lighter up to his face.

'Keep your noise down,' Stuart said firmly. 'Let's see if you're more than just talk.'

Dylan was desperate to soothe his burned thumb under the cold tap, but he got tugged off the bed and took a punch to the back of the head as Stuart pushed him out into the courtyard.

'All clear,' Freckles said, as Dylan realised he'd been posted on the door as lookout.

Stuart marched Dylan across the courtyard, past the vending machines and along the short hallway into unit 1B. They took a sharp right into the second cell, where a muscled black dude called Elvin sat on his bed, shirtless.

'Are you shitting me?' Elvin said anxiously, as he jumped up. 'Bring the whole damn posse into my cell so the feds come running!'

Stuart told Freckles and Fat Man to bounce, then shoved Dylan up to the back of the cell, tearing one corner of a poster of Yaya Touré in his Ivory Coast strip.

'Watch it,' Elvin warned.

Dylan's thumb was excruciating as Stuart's evil-smelling breath hit his face.

'What's your bitch's number?' Elvin asked as he reached under the bed.

'What?' Dylan asked.

'Your girl, Summer,' Stuart explained.

'I dial the number so there's no overseas calls or shit burning my credit,' Elvin explained, as Dylan saw the primitive little Nokia he'd taken from under the bed. 'Is that Summer Smith off *Rock War*?'

'Sure,' Dylan said.

Elvin laughed. 'That was some *hilarious* shit when she got run over on live TV. I watched that like fifteen times.'

'Never saw it,' Stuart said. 'Been in here since before it started. Now give Elvin the number.'

Summer wasn't a social animal so Dylan was pretty certain she'd be home on a Sunday morning as he recited the number he'd memorised the night before sentencing. She answered suspiciously after a couple of rings and her voice made his whole body yearn.

'Hello?'

'Summer, it's me,' Dylan gasped, as Elvin held the phone up to his face.

'Good to hear your voice,' Summer gasped. 'How are you doing?'

'It's really not my idea of fun,' Dylan said anxiously, as he clenched his thumb to try stopping the pain. 'I haven't got long and there's something important I need you to do. Have you got a pen and paper handy?'

11. Blue Monday

'Mr Thomas!'

Jay opened one eye and saw ink stains on his white shirt-sleeve. Face planted against a desk top and a whiff of chemicals and sewage coming out of the sink close by. As he bolted upright, there was laughter from classmates and a ringtone peeling from his backpack.

'Shit,' Jay blurted, wiping drool on the back of his wrist as Mr Huddy glowered through specs that made his eyeballs look huge. 'Sorry.'

'Is my lesson less than fascinating to you, Mr Thomas?' Huddy asked. 'Or perhaps you need to adjust your late night habits? Your phone should be off and I do *not* appreciate that sort of language in my class.'

'I was in America with my band,' Jay explained. 'I landed last night and I never slept . . .'

Mr Thomas thumped the desk. 'Give me your phone.'

Jay's head was foggy and he stifled a yawn. 'I just left it on by mistake.'

'You know school policy. You can collect your phone from your head of year at the end of the day.'

Jay had been through this once before. His head of year always made you wait for ages outside her office, then you got a lecture. He wanted to go home and sleep, so getting held back was the last thing he wanted.

'It was a mistake,' Jay insisted as he started burrowing down his backpack to find his phone.

He'd packed in a hurry, so it was even more of a tip than usual. The phone's screen lit up inside the backpack, but it had got stuck between the pages of a textbook. As he pulled out the textbook, a black banana and keys hit the desk. The balled-up gym socks he'd been unable to find the previous Tuesday rolled across the desk top and into the sink.

'Gross,' a girl sitting on the opposite side of the sink said, as she shot backwards.

'Biohazard!' her neighbour added.

Huddy was so pissed off he was starting to shake. 'Cut the drama, ladies,' he yelled.

There was more laughter as Huddy picked up the socks with the end of his pen and lifted them, dripping, from the sink with a look of mock horror.

'It's dropped down the bottom,' Jay explained, as he plunged his arm deeper into the bag.

But Mr Huddy had lost patience. 'You've already wasted enough of everyone's time. Go stand in the hallway. We'll speak after class.'

Jay's phone had stopped ringing, but he finally had it in his grasp. He looked at the dripping socks, crumbs, paper-clips and black banana, wondering if he was more likely to get yelled at for leaving the mess, or for wasting more class time picking it up.

'Move, move,' Huddy urged, clapping Jay out of the room as a couple of classmates jeered.

The hallway was empty and the lights had been dead since rain came through the previous term. Jay slumped against a peeling wall, and in his tired state it took a couple of seconds to register that he was still clutching his phone. He was surprised to see 12:22 on the display. Jay thought he'd dozed for a few minutes, but the lesson was almost over.

Below the clock were two message boxes:

12:19 Missed Call – Summer.
12:21 Voice Message – Dial 333.

Jay hadn't spoken to Summer in the year since he'd cheated on her. Maybe she'd butt-dialled, but then surely there wouldn't be a message? After a sneaky glance into the classroom, where Huddy was writing homework on the whiteboard, Jay turned to the wall and dialled 333.

Summer's voice evoked memories of being on *Rock War*, and in particular the last weeks of boot camp when they'd been an item. But it wasn't her regular voice. The pitch was high and the words tumbled out.

'Jay, listen, sorry . . . I know it's been a really long time.

You're probably in school right now. I'm sorry I hit you and stuff. But, I need a number for Theo. I had one, but I guess it changed when he moved to America. Call me back, it's urgent.'

Summer's burst of emotion blew Jay's tiredness in a way that Monday third period science had failed to. Trouble was, there were eight minutes until lunch break and when the bell went Huddy would confiscate the phone.

Jay had risked listening to a message in the hallway. But a call would last much longer and there was a fair chance a staff member would come by. After a glance to make sure Huddy was still occupied, Jay strode off, looking for somewhere out of sight. Pupils had to go to the office and get a key to use the toilets during lesson time, but he noticed there was nobody inside the old sports hall and the double doors weren't locked.

The school opened a new sports hall when Jay was in year seven. Money was being raised to convert the old one into a dance studio, but for now it was a refuge for burst gym mats and stacking chairs.

After making sure nobody saw him go in, Jay propped himself against the lid of a battered piano before dialling Summer. She took a while to answer, but that was no surprise, since she was probably in school and had to be careful too.

'What's the matter?' Jay asked, half whispering. 'I called straight back. You seemed upset.'

'I'm really sorry,' Summer began, close to tears.

'I'm listening,' Jay said, feeling that it was cool to be speaking to Summer again, even if the situation mystified him.

'You heard what happened to Dylan? Getting eight months.'

'All the *Rock War* people were talking about it online,' Jay said. 'What's that got to do with Theo's number?'

'I can't talk to my nan about this,' Summer explained. 'She's not been a fan of Dylan since he got busted and any kind of stress affects her asthma.'

'Talk to me,' Jay said, trying to soothe Summer, while simultaneously worried that a teacher could walk in and bust him at any moment. 'Everything went wrong between us. But I'm happy to help.'

'Dylan called,' Summer began, before sniffling. 'But from some guy's mobile, not the proper prison number.'

'Mobiles are banned,' Jay said.

'I know, let me finish. First these guys put Dylan on. He was trying to keep it together and said he was OK, but I could tell he was scared. He told me that these guys had offered to protect him. He gave me details for a bank account and asked if I could transfer seven hundred and fifty up front, then three hundred pounds a week after that.'

'Shit,' Jay gasped. 'You don't have that kind of money.'

'It's not the money,' Summer said. 'I've got over twenty grand left out of my advance from Wilton Music, and Dylan said he'll pay me back anyway. But when I tried talking to Dylan properly, this scary guy snatched the phone. He said that if I didn't get the money sorted fast Dylan would get beaten and stabbed. Then he said he had four cousins, and if I breathed one word they'll come find me in Dudley and that *I didn't even want to think about what they'd do to a pretty girl like me.*'

Jay's mouth dropped as Summer started to sob.

'I've got the money in my savings, so I think I should probably pay,' Summer said. 'Though I did some Googling. Most of the info about prisons was American. But they said extortion is really common in prison, and most of the time once it starts the bad guys try and bleed you dry by asking for more and more.'

'Nightmare,' Jay said, feeling so shocked that his hands were clenching.

'So I've been thinking and thinking,' Summer said. 'I remembered that Theo did time in young offenders'. I thought if I could talk to him, he might know the best thing to do.'

'Makes sense, I guess,' Jay said.

'Do you think he'll mind?'

'Of course he won't,' Jay said. 'I have no idea if he'll be able to help, but I'll text you his US mobile number as soon as I hang up.'

'What time is it in LA?' Summer asked.

'Eight behind, but don't stress over that.'

'I can pay the money using my nan's internet banking,' Summer explained. 'But I have to go to the branch to transfer the seven hundred and fifty from my savings account first. The branch closes at four, so I'll have to ditch school to get there in time.'

'So you're paying these bastards?'

Summer sounded frantic. 'I'll try and speak to Theo first, but what else can I do? The guy was so cocky. Dylan sounded so scared, and his parents are worse than useless. At the very least, paying will buy him some time. And they *might* hold up their end of the bargain if they're expecting regular cash.'

Jay's heart was thumping. 'They don't exactly sound like stand-up blokes.'

'What else can I do?' Summer screamed, making Jay wish he'd been more tactful.

'So I'll text the number and you can get Theo's opinion before you go to the bank.'

'You think he'd answer his phone in the middle of the night?'

'Probably,' Jay said. 'I leave mine on charge beside my bed.'

'Me too,' Summer said hopefully. 'And you're not going to spread this around, are you? Dylan's with these shits 24/7 so they could hurt him so easily if word gets out.'

'No way.'

'Do you swear?' Summer said.

Jay found this slightly childish, but Summer was clearly anxious. 'I swear on my little sisters' lives.'

A crash made Jay jump, but he was relieved to see it was just a year seven kid who'd been shoved through the gym doors by his mates.

'I'll text right away,' Jay said. 'And I know you're on your own. So stay in touch. Let me know what's going on, yeah?'

'I will,' Summer agreed. 'You're a good guy, Jay.'

'Oh, but my phone rang in class, so I have to go and hand it in until the end of the day. But I'll have it back after three fifteen.'

'Sorry, I got you into trouble,' Summer said guiltily.

'It's nothing,' Jay said. 'You've got bigger problems. Speak soon, yeah?'

Jay couldn't stop his fingers drumming as he found Theo's number and pasted it into a message for Summer. He was so caught up trying to think through Dylan's situation that he hadn't noticed the bell go for the end of lessons. He was barely aware of the scrum of year sevens messing around in the doorway, until he had to yell at them to get out of his way as he exited.

He headed back to Mr Huddy's room, fighting a tide of uniforms going the other way for lunch. He was worried for Dylan, but it was thoughts of Summer being on her own and of guys tracking her down that made him queasy. There was a good chance it was just scare tactics, but Summer was clearly freaked out.

Huddy was cleaning chemical reactions off his whiteboard and swung around furiously as Jay walked in.

'I told you to wait outside,' he snapped. 'How *dare* you go walkabout.'

Jay would have loved to tell Mr Huddy to kiss his ass, but battles with teachers are hard to win, so he bit his tongue and meekly held out his phone.

'Where did you go?'

'The call was important,' Jay said.

'There are very few things more important than a good education,' Huddy said pompously. 'I'm not just going to hand this phone over. You disobeyed my instructions.

I'll be talking to Mrs Stourbridge and you can expect there to be consequences.'

Given Dylan's situation, detentions and lectures seemed pretty inconsequential as Jay moved stroppily down to where he'd been sitting, grabbed his pack off the floor and started packing his stuff away.

'Whatever,' Jay said, just loud enough for Huddy to hear as he walked out.

Bailey was waiting, cheerfully wagging a finger of rebuke. She didn't know about the Summer/Dylan stuff, so she was just seeing the funny side of her boyfriend falling asleep in class.

'You got in trouble,' she teased.

She was just the right height for her head to nestle under Jay's chin when they hugged. She'd washed her hair in some weird fruit-smelling shampoo and Jay felt calmer as he breathed that in.

'Bad little Rock Star,' Bailey said. 'And we'll be dead last in the lunch queue.'

Jay managed a half smile, but Bailey sensed something was up as they started to walk.

'You're all clammy,' she noted.

Jay trusted Bailey, but he'd sworn not to tell, so he just shrugged. 'Jet-lagged, gotta deal with that bitch Stourbridge after school. Bet she gives me detention . . .'

'Oh well,' Bailey said, smiling. 'Look on the bright side, babes, it's only four and a half days till the weekend.'

12. Tilt

While Terraplane's global tour has attracted a mixed critical response, the demand from fans of the Edinburgh-born rock dinosaurs has proved insatiable.

Tickets for Terraplane's London gigs are selling at up to seven times the original £120 price, while scalpers are offering a pair of VIP tickets for October's shows in New York's Central Park at $6,000.

Now residents living close to Murrayfield Stadium are up in arms over plans to add an extra night when the band plays the Edinburgh rugby stadium next month. Many claim that the unprecedented four-night run would breach a long-term agreement between residents and Scottish Rugby Union.

Wilton Music have also announced that last year's Rock War winners, Half Term Haircut, will be Terraplane's support act during the UK leg of their tour.

Edinburgh Star, 17 April

Crash Landing

Dylan was in a unit for fourteen- to sixteen-year-olds, but the majority of Whitburn Youth Training Centre's inmates were seventeen- to twenty-year-olds, housed in units A and C. The education department had assessed Dylan as someone of high ability, so there were mostly older kids in his Monday afternoon Core Skills class.

The idea of Core Skills was to teach stuff like how to handle job interviews, or fill in forms to open a bank account. There were nine lads in the class, and the tutor had them in three groups of three. They'd watched a video of a young bloke serving customers in a hardware store and now the teams were supposed to work together to *list good and bad elements of his customer interaction.*

The other two guys in Dylan's group were unit C guys in their late teens. They were mates, who ignored him and started talking about cars. After writing a title, followed by *(1) Smart appearance, (2) Made a polite greeting to customer,* Dylan realised he was the only person in the room following the teacher's instructions and zoned out.

Dylan twirled his pen, tipped back his plastic chair and stared at the ceiling. The teacher seemed content to sit on a desk up front, flicking through a power tool catalogue, while Dylan calculated that the red LED on the smoke detector flashed every twelve seconds and found himself anxiously wondering what Summer was up to, and if she was going to pay, and how soon Stuart and his crew would lose patience if he didn't.

He was dragged back to reality by a sharp crack. A quick

save from one of his team-mates stopped Dylan from falling backwards off his chair.

'Thanks,' a startled Dylan said.

'No worries, pal.'

The teacher glanced up, before going back to lust after an eighteen-volt cordless drill. When Dylan looked behind, he saw that the back of his chair had cracked.

'So many guys kick off and throw shit,' the guy who'd saved him explained.

'Chairs here get mashed to shite,' his mate added.

Dylan had got used to being blanked by the population of unit B, but Stuart's authority didn't extend to older boys in units A and C. It felt really good having someone talk to him, and he looked away to hide an involuntary smile.

'Sir, my pencil broke,' a kid in another group shouted, as Dylan realised he was now sitting lop-sided.

He peered under his chair, and saw that besides the back cracking, the tubular metal chair legs had popped out of a clasp that held them to the orange seat. He figured the legs would clip back into the slot if he stood up and sat down hard. But instead, his jolt broke the clasp holding the legs on the other side of the chair. Teacher and classmates turned towards the noise and watched as seat parted company with legs.

Dylan tried grabbing the desk top, but couldn't save himself as he went off backwards. The floor jarred his back, but he was far enough from the rear wall that his hair only tickled it. One leg flailed, while the other got tangled with the metal legs, and the whole room broke into cheers and laughter.

'Bloody hell,' Dylan gasped, as he realised the floor was filthy.

A kid at the next table scraped a grubby Fila trainer on his thigh as he tried to get up, but it was light-hearted rather than nasty.

The teacher was chilled and grabbed another chair as he walked over. 'You hurt?'

'All good,' Dylan said, as he got up on one knee.

'You should sue,' someone across the room said, as the teacher put the chair down and grabbed two halves of the broken one.

'Bit less noise, guys,' the teacher said.

'You dumb shit!' the guy who'd saved Dylan first time around told him happily.

Dylan brushed floor dirt off his crappy prison-issue tracksuit and realised his pen had rolled off the desk as he settled warily into his replacement chair. As he stretched for the pen he noticed something else: a shard of broken plastic from where the broken chair once met the legs. It had a piece of jagged metal sticking out, which Dylan realised was a rivet that had sheared when the legs broke away.

Before anyone else saw, Dylan scooped it quickly and pushed it down into his pocket. As the room settled back into banter, he rubbed his thumb over the rivet inside his pocket and felt its sharpness.

*

Boxers have to run to build stamina. In London Theo hated it: rain, monotony and dog shit. In Santa Monica he found it cleared his head. Setting off as the sun came up, downhill to the sea and along the boulevard to Venice, with an ocean breeze and Motorhead in his ear buds.

Halfway point was a set of chin-up bars and a wave from the cute girl opening the shutters of a beachfront juice bar.

'Great show Saturday,' she yelled.

Theo returned the compliment with a thumbs-up.

If the tide was out, he'd run back through sand, which was slower but great for building stamina. His Under Armour vest was sweated through as he sprinted the last stretch, trailing wet sand as he neared the gates of his house. You can get celebrity addresses off the web and a fan snapped Theo from inside her minivan as he tapped the entry code into his side gate.

He drank water from a bottle he'd left out on the doorstep and was peeling sandy running socks as his music cut out. *Who the hell calls at seven a.m.? Most likely Mum, got the time difference wrong again.*

'Hello?'

'Theo? It's Summer, do you remember me?'

'Remember you kicking Jay's ass!' Theo said brightly. 'What up?'

'You sound . . . I mean, I hope I didn't wake you up.'

'I'm out of breath. Ten K along the seafront.'

'You're liking it out there?' Summer asked.

'Life's good.'

'Jay gave me your new number. I take it you heard about Dylan?'

'Tough break, getting sent down for a first offence.'

'I need some advice.'

Summer explained the situation as Theo headed barefoot into his kitchen, ticked a box on the training chart attached to his fridge, then opened it up and took out a protein shake. He'd downed half and sat dripping sweat on the dining table by the next time she'd finished.

'You clearly love the guy, but I wouldn't pay.'

'Why not?'

'Dylan's got to fight his own battles,' Theo explained. 'It's all about face. He just arrived and everyone will be sizing Dylan up. A crew like the one you're describing probably has more enemies than friends. He's got to suss out who those enemies are and make nice with them. Most guys in young offenders' will be doing short stretches, so the balance of power changes as people come and go. But if they see that Dylan's weak now, he'll never get off the bottom of the pile.'

'I've just been into the bank and transferred my savings into my nan's current account,' Summer explained.

'You paid already?' Theo said, irritated.

'No, no,' Summer said. 'I can't do electronic transfers from my savings account. But I can do it using my nan's internet banking.'

'Hold on to your cash.'

'Won't it buy him time if I buy them off now? If they lay off Dylan for a week or so, maybe he'll make friends like you say.'

Theo snorted. 'I was the bad guy back in the day, part of a little crew. You've got a bunch of guys with no internet, no girls, no video games, two hours a night TV and you can't even pick the channel. We were bored off our heads. When a new freak rocked up scared, messing with his shit was the most fun you could have.'

'So *you'd* have beaten someone like Dylan up?' Summer asked warily.

'I was a fourteen-year-old dickhead,' Theo admitted. 'I'm not proud of a lot of things I've done in my life. I saw one guy we were messing with get taken out of the cell opposite mine after slashing his wrists. Total bloodbath. I felt crappy and I backed off. But I was the youngest on my block and the older guys started calling me a fag and a pussy. So I raided the poor kid's cell and battered him to prove that I wasn't.'

'That's awful,' Summer gasped, close to tears again. 'Isn't this supposed to be a civilised country? What are the staff doing while all this is going on?'

'You take all the worst one per cent of kids and stick them in one place, it's not gonna be nice no matter who the staff are,' Theo said, sensing that Summer hadn't grasped his argument.

'Here's another way to explain it,' Theo began. 'Imagine I'm the bully. There's two guys I can pick on. One kisses my ass, gives me all his chocolate and his best Nike hoodie. He pays me money and offers to do my laundry if me and my boys stop hurting him.

'Now imagine a second guy. He's no tougher than the first one. I can still beat his ass, but he spits at me. Flushes his Bounty bars down the toilet rather than let me get my hands on 'em. Threatens to stab me after I've given him a bloody mouth. Takes the odd swing, tries to make friends with my enemies, maybe even snitches to the guards on the sly. This guy's gonna have it hard to begin, but in the long haul, I'm gonna find an easier target.'

'What about the threat to me?' Summer asked.

'That's all talk. They're not the Mafia. They're a bunch of gobshites, who got sent down for mugging old ladies or joy-riding.'

'But they can't be completely dumb,' Summer said anxiously. 'They had a bank account set up and they've got a cellphone in the prison. And it can't be that hard to find where I live. Journalists find me all the time.'

'I'm just trying to give you my honest opinion,' Theo said.

'I appreciate that,' Summer sighed. 'I just wish there was an easier answer.'

13. After Skool

'Sorry I didn't get your message,' Jay said, holding his phone up to his face, while his free hand blipped his Oyster card on an exit gate at High Barnet Underground station. 'Two girls in my year had a punch-up, so I wound up waiting over half an hour to get my phone.'

'I get what Theo's saying,' Summer said, as Jay went left out of the station lobby for the eight-minute walk home. 'But Theo's a tough guy. I don't think he sees life from the perspective of someone like you or Dylan.'

Jay dodged traffic and crossed a main road. 'I think Theo's probably right,' he said.

'Would you feel the same if you were in Dylan's shoes?' Summer asked.

'Maybe not,' Jay admitted.

'I'm just frustrated. I can't stop thinking about what to do. And I skipped school to go to the bank, so I'll have that to deal with tomorrow as well.'

'Head of year said she wants a meeting with my mum,' Jay said. 'And she was only there this morning dealing with Kai, so she'll be in a right mood when she finds out.'

'It's good to have someone to talk to, anyway,' Summer said, sighing. 'I'd better go start dinner.'

'Anytime,' Jay said. 'I've missed having you around.'

Jay was on tenterhooks as he went in the front door, glancing around, half expecting a maternal onslaught. But all he found was Hank watching *Nexo Knights* in the living room, while Patsy and June were a picture of girlhood, making muffins with their dad in the kitchen.

'Jay, buddy,' Len said cheerily, as he wiped giant floury hands on his *No1 Dad* apron. 'I think you poked the hornets' nest.'

'How so?'

'Sean Cox is seriously unhappy with your performance on *Jennifer Moon*,' Len explained. 'He called me this afternoon. Then I had Harry Napier bending my ear after that.'

With jet-lag, school hassle and Summer calling, Jay had spent the day thinking about everything except his band.

'Sean Cox is a *total* bell-end,' Jay groaned. 'Erin doesn't sound like Theo, how hard is that to grasp?'

'What's a bell-end?' seven-year-old June asked.

Len narrowed his eyes at Jay. 'You gotta talk like that in front of my girls?' he growled. Then he sounded stressed. 'So Harry Napier is in London next week. He wants some big showdown meeting about the future of Jet. He's all for Sean Cox's idea to replace Erin with a male vocalist.'

Jay gawped. 'That's idiotic. What did *you* say?'

'Napier's a bully,' Len explained. 'And he's never liked me.'

'How come?' Jay asked.

'Napier's dad was some big-time Glasgow thug. First time I met Napier was in eighty-seven at my office inside Lovegroove studios. He was dressed up in gold rings and this ridiculous coat with fox fur lapels. He opened a briefcase, paid for Terraplane's studio time with a wodge of twenty-pound notes and told me not to bother with a receipt.

'The producer he'd hired to work with Terraplane on their first album was a novice. My job as studio manager was basically a caretaker role, but I wound up spending a lot of unpaid hours helping them put the album together. The lads in the band seemed to appreciate my help. But when I asked for a co-writer's credit on "Grace", Napier laughed in my face and told me he'd have my fingers cut off if I messed with him.'

'But didn't "Grace" sell like a zillion copies?' Jay asked. 'Even a partial songwriter's credit would have made you a bundle.'

Len sighed, then smiled ruefully. 'But I'd have led a different life if I had money. So I wouldn't have met you or your mother. Wouldn't have my three beautiful kids. I guess it's fate, though I still want to give Napier a good crack every time I hear "Grace" played on the radio.'

Jay laughed. 'So when's the meeting?'

'Saturday,' Len said. 'But Napier already lost it on the phone, telling me he wouldn't throw good money after bad and that he'd shelve all plans for promotion and new recordings if we don't follow orders.'

'Why's life never simple?' Jay grumbled, as he grabbed a can of Diet Rage from the fridge, then cheekily dipped his pinkie finger in the cake mix.

June gave his knuckles a crack with a wooden mixing spoon, and the girls laughed as Jay backed off with a yelp.

'Serves you right,' Patsy said.

It was a nice family moment, but Jay's smile expired three seconds later when his mum, Heather, came in.

'I just got off the phone with Mrs Stourbridge,' Heather said, placing hands on hips. 'What the hell, Jayden?'

Patsy smirked as Jay decided to go on the attack. 'I was knackered. Salman's mum gave *him* the day off to sleep off his jet-lag.'

'Get here,' Heather said, backing down the hall and pointing into the living room.

'Mum, I'm watching telly,' Hank protested, as Jay reluctantly entered behind his mum.

'Scoot!' Heather shouted to Hank, as she grabbed the remote and switched the TV off. 'And close that door behind you.'

Hank slammed the door and raced upstairs, leaving Jay facing his mum in front of the line of old school photos on the mantelpiece. Even Theo was cute when he was six, with two front teeth missing.

'We made a deal when you signed up for *Rock War*,' Heather began. 'You *have* to carry on working hard at school. I told you the same thing again when we agreed to take you out of school for the LA trip and now you've got the cheek to toss it back in my face.'

'I left my phone on and fell asleep,' Jay said. 'Compared to some of the stuff Kai and Theo got up to . . .'

'No, no, no!' Heather interrupted, frantically wagging a finger. 'You are a smart kid. Comparing yourself to two brothers who don't have your god-given abilities is not a defence.'

'Theo's doing all right,' Jay pointed out. 'Maybe you should take a chill pill for once.'

This went down like a brick through a flat screen. 'How about I ground you and that chopsy mouth for two weeks? *Including* band practice.'

'No way,' Jay said, his voice going high from shock. 'The band is my life. It's not a joke.'

'I tell you what's not a joke,' Heather yelled. 'Your education. I get that you were tired. I might even forgive you for falling asleep and forgetting to put your phone on silent. But that's *not* why your head of year is calling me. She said you disobeyed an instruction to wait outside a classroom. Then you had the cheek to return the call and were rude to your science teacher.'

'I wasn't rude . . . A bit moody, maybe.'

'What was this super-important call?' Heather asked. 'Was it Bailey mucking around? Whoever it was, was it *really* worth getting yourself into a heap of trouble?'

Jay kept quiet, knowing that Summer's name would just lead to more questions.

'Well, who was it? Are you buying drugs or something?'

'Jesus, Mum,' Jay gasped. 'Do I look like I'm on drugs?'

'Who knows what was going on at Rock War Manor?' Heather sighed. 'Dylan just got sent down. Got so crazy he almost stabbed some poor kid to death.'

'The *poor kid* was a twenty-two-year-old drug dealer who tried to rob him,' Jay said. 'You know how the press distort everything. And you *liked* Dylan. He came to the shop and told you your fish and chips were the greatest.'

Heather paused to think about this before wagging her finger in Jay's face. 'I need to understand, Jayden. You've got someone calling you. It's so important that you have to take the call. And when I ask who that person was you won't tell me.'

'Am I not entitled to any privacy?' Jay asked.

'Have all the privacy you want,' Heather said. 'But seeing as you're still a child, who lives under *my* roof, and eats *my* food, you can have privacy in your room while you're grounded for two weeks.'

'I'll just go stay with my dad.'

'You wanna play that card?' Heather laughed. 'Go call your dad, tell him you got in trouble and see how far you get.'

Jay sighed. A lot of kids played separated parents against each other, but with a tough mum and an ex-cop for a dad, he'd never wrung much out of it.

'Summer Smith called me,' Jay finally admitted. 'You wanna see the call logs?'

Heather seemed surprised. 'Since when are you two back on speaking terms?'

'Just since this morning.'

'I hope she was worth getting grounded for two weeks.'

'Aww, come on!' Jay blurted. 'I thought you were grounding me for not being honest.'

Heather smiled. 'Now I'm grounding you for being an idiot. Why didn't you just call Summer back *after* school? You've got another girlfriend anyway.'

Jay had sworn not to blab, but being grounded did his head in and since two of Heather's sons and her first husband had been behind bars, she was the last person on earth who'd go snitching to the prison authorities.

'Summer was in a state,' Jay explained. 'Dylan called her from prison up in Scotland. He's having a really bad time, getting bullied and stuff. Summer wanted to talk to Theo because he's done time and she wanted advice on how to help him.'

Heather shook her head. 'Knowing Theo, his advice will be how to make a shank.'

'So that's why I got into trouble,' Jay said. 'I returned the call because Summer sounded really upset.'

'There's not much Summer can do,' Heather said thoughtfully. 'Poor girl. I know she made a bit of money, but it's still tough having her nan to look after.'

'So, am I grounded?' Jay asked.

'Dylan *was* a nice kid,' Heather said. 'That's why you've got to stay away from drugs.'

'Mum, I've never even puffed on a joint,' Jay lied, then gave his most pleading expression. 'So?'

'You're not grounded,' Heather said, as she pulled Jay close for a kiss.

'Best mum ever!'

'Ain't such a bad kid, either,' Heather said. 'Did you pick up the extra work for the two days you missed?'

'Heaps.'

'Better get your butt up to your room and crack on then, hadn't you?'

14. New Kicks

Crashing off the chair had broken the ice with Dylan's Core Skills group. The afternoon's second exercise was a role-play. One character had just landed a job as a waiter in a busy restaurant, while Dylan and another inmate played customers fighting over the last available table.

The teacher had discussed strategies the waiter could use to keep both customers happy, but the role-play went off message, with Dylan and the other two role-players joking around threatening to knock one another out, before the waiter stormed off, made a gun with his fingers and told everyone that he was quitting *this shitty minimum wage job* to go rob the bank across the street.

Everyone was laughing as class filed out. Unlike regular school, lesson times were staggered so only a few inmates were on the move at once. The older inmates headed for A and C units, leaving Dylan walking down a hallway that overlooked a basketball match taking place in the drizzle outside.

Dylan's mood sagged when he reached his little cell and started taking a long piss. There were four and a half hours until lockdown and at some point Stuart and his crew were sure to visit. He splashed water on his face and squeezed a zit on his shoulder, then sat on the edge of his bed, taking a proper look at the piece of broken chair.

If he gripped it inside his fist, he could leave the sharp end of the rivet sticking out between two fingers. But he remembered the community cop who'd visited his primary school back in the day. He'd warned the kids off drugs, and Dylan certainly now wished he'd taken *that* advice. Then the cop told all of year five and six that it's dumb to play on train tracks or construction sites and that people who carry knives wind up getting stabbed themselves.

Dylan let the nostalgia wash over. It was just before his parents split. Jumping out of his dad's Land Rover and running into the rural three-room school at the top of the hill. The Kermit-green school shirts, the brown Plasticine and getting partnered with the double-jointed, pee-smelling Polish kid for forward rolls in gym class.

'Daydreaming?' Nash asked.

The chunky officer stood with his hands up on the door frame. Dylan panicked, until he was certain his excuse for a weapon was back down his pocket.

'Something like that, sir,' Dylan said.

'Got a package for you in the office. You wanna come sign for it?'

Dylan was mystified. 'Where from?' he asked, as he stood up.

'I emailed your dad's office, asking for someone to call me, and saying you could do with a few things,' Nash explained. 'Tried your dad's personal number too, but I struck out.'

'He's barely spoken to me since I ran away,' Dylan said.

As Nash led Dylan between the bench seats in the courtyard, Archie was walking away from the vending machines holding a Fanta. His polo shirt had the collar hanging off and he had a massive black eye.

'Claims he tripped on the stairs,' Nash said, shaking his head as they reached the guards' office. 'Nowt I can do to help if a boy won't talk.'

Radio X was playing low. A chunky female guard sat doing paperwork up back, as Nash grabbed a grey plastic tray, exactly like the ones you feed into X-ray machines at airports. All the gear was new, with JD Sport tags hanging off. A pair of Nike Free Run trainers, retro style Pumas, slip-on pool shoes for the showers, two tracksuits, T-shirts and underwear. Besides clothes there was gum, deodorant, two packs of biscuits and a bag of fun-size Snickers.

'Not a bad score,' Nash said, as he grabbed a *Rub-A-Dub* laundry marker out of a pen pot. 'Write your surname and trainee number on everything that'll take it. Especially those shiny new trainers.'

Dylan was safe in the guards' office, so he took his time writing his ID on tongues, pocket linings and even inside the waistbands of boxer briefs. A new arrival in the suicide cell was bawling and Nash sat in the cell comforting the poor kid as Dylan headed out.

Everyone was back from lessons, but luckily Stuart and his boys were in a kick-about on the all-weather pitch. Dylan wouldn't normally be seen dead in sportswear, but he was happy to switch his five-day-worn prison-issue tracksuit for Adidas bottoms and a hoodie.

When he went up to dinner, Archie stepped up and whispered while ladling mashed potato.

'Don't look at me,' Archie said. 'They won't pull shit while Nash is on duty. But your girl didn't pay, so you'd better prepare for a visit when the night staff clock in.'

'Are you sure?' Dylan asked, fighting the basic instinct to look at the person you're talking to.

'I heard them in class earlier.'

'What happened to your eye?' Dylan asked, but Archie bolted before answering.

Impending doom spoiled Dylan's appetite and Summer's apparent failure made him question how much she really cared. For all the messages and hanging out, he'd only kissed her once . . .

Rather than go back to his cell after dinner, Dylan sat in the indoor courtyard watching a quiz show followed by the BBC News. He started feeling sick as the night staff came on duty, jiggling his new trainers and shutting hands under his armpits to stop them shaking.

Stuart sat across from him barely a minute after Nash clocked out. Two minutes after that, a kid who existed on the fringes of Stuart's crew approached the guards' office and started distracting them with a story that he'd just been sick and needed to see the medical officer.

'Your girlfriend didn't pay,' Stuart told Dylan, as he beckoned Freckles and Fat Man.

'Tomorrow, I'd bet,' Dylan said, as he looked for the best escape route. 'You heard the call, she said she'd pay.'

'Tomorrow wasn't the agreement,' Stuart snarled, as his henchmen closed up.

Before Fat Man could grab hold, Dylan jumped on to the bench table and hopped across to the next one before leaping down. The obvious next move was to run towards the safety of the guards' office, but Stuart had another henchman blocking that route.

The last thing Dylan wanted was to get dragged into a cell where the bad guys could take their time, so he backed up to the ping-pong table beneath the TV where everyone would be looking at him.

As Stuart lunged, Dylan scrambled left, dodging an outstretched ankle, sprinting towards the vending machines and the short corridor into unit B2. He hoped a chase in the busiest part of the unit would get spotted by guards watching CCTV, or maybe he'd get as far as the B2 guards' office on the opposite side of the unit.

But while cocaine and stress meant Dylan had lost most of his puppy fat, he still wasn't very fit. Stuart barged him into a wall, locked muscular arms around his chest, then bundled Dylan head first into the illuminated panel of a vending machine. Dylan was dazed as Stuart doubled him up with a gut slug, then grabbed the back of his hoodie and started dragging him towards the showers.

'You're a dead man, Wilton.'

Stuart tried getting a hand over Dylan's mouth to stop him yelling, but Dylan snared his little finger and bit down until he tasted blood.

Trainers sploshed as they entered the shower room. The steamy space had doors at either end and Freckles, Fat Man and a couple of hangers-on formed a crowd as Stuart forced Dylan into a corner back by the shower heads.

As Dylan defended another punch, Stuart got the ball of his foot on the edge of a rubber mat. At walking pace, the mats stopped trainees slipping on shower tiles, but when Stuart turned swiftly, the edge of the mat arched up. His foot slipped back and he wound up hitting the puddled floor hard as Dylan stumbled on top of him.

A splash of water was soapy enough to sting Dylan's left eye. Stuart started wriggling out, as Dylan grasped the makeshift weapon in his pocket. Freckles was stepping in to give Stuart a hand as Dylan swung.

The sharp edge between Dylan's knuckles hit Stuart hard and gouged upwards, from the lower part of his cheek to the edge of his eye socket. Blood smeared Dylan's hand as he took a second jab. It grazed just below Stuart's ear, but before it got deeper, Fat Man grabbed Dylan under the arms and swung him around, enabling Freckles to punch him in the face.

As Stuart clutched his bloody cheek, Fat Man let Dylan go and stomped his ribs. Three more guys closed in and Dylan got a vicious Air Max under the chin as an alarm sounded. He took a dozen more blows before three guards charged in, shouting.

'On your knees, hands on heads.'

One burly guard splattered Fat Man into the wall behind Dylan as the rest of Stuart's crew did what they were told. Everything was still fifteen seconds later, when a second batch of guards arrived. This five-person response team wore helmets and body armour and carried circular elbow shields and half-metre-long batons.

'Nobody move,' they shouted repeatedly, dominating the shower room while the regular guards backed out and started herding the rest of the inmates to their cells for a lockdown.

Only one of the response team was female, but she made up for her lack of size with ferocity, first smashing her baton into Freckles when he dared to take a hand off his head, then standing over Stuart as he writhed in his own blood and ruthlessly booting him in the ribs.

'Did little Stew-pot get a taste of his own medicine?' she teased, unveiling a grin as she flipped up her helmet visor.

Dylan was soaked in cold, soapy water, with his vision blurred, a wobbly tooth and his ears ringing. He flinched as the female response officer crouched in front of him.

She held up gloved fingers. 'How many?'

Dylan squinted and saw three fingers, but when he tried to speak his tongue just pushed a stream of blood over his bottom lip and down his chin.

'Two for the medics,' the officer said, as she stood back up.

'Put the rest of these dicks back in their cells and get the paperwork done *before* they can talk to each other.'

15. Big Important Futurey Stuff

When school kicked out on Wednesday, the five members of Jet, along with former band mate Tristan, piled into an Uber XL for a twenty-minute ride up to Alfie and Tristan's detached Hampstead home. Mrs Jopling held a tray with a pot of tea as she led the band around the side of the house, to a swanky cabin at the end of the garden.

It had been built as a playroom when Tristan and Alfie were little, but since *Rock War* ended it had become Jet's permanent rehearsal space. Besides the band's instruments, there was a big screen, a fridge stocked with snacks and drinks, games consoles, and enough microphones and recording gear to make a decent demo.

As Jet's manager, Big Len sometimes dropped in on after-school rehearsals, if he wasn't occupied with his day job running bingo and sing-alongs in old folks' homes. Today he was joined by Erin's mum, Rachel, Salman's older brother and both of Babatunde's parents.

The space wasn't huge and it was a mild afternoon, so the gathering sprawled through sliding glass doors and on to the outside decking. Mrs Jopling dealt with tea and coffee, while Tristan grabbed cold cans from the fridge and lobbed them to his mates.

'Everyone here now?' Len asked, as Babatunde's dad jogged across the lawn after a trip to the toilet. 'I really appreciate all of you taking time to come out here at short notice. I'm sure everyone has heard about the dispute with Sean Cox that took place after the *Jennifer Moon* rehearsal. I've been dealing with the blow-back from that ever since, spending hours on the phone with various people at Wilton Music.

'Before I get into the nitty-gritty, I'll butter you all up with a few bits of good news. First off, I've heard unofficially that *Tenured* has been picked up for a second twenty-episode season by the network. The first season is starting on Sky here in a couple of weeks, which should give us a boost here in the UK. Sales-wise *Jennifer Moon* has done what we hoped it would across the pond: "Strip" was up to number nine on the US iTunes site, and thirteen in the Spotify USA singles chart when I looked this morning.'

'Nice,' Salman said, leading thin applause before Big Len carried on.

'And just to get all of the good news out of the way in one go, Mairi at Wilton Music in Edinburgh says we can have as many tickets as we want for Terraplane's gig at Wembley Stadium in a couple of weeks. If you're really lucky, we'll arrive late enough to miss Half Term Haircut.'

This earned a few laughs.

'All the talk between me and Wilton Music since the weekend boils down to us having two options.

'The first is to run with what Wilton Music are putting on the table. Sean Cox and Harry Napier want to hire a full-time publicist, here and in the USA, to raise Jet's media profile. They want to get you in the recording studio soon, to record a couple of new tracks to keep momentum building. Then record an album during your summer holidays, with a view to releasing for Christmas. The biggest cherry on this cake is that Napier is offering Jet the chance to play as the opening act during the North America leg of Terraplane's world tour. That would mean live exposure in front of half a million rock fans, and money in our pockets too.'

'Awesome,' Salman said, followed by similar comments from his band mates.

'I'm not sure about touring,' Babatunde's mum said. 'Didn't these kids miss enough school last year when they were in *Rock War*?'

Salman's brother spoke up, shaking his head. 'Education's not all that it's cracked up to be. Everyone I know has qualifications sticking out of their earholes. I dated a girl with a master's degree who works on checkouts at Lidl.'

'OK, OK,' Len said, keen to get the whole story out before his audience lost focus. 'I know all parents are concerned about education and that's something we must think through very carefully before agreeing to any kind of overseas tour. But before we get to that there's a *major* catch.

'Wilton Music want Jet to sound like they do on "Strip". Now there's no way Theo can come back with all his television commitments, so they want us to audition a new, male, lead vocalist.'

'Screw them,' Jay said instinctively, as he loyally put a hand on cousin Erin's shoulder.

'Where would that leave my daughter?' Rachel asked.

'I've been able to twist Wilton Music's arm somewhat,' Len explained. 'At first they were talking about replacing Erin, but they're amenable to her staying in the band as a backup singer. Or even retaining a female lead on certain tracks.'

'We're playing our best music right now,' Alfie noted. 'We've developed a new sound since *Rock War*.'

'A better sound,' Jay added, to broad agreement from his band mates.

Mrs Jopling spoke next. 'What happens if we turn down Wilton Music's offer?'

'I spoke to a music lawyer who I've known for years,' Len began. 'Normally, a band is contracted to a record label and getting out of that contract is very hard. But, since none of the current members of Jet are adults, there are no legally binding contracts in place between the band and Wilton Music.'

'Sweet,' Babatunde said.

'However,' Len continued. 'Wilton Music will still retain rights to everything you've recorded in the past, including "Strip". Venus TV also owns rights to things like your band logo. They also control the band website and social media accounts that were set up for the TV show. There's also a big question mark over whether we can still call the band Jet.'

'They own our name?' Jay gasped. 'That sucks.'

'They probably *don't* ultimately own the name,' Len explained. 'But we would have to prove that the band existed under the name Jet for a reasonable period of time before you signed up for *Rock War*. My lawyer pal said that we could easily wind up getting sued if we used the name Jet. And even if we ultimately won, it could take a couple of years to win, and cost us tens of thousands in legal bills.'

'So they've got us by the balls?' Salman asked. 'We either accept some crappy Theo sound-alike and play crash-and-bang stuff we no longer want to play, or we're screwed.'

'I don't care,' Jay said. 'I'd rather build a great band from scratch than kiss the asses of scumbags like Sean Cox.'

'Easy for you to say,' Babatunde noted. 'You're coining dollars in songwriting royalties from *Tenured*. All the rest of us get is a hundred and twenty bucks an episode for playing on the title track.'

'Me and Erin didn't even play on "Strip", so we don't even get that,' Alfie reminded him.

Jay had assumed Babatunde would take his side and scowled. 'You want our music dictated by these assholes?'

'Of course I don't,' Babatunde said defensively. 'But we all know how tough it is for a band to succeed. So maybe it's better to take a long view. Eat some shit from our record company right now, if it means we're getting in the charts and gigging with Terraplane.'

'I think we should listen to Wilton Music,' Mrs Jopling

suggested. 'They're supposed to be experts. And I don't know this Sean Cox guy, but Harry Napier didn't get to be the richest man in Scotland by not knowing anything about music.'

Len smiled. 'With respect, Jane, Harry Napier is an opportunist. He made his first fortune in the eighties and nineties as the manager of Terraplane. For the last two decades, he's made an even bigger fortune as a property developer. He only got back into the music business when he saw Venus TV going broke and sniffed an opportunity to make big bucks.'

'Do you guys really want to take advice from the guy who flushed Summer Smith's career down the shitter?' Tristan added.

'Tristan, language!' Mrs Jopling yelled.

'He's *right* though,' Jay said pleadingly.

'I've explained our two options as best I can,' Len said. 'The usual thing with a band is for every member to have a vote. The only question is, do we vote here and now, or do we want to think it over for a day or two?'

Jay was tempted to be dramatic and say that he'd quit Jet if they voted to follow Sean Cox's plan. But he'd made a similar threat in this cabin two years earlier, and it wound up getting him kicked out of his first band, Brontobyte.

'It's not *that* complicated,' Salman said. 'Everyone's already here.'

'I say we vote,' Erin agreed.

A murmur of agreement went around the cabin, as Mrs Jopling crossed the room and started some conspiratorial whispering in Alfie's ear.

'I vote we tell Sean Cox where to go and make our own path,' Jay said.

'There's a surprise,' Len laughed. 'Erin?'

'I don't want to be selfish,' Erin said. 'A new male vocalist would mean I'd have a smaller role in the band. But I'd rather have a small role in a band that's selling records and playing gigs with Terraplane, than be lead vocalist playing to a hundred people in some dingy pub.'

Jay felt doomed. Erin was the one person he felt was sure to take his side.

'One each,' Len said. 'Salman?'

'I'm seeing both sides of the argument,' Salman admitted. 'But we're not the Jet that played in *Rock War*. Plus, the album Sean Cox made Summer put out tells me all I want to know about his level of expertise.'

'Two-one in favour of quitting the label,' Len said. 'Alfie?'

'I vote we stay with Wilton Music,' Alfie said stiffly, before his mum whispered something else in his ear. 'Also, my mum suggests that Tristan could come back in the band and be our new male vocalist.'

Tristan shot up from where he was squatting at the back of the cabin. 'Mum! You're so embarrassing.'

'Why not, honey?' Mrs Jopling asked. 'You're a great-looking kid. And Erin's your girlfriend, so you'd have chemistry for duets.'

'Only my total inability to sing stands in my way,' Tristan noted, shaking his head. 'And no offence, everyone, but I am so over the band thing . . .'

'I'm just thinking out loud,' Mrs Jopling said grumpily. 'Trying to solve a problem without bringing in a stranger . . .'

'Two votes each,' Len said. 'Down to you, Mr Okuma.'

Jay wasn't optimistic, based on Babatunde's comments a few moments earlier.

'This is no fun,' Babatunde said, shaking his head. 'I've got the casting vote, so half of you will hate me whichever way I go.'

Tense laughs went around the cabin.

'I think my parents brought me up a certain way,' Babatunde continued, after a pause. 'They worked hard to get where *they* are. So even if it's going to be a tough road, I'm loving the way Jet sounds with Erin's vocals and me and Jay writing songs together. So basically, Sean Cox can go kiss my big black balls!'

'Nice one!' Jay said, wrapping arms around Babatunde and planting a deliberately wet kiss on his cheek. 'You won't regret this.'

But Len didn't seem so sure. 'I'll certainly guarantee fireworks when Harry Napier finds out.'

16. Tooth Fairy

Stuart got dibs on the ambulance. Since Dylan's injuries were less serious, he wound up rattling through rural Scottish darkness in a Transit van with bars at the windows. Pain all over, but mostly in his mouth. A dozen faces cut sly glances as he sat in casualty. He wore a neon orange bib with *prison transit* written on it, clutched a wodge of paper towels to his bloody mouth and had a uniformed guard sat alongside.

Dylan waited an hour to get examined. While he sat on a padded hospital trolley, getting dabs of disinfectant and sticking plasters from the nurse, his guard stood on the other side of the cubicle curtain, listening to a colleague explaining how Stuart had whined when the nurse put a needle in to numb his face and spewed on himself after it pierced his cheek.

The prison staff clearly thought Stuart was a nasty piece of work, and Dylan hoped that would work in his favour when punishments got dished out. He was less sure how it would affect his status with the other inmates.

'You can get dressed,' the nurse told him. 'I don't think there's any need for X-rays, but you'll have to go up to three and get that tooth looked at.'

It was two a.m., and the hospital's top floor was spookily barren. Dylan spent ninety minutes on a lime chair, in front of an unstaffed reception desk, with windows overlooking a deserted hospital car park. There were eight dental suites, but the only sound came from the one at the far end. The guard had a box filled with carrot and celery sticks. He told Dylan how he'd gone down two trouser sizes since new year and that digesting celery actually burns more calories than it contains.

'Negative food,' he said, cracking a laugh that echoed down an unlit Audiology corridor.

The dentist had a Hollywood smile and a Nigerian accent. 'Been at the wars then, young man?' she asked. 'Hop on through.'

Dylan hoped she could set the tooth back in place. But she said it was practically out already and tugged it free before numbing the area with an injection. The dental assistant kept vacuuming Dylan's mouth, but he still reckoned he'd swallowed half a litre of blood by the time the dentist finished digging into the gum to retrieve a buried tooth fragment.

'You can discuss options with your regular dentist once it heals,' she explained. 'Dental plates, bridgework, or even a titanium implant if you're feeling rich. It'll take four to six weeks before it's ready for any further treatment.'

'Maybe a gold tooth like a gangsta rapper,' Dylan joked,

words slurred because his tongue felt like an airship.

He got out with instructions to bite down on a lump of gauze for the next hour, and a white paper bag containing three days of pain-killers, seven of antibiotics and two pages of A4 telling him to gargle salt, avoid hot drinks and a bunch of other stuff.

With all the pain and his brain scrambled, Dylan only now fully realised that he wasn't spending the night in hospital. He got goose bumps as he got into the custody van. Back through four a.m. dark and winding tree-lined roads, to a place where he reckoned he was in more danger than ever.

*

Summer was battling the bedsheets. The duvet kept falling off, the pillows were all wrong. Her train of thought was a TGV doing three twenty KPH. She wanted to know how Dylan was feeling. *Have I got it all wrong? What if they hurt him because I didn't pay? What if he thinks I've abandoned him?*

The mobile banking app was 24/7. She could log in and do the transfer now and gain the satisfaction of having done all she could. But she still saw the sense in what Theo said. Paying now could make it worse down the line and Jay had seemed to agree.

Jay had hurt Summer when he cheated on her, but now some time had passed, she grasped the pressure his band mates put on him to be one of the lads and lose his virginity. Summer was surprised by how welcome she found Jay's voice, just like the way he'd calmed her down before her early appearances on stage.

But what kind of person does this make me?

Beating Jay up in front of everyone, not talking to him for over a year, then calling out of the blue when she needed something? *What do Jay and Theo really think of me? And the way I ditched my band mates for a pile of money. Probably all thought I got what was coming when my album tanked . . .*

More than anything, Summer wanted to speak to Dylan. Hear his voice in person, or better still dig fingers into the fat over his shoulder blades, sniff his hair and tell him how much she cared. The hopelessness made Summer angry. She shot up in bed, throwing hair off her face and peeling the T-shirt stuck to her back.

She wasn't thirsty, but she sauntered to the kitchen, dragging one hand along the wall just to feel it. Maybe if she opened a window, straightened the sheets, flipped the sweaty pillow she could make a fresh stab at sleep. Maybe get enough that she wasn't totally fried when she got to school and had to deal with bunking the previous afternoon.

Eileen was coughing as Summer passed her bedroom door. She put her ear to the door and recognised the gentle hiss from her oxygen cylinder. Since she wasn't thirsty herself, Summer fixed a glass of cold water and put her head around her nan's door.

'Thought you'd like this,' Summer said, then jolted.

Eileen's asthma was worse when she laid flat, so she had an electronically adjustable bed on which she always slept slightly upright. The oxygen cylinder was hissing, but the mask had dropped to the carpet, and Eileen was on her chest, hanging breathlessly off the side of the bed trying to reach it.

'Nan!' Summer gasped, putting the water down and rushing in. 'Why didn't you press your emergency bracelet?'

'You need your sleep,' Eileen gasped, as Summer gently rolled her back to her regular sleeping position. 'Can't keep on disturbing you.'

'You *must* press it when you're in trouble,' Summer said firmly, as she bent down and picked up the mask. 'Do you think I'll ever sleep if I'm worried you're not OK?'

After checking the level gauge on the oxygen cylinder's neck, Summer placed the mask and stretched the elastic around the back of her nan's head. This settled Eileen's breathing, but as Summer backed up to replace her nan's water with the cold one she'd left by the door, she noticed a dark patch in the corner of the sheet.

'I need to put the lamp on,' Summer said warily.

Summer squinted as the bulb came on, but as her eyes adjusted she saw a glistening stain, made of spit flecked with blood. A few spots of blood weren't unusual, but this was the most Summer had ever seen. There were a dozen bloody tissues scattered about and when Summer touched her nan's arm the skin was roasting.

'Do you feel hot?' Summer asked.

Eileen pulled her mask off to speak. 'I'm shivering. I've put the extra blanket on.'

On doctor's advice, Summer kept the bungalow at a toasty twenty-three degrees day and night and only aired the place when her nan went out.

'Let's have your hand,' Summer said.

She fumbled in a bedside drawer. Eileen started another round of hacking as her granddaughter located a little plastic gadget and placed her nan's finger into the hole at one end. After a series of bleeps, a display flashed up with a racing heart rate of a hundred and twenty and a blood oxygen level that set off a ringing tone and made *LOW* flash on the backlit screen.

'I'm calling an ambulance,' Summer said, knowing her nan wouldn't like it.

'I'll just lie on a trolley for hours before they send me home,' Eileen croaked.

'I've never seen you cough up this much blood,' Summer said firmly, as she looked around the floor for a pre-packed bag filled with clothes, toiletries and medication. 'I don't think you'll be coming home.'

'I'm playing cards tomorrow.'

Summer half smiled, but kept her tone firm. 'Nan, the state you're in, how are you even gonna make it to the loo?'

Then she grabbed the phone and dialled 999.

17. Admit Nuffink

It was almost five by the time Dylan got back to his cell. When he tried lying flat, blood would pool in the back of his mouth and make him cough. He propped himself up, but the prison-issue pillows were pathetic and the metal bedframe jarred his back.

His light came on at seven, but his door didn't unlock. He heard the other trainees move off to breakfast, and was examining his missing tooth in the shatterproof mirror above his sink when Nash came in. He had a clipboard, and a Ziploc bag containing the plastic piece from the chair.

'How's my wounded soldier?' Nash chirped.

Dylan shrugged. 'Been better.'

Nash smiled, as he aimed a hand at the bed. 'Better than Stuart, for sure. Can I sit?'

'Sure,' Dylan said.

'You realise you could be out of here in just over fifteen weeks?' Nash asked. 'But if you mess up you could end up doing the full eight months. Maybe even cop a charge for assaulting Stuart and get extra time tacked on.'

'I love my life,' Dylan said sourly.

'Stuart doesn't have a lot of fans amongst the staff. We can't wait for his eighteenth so we can ship him off to C block. There's no CCTV in the showers, but there is in the courtyard, so there's no disputing that you got chased and dragged in there by Stuart. The problem is this.'

Nash tapped the bag with the plastic inside.

'They'll question you later . . .'

'Who will?' Dylan interrupted.

'It'll be a senior officer, upstairs in the office. Now here's the thing. *If* you tell them you were carrying this weapon before the incident, they're going to say it was a deliberate act and pin Stuart getting cut on you. The CCTV proves that you were provoked, but if you say you were carrying a weapon you're still going to be looking at a *big* loss of remission time.'

'So what do I say?' Dylan asked.

Nash smiled. 'It was dark. You were confused. You don't know where the weapon came from. You grabbed it off the floor during the tussle and used it because you feared for your life.'

'Right,' Dylan said, though in the back of his mind, he wondered if an investigation might link the piece of sheared plastic to the chair he'd broken the previous afternoon. 'What if one of Stuart's boys says they saw me pull it out?'

'I'd be astonished,' Nash said. 'They'll want to settle their own scores.'

'Something else for me to look forward to,' Dylan said.

'I'll do what I can to look out for you,' Nash said. 'Stuart's no genius, but he's smarter than the others. His crew tends to be rudderless when he's out of circulation. So watch your back, and there'll be extra random searches after last night's incident, so make sure you and your cell are clean.'

*

Early sun made the hospital corridor dazzle as Summer blinked a ginger-bearded nurse into focus. She had a crick in her neck and her tongue felt like a scouring pad, pushing its way round a chalky mouth.

'Summer Smith?'

'Ugh,' Summer said, stifling a yawn.

As she moved, a note-pad slipped between her legs and the nurse dashed off to catch the biro that began rolling across the floor. Summer had bought a Hello Kitty note-pad and pen set from the hospital's twenty-four-hour shop and scribbled lyrics for a song until she'd finally grasped some sleep.

'What time is it?'

'Fourteen past nine,' the nurse said. 'I'm sorry to wake you, but I know you wanted to speak to the doctor.'

'Thanks,' Summer said, smiling.

Summer noticed smears of Eileen's blood down her arm as she stood up, rubbing her neck. She wore the oversized nightshirt she'd been trying to sleep in, tartan leggings and All Stars she'd rushed on in the dark. One was from her old battered pink pair, the other one of the almost-new yellow ones which were two sizes bigger.

'Can I get a cup of water?' she asked, clutching her throat.

Summer had left her nan in the respiratory ward, but after stopping by a water dispenser, the nurse led her up two flights of chilly stairs to a single room. The doctor was a young Pakistani man, with a crack in the right lens of his glasses that made him look slightly mental. Eileen had been sedated to control her coughing. Each breath came with a gentle whistle through her oxygen mask and a drip had been inserted into her arm.

'It's highly likely that your grandmother has a lung infection, so she has been moved here to prevent transmission to other patients,' the doctor explained. 'You were correct to be concerned about the quantity of blood in her mucus. We don't yet have lab results, but I have begun a precautionary course of antibiotics.'

'So she'll be OK?' Summer asked, as she drained her plastic cup and scrunched it.

'Raised body temperature and presence of blood suggests that the infection is fairly serious,' the doctor explained. 'Has your grandmother been admitted with breathing difficulties before?'

'Regularly, since I was eight,' Summer explained. 'Though she's actually done pretty well for the last eighteen months.'

The doctor wrote something on Eileen's notes and clicked his pen.

'The predictability with these situations is difficult,' the doctor explained. 'Everyone's immune system handles infection differently. An apparently strong and healthy person can get a lung infection and become extremely sick. Someone older and weaker can get an identical infection and recover quickly.'

'Is there any way to tell?' Summer asked.

'The lab results will enable us to identify the pathogen and help us choose the best course of treatment. Since you have been in close contact with your grandmother, I'd like to take some throat swabs from you.'

'How does that work?' Summer asked angstily.

'It's basically a long cotton bud,' the nurse explained. 'I'll scrape some cells from the top of your mouth and the back of your throat. Then it goes to the lab, to see if you've picked up any infection.'

'It is a routine precaution,' the doctor added. 'On a more serious note, your grandmother's chest X-rays show signs of blood clotting in the inferior lobe of the left lung. I'll have to speak with my senior colleagues, but it's likely your grandmother will need surgery.'

'The clot won't clear on its own?' Summer asked.

The doctor shook his head. 'The inside of a lung contains hundreds of thousands of very fine tubes that absorb oxygen from the air. When a large quantity of blood settles in the lung it clots into a hard mass, much like the scab you get if you cut yourself. The only way to contain this kind of infection is to remove a portion of the lung.'

'Damn,' Summer said, as she glanced mournfully at her nan.

'I'm sorry I can't give you more positive news,' the doctor

said. 'But you were very smart to call the ambulance last night.'

Summer sat beside her grandmother's bed, feeling slightly tearful as the doctor left and the nurse grabbed a pack of throat swabs from a trolley parked at the end of the bed.

'Tilt your head back slightly and open up wide.'

The cotton swab felt scratchy and the sample from the back of the throat triggered Summer's gag reflex. Fortunately, she'd not eaten so nothing came up.

'Do you have another adult carer?' the nurse asked, as he dropped the swab stick into a plastic sample tub and started writing out a label with Summer's name on.

Summer was capable of looking after herself, and shuddered at the thought of the hospital getting social services involved.

'My cousin lives across town,' she lied. 'I'll stay there until Nan's better.'

18. Chainsaw's Ex

Nash got a breakfast tray brought downstairs to Dylan's cell.

'Good news is, your phone contact with Summer Smith has been approved,' Nash said, as Dylan sucked mashed-up Weetabix to the back of his mouth. 'The bad news is, all inmates on this unit have had their communication privileges suspended until the investigation is complete.'

'Perfect,' Dylan slurred, getting a smile from Nash as he shook his head.

An hour later, Dylan was upstairs in an interrogation room. He got introduced to Keith, who was Whitburn's deputy director, along with a non-uniformed admin assistant, who took notes and switched a tape recorder on and off.

Dylan told them that he was new in the unit and didn't know the names of any of the people who'd attacked him. He said he grabbed the weapon off the floor in the shower room out of desperation. Then he had to answer a list of standard questions, on how prison staff had behaved during and after the incident, rating them from one to five on things like *speed of response* and *did members of staff use proportionate levels of restraint at all times?*

After ten minutes, Dylan realised that the investigation had more to do with staff covering their butts against accusations of abusing inmates than a proper investigation of what went down the night before.

At the end, Keith read a prepared statement for the benefit of the tape recorder.

'Based on the evidence given by trainee Wilton, I have no grounds to believe that further action against him is necessary at this time. Notes relating to this incident will be placed on his trainee record and may be taken into consideration in the event of similar incidents in future. The trainee has also indicated that he has not been mistreated by staff and has no wish to raise any complaint against them at this time.'

Dylan's gum was still bleeding slightly and the assistant looked horrified as he spat bloody gauze into a tissue. Outside, he was relieved not to be facing a formal hearing, or loss of remission, but grimly aware that his battle with Stuart's crew wasn't over.

The hallway from the office led to the rear of the dining area. Lunch was fifteen minutes away and the first trays of food were being brought out to the stainless steel serving counters as Dylan crossed the dining area, aiming for the stairs down to B1.

'You Dylan?' a trainee holding a metal tub filled with steaming carrot slices asked.

He was a solidly built black trainee from unit A. Dylan backed up, fearing a clank of metal and a face full of boiling veg, but the carrot tray got dropped into a slot in the serving counter and the teenager yelled towards the kitchen.

'JJ, the boy you're after is out here.'

The aproned trainee clanked a metal lid on to the carrots as JJ sauntered out from the kitchen. He was dressed in a white button-up chef's coat and thick rubber gloves that glistened with soap bubbles. He was shorter than Dylan, but had arms like railway sleepers.

'Fifty-two stitches in Stuart,' JJ said, with a near-incomprehensible Glasgow accent. 'You a bad boy, Dylan Wilton?'

Dylan knew Stuart was from Glasgow. He imagined a thirty-centimetre paring knife carving his guts as JJ's powerful frame closed up. He thought about running, but JJ's tracksuit bottoms stretched over huge sprinter's thighs.

'I . . .' Dylan spluttered, slightly relieved when one of the non-inmate kitchen supervisors came out.

'JJ, are you messing with me?' the supervisor shouted. 'Got service in ten minutes and dirty pots piled up to the ceiling.'

'Checking in with my boy here,' JJ said, all friendly. 'I'll make your pots sparkle, Mr Deane. Just give me a few ticks.'

'One minute,' the supervisor shouted.

'I'm not as scary as I look,' JJ told Dylan, as he peeled one rubber glove and offered a meaty hand.

Dylan tried not to moan as the hand crunched his knuckles. And since Summer hadn't cared enough to pay up, maybe being a dead man was better than living through more of this shit . . .

'I hear you know the Chainsaw's ex-old lady?' JJ said. 'You ever meet the legend himself?'

'Chainsaw?' Dylan stuttered, sure that people in other countries could hear his heart drum. Where had he heard the name Chainsaw? 'Have you got the right person?'

'You Dylan Wilton?' JJ asked.

'Sure,' Dylan agreed. 'But I don't know about this Chainsaw, or his ex-old lady.'

'Vincent Chainsaw Richardson. Bad boy outta north London.'

Now Dylan remembered a newspaper article that had been published during his time in *Rock War*. It implied that Theo and Jay's family were a bunch of serious villains. Chainsaw Richardson was Theo's dad, which meant that his ex-old lady was Jay and Theo's mum.

'I've met Heather Richardson a couple of times,' Dylan said, as he wondered if Summer could have contacted her. 'She ran a chip shop in London.'

JJ shrugged. 'That lady has a hard-on for you, cos she spoke to Chainsaw. He's pals with some of Glasgow's finest. So I got a message through one of the guards, and now I'm told that if anyone else hurts you in here, me and my pals will have to answer for it when we're released.'

Dylan collapsed against the serving counter, smiling at the idea that this fearsomely solid eighteen-year-old had his back.

'You're serious?'

'These people aren't renowned for their sense of humour,' JJ explained. 'I'll introduce you to my boys later on.'

'You can stop Stuart's crew kicking my ass again?' Dylan asked.

JJ laughed. 'Stuart will be in my unit once he turns eighteen in a few months. He'll do as he's told. And anything else you need, just let us know. Weed, clothes, pillows?'

'Pillows in here are shite,' Dylan said, as the supervisor came back out of the kitchen, scowling. 'But what I really want is a proper talk with my girl.'

'JJ,' the supervisor shouted, as he rapped his wedding ring on a steel counter. 'Quit talking to your boyfriend, unless you wanna spend the afternoon scrubbing the fryers.'

'I gotta run,' JJ said, smiling as he backed away. 'But once I get word out, you'll have no worries.'

19. Missed Calls

The main hall of St Mark's Catholic Community Centre had 'Cotton Eye Joe' blaring from bashed-up Tannoy loudspeakers. Two rows of elderly women copied gentle line dance moves from Big Len, who stood on a low stage, wearing a silken red shirt with seventies-style jumbo collar.

'Ladies that was beautiful,' Len said cheerfully, as he faded the track on his iPad screen. 'But maybe you can drag a few more lazy husbands out of their seats next week, yeah?'

Some of the women laughed as they pottered back to their seats. Most of them started putting on coats, or taking empty cups and saucers to the serving counter up back.

'We've got the after-school club waiting to get in,' Len announced. 'But before that, would Dolly kindly pull today's raffle winner?'

Len stepped off stage and held a cloth bag in front of a large lady squeezed into a wheelchair.

'The winner of the tin of Quality Street, is number twenty-one. That's the key of the door, twenty-one. Have a great day everyone, and careful on the steps. You know how slippy they get when it's raining.'

Len got smiles and pats on the arm as the elderly dancers and bingo players headed out.

'That Indian lady is stealing biscuits,' one outraged woman warned. 'Scooping up great handfuls and putting them in her handbag.'

'I'll look into it,' Len said, stifling a smirk. 'Mind the step. See you next week.'

Len helped the Dial-a-Ride lady wheel Dolly and a couple of others out to her double-parked bus, then rushed back to unplug his speakers before after-school club unleashed hell. He just had to wheel his speakers and bingo blower out to the van when he decided to take his phone off silent and check his messages before the half-hour drive home to Barnet.

36 Missed Calls.

'Blimey,' he mumbled.

Len instinctively assumed something bad had happened to one of his kids. But Heather's number wasn't amidst the missed calls, and the only name displayed among unrecognised numbers was *Sue Willoughby*. She'd been an entertainment correspondent for the BBC and several newspapers, but now worked as an independent publicist – getting publicity for those who wanted it, or burying stories for those trying to avoid it.

She picked up on the first ring. 'Leonard,' Sue said brightly, with a smoker's croak. 'Long time no speak.'

'I've had a heap of messages over the last two hours,' Len said. 'What can I do for you?'

Sue laughed. 'I thought you might need me to do something for *you*,' she said. 'And since I've known you for thirty years, I might even charge mate's rates.'

Len was baffled, and also kept one wary eye on a bunch of six- to ten-year-olds who'd just come in. A few were chasing around, but the majority had formed a lively line by the serving hatch, buying Monster Munch and juice boxes.

'Sue, you clearly know something I don't,' Len said. 'Why is half the world trying to call me?'

'Alfie Jopling put up an Instagram post, showing him and Erin giving two-fingered salutes and saying that Jet are ditching – and I quote – *Get lost you arrogant dickholes like Sean Cox who run Wilton Music. You ruined Summer Smith's career, now Jet are going our own way so you can't do the same to us.*'

'Instagram,' Len said. 'I don't think I've heard of that one. Is it new?'

'Not really,' Sue laughed. 'You're not up on social media?'

'I told the kids to keep this quiet,' Len said. 'And little Alfie's the *last* one I'd expect to stir it.'

'Well it's out there,' Sue said. 'Like it or not.'

'I haven't even spoken to Wilton Music yet,' Len sighed. 'Harry Napier's never liked me and this won't make my life any easier.'

'At least you're too big for him to thump you,' Sue joked.

'He'll find a hundred other ways to get at me,' Len said warily. 'But Jet are lucky to get crowds of a hundred right now, so why is Alfie's Insta-wotsit even a story?'

'The media moves in cycles,' Sue explained. 'A year ago, *Rock War* was the plucky underdog show. Summer Smith's voice-in-a-million, crazy Theo. A show nobody expected to do well all over the news and getting the biggest ratings of the year. Terraplane reuniting for the final and causing the revival of Karen Trim's *Hit Machine* to be cancelled after one season.

'But once the media has something up on a plinth, the only way to keep it newsworthy is to knock it down. *Rock War* season two contestants aren't capturing the public's imagination in the same way that people like Summer and Theo did. Viewing figures are down by a quarter. Summer's album was a disaster. And Half Term Haircut may be selling out arenas and topping the download charts, but since the show ended, they've given up whatever pretence they ever had of being a rock band.'

'I'd read some of the recent stuff about *Rock War*,' Len said. 'But I didn't realise that Jet quitting the label would be a big story.'

'I bet you'll have three more missed calls by the time you finish speaking to me,' Sue said, laughing. 'There *will* be publicity. Any story knocking *Rock War* is hot right now. The question is, how can we make sure that it's the right kind of publicity for your band? If you let your band members run the story through their social media, it'll end up being back and forth mudslinging with Wilton Music and everyone will get bored very quickly.

'But if you play this right, you can portray the band as

victims of *Rock War*'s callous management. I can set you up newspaper interviews, possibly even TV news. I know all the big rock music vloggers. If we play this right, we can build a terrific platform for relaunching the band in the UK.'

Len paused for thought. He was an overweight ex-studio musician, who put on a shiny shirt and ran bingo and dancing in community centres. Now he was going into battle against a record company owned by a billionaire . . .

'Am I out of my depth here?' Len asked Sue warily, as two brats chased by, almost clattering into the bingo blower. 'I appreciate your call, but how much is this gonna cost?'

'A lot less than your lawyers' bills if Wilton Music take you to court,' Sue said. 'But you're not out of your depth. You've been in the biz since the late seventies. You've always been a decent person. You've got a lot of experience and a ton of friends in the biz.'

'I appreciate you saying that,' Len said, as he ran a hand through his hair. 'But I'm not some big management company. If we have to get lawyered up, I've basically got to go to Heather and the other band members' parents asking for thousands of pounds . . .'

'One day at a time, eh?' Sue said. 'Since you're a mate, I'll make some calls and deal with the current situation for free. But when you've got that million-pound recording contract in a few months, I want the paid publicist gig.'

'You've got it, Sue,' Len said, relieved to have someone he trusted on his team.

'Three things for starters though,' Sue said. 'First, talk to those kids and their parents and drill them to shut their mouths, in person and on social media, until I've sorted our media strategy. Second, get a proper legal notice drawn up, severing the band's ties with Wilton Music. Third, if Wilton Music own the name Jet, we have to get the new band name out there in my press releases and in any interviews we give. Is all that clear?'

'Sure,' Len said. 'I've already got a lawyer friend drafting the notification. The rights to the band name are a grey area, for sure.'

'Well maybe that's a news story in itself,' Sue laughed. 'Harry Napier's evil record company force teen band to change their name.'

Len laughed uneasily. 'I'd better get home and talk to the band.'

'And be confident,' Sue said. 'I'm not just doing this because you're a pal, Len. I watched Jet's *Jennifer Moon* performance on YouTube before I called earlier, and they're sounding *properly* good.'

20. Costco and Wilfred

'Dead man,' Freckles hissed, giving Dylan a shove as he brushed past on the way to class.

JJ told Dylan that he'd have no hassle *once word gets out*, but a beast like Fat Man could stab Dylan or crack his skull on the floor in a second. Dylan was sure he'd be safer in class than alone in his cell and the lesson might take his mind off his injuries.

There were eight kids in his advanced maths group, but at Whitburn, advanced basically meant anyone capable of sitting still with a pen in their hand. There was too much noise to focus on his standard grade book, and Dylan wound up explaining basic fractions to a shy kid called Matt, who kept getting ignored by the teacher.

JJ and a couple of tough-looking dudes were waiting outside after lesson.

'This is Wilfred and Costco,' JJ explained.

'Costco?' Dylan asked.

'He was on the TV,' JJ explained. 'Hid up on the shelves in Costco at closing time and stole all the laptops and fags.'

The story took a dark turn as Dylan laughed.

'Then the ass killed some chick with a pram during the getaway,' Wilfred added. 'So Costco is doing eight years.'

'Out in two,' Costco said, shrugging. 'That ain't shit.'

'You ever do weights, Dylan?' JJ asked.

Dylan wasn't the type, but he was offended that the mere question made Wilfred and Costco smirk.

'We're heading into the fitness centre,' JJ explained. 'I need you to hang back and join us in two minutes.'

'Why?'

JJ failed to answer as he led Dylan down an unfamiliar hallway. As JJ led Costco and Wilfred through swing doors, Dylan peeked into brightly lit space, with a mirrored back wall and a line-up of treadmills and rowers.

Dylan imagined a knife attack as he waited outside the gym doors, reading a notice about how all trainees needed an induction session before using gym equipment, and that anyone who came in with wet or dirty shoes would be banned for a month.

A couple of big guys eyed Dylan suspiciously as they headed in. When Dylan's two minutes were up, he stepped in. The gym was clearly a major hangout. There were four guys using resistance machines or pull-up bars and a dozen more with backs to the wall.

Alarmingly, Dylan saw no sign of JJ, Wilfred or Costco. But Freckles stood up by the back wall, along with a couple of

Stuart's other hangers-on. One of them whooped with outrage.

'Are you shitting me?'

'Can I believe my eyes?' Freckles shouted, as he jumped away from a leg press machine.

Dylan tried to back out, but someone cut off the door. Five seconds later he had Freckles striding towards him with his fists bunched, two more closing behind, while Fat Man was hauling himself off the floor with a jelly donut in one hand.

So JJ was messing with me, and now I'm dead.

Dylan heard a door bang off to one side. JJ and four other guys piled out.

'You got a beef with my boy?' JJ shouted, leading the charge.

JJ had a seven-kilo kettle bell in one hand. Freckles ducked the first swing, but caught a kick to the face before JJ smashed the weight into his back. As Freckles hit the rubber floor, the two guys behind Dylan bolted for the exit.

'Nobody touches him,' JJ shouted, pointing at Dylan. 'Make sure *everyone* knows that.'

None of Stuart's cronies had an appetite to fight the older crew. Fat Man backed up, trying to make himself invisible.

'Right now I've got no problem with anyone in this room,' JJ shouted. 'Is that gonna change?'

The only sound was Freckles gasping on the floor. JJ signalled Costco.

Dylan only now realised that Costco had been holding the door to the equipment room JJ and his crew had emerged from. Another guy jumped down off a chair, and dropped the yoga mat he'd been holding in front of the gym's CCTV camera.

As trainees jogged back to the equipment and acted like nothing had happened, a moustache and tracksuit marched out of the equipment room yelling, 'What the bloody hell? *Who* held the door shut? *Who* held that bastard door on me?'

But everything seemed normal. Freckles had been given a kick up the ass and sent limping to the sick room, and while the gym teacher knew something had happened, he'd taught at Whitburn for long enough to know he'd make an ass of himself if he tried getting to the bottom of it. And he had no interest in making a report, because he'd come out badly for letting a bunch of inmates barricade him inside a cupboard.

'All right, back to it,' the teacher shouted.

Dylan stood in the middle of the room looking lost and the teacher strode up with a comically pompous strut. 'And who are you?'

JJ answered for him. 'This is my boy Dylan, sir. He needs you to show him the ropes, so he can bulk those weedy biceps.'

'Fitness, excellent!' the instructor said. 'I'll go fetch an induction form.'

Dylan looked at JJ warily. 'This really isn't my scene,' he whispered.

'Train if you want, plant your ass in the corner if you don't,' JJ said. 'But I'm in serious trouble if shit happens to you, so you'll stay in my sight.'

'Appreciated,' Dylan said thoughtfully. He'd always hated sport, but weight training didn't involve freezing your ass off in mud, and he wasn't in love with what he saw in the mirror when he took his shirt off.

'Got you some feather pillows coming,' JJ said. 'And phone privileges should be back on your block by this evening, so you can call your bitch.'

21. What's In A Name?

Summer sat in the chair beside her nan's hospital bed, with a tatty book in her lap called *Children of the Bible*.

'Shall I read another one?' Summer asked.

'You read so nicely,' Eileen said, her voice muffled by the oxygen mask. 'Where on earth did you find it?'

'I found the book when we moved out of the flat,' Summer explained. 'I think a couple of pages are missing, but I didn't throw it out because I always remember you reading the stories to me when I was little.'

'"The Great Flood" was your favourite,' Eileen said cheerfully. 'I bought the book for your mother when she was small, but she was never interested. I must have read it to you a thousand times.'

'May next door took my Amazon parcel in,' Summer said. 'I spoke to her when I went home to get your extra clothes. She said she'll let the others know you're not well, and maybe come and visit if you're in for a while.'

'I don't want a fuss,' Eileen said.

'Let's see what the surgeon says tomorrow morning,' Summer said, as she gave her nan's hand a reassuring squeeze. 'You look a lot better this evening. Your colour's back, so maybe it's not as serious as they thought.'

'Maybe,' Eileen said, as she turned to look at Summer. 'I'm just so tired of being weak all the time. And you're missing more school with your exams in a few weeks.'

'It's OK,' Summer said. 'But I have got a history mock tomorrow. If you've got everything you need, I'll go home and do a bit of revision in a while.'

'Go right now,' Eileen said. 'I'm fine. And make sure you eat something.'

'I had a pesto pasta thing in the restaurant downstairs when you took your nap,' Summer said, not adding that she'd barely touched it because she was stressed out. 'It was nice.'

'And get a taxi home,' Eileen said, as firmly as her limited lung capacity allowed. 'It's getting dark and that bus goes through some right dodgy areas.'

*

Len tried to set up another band meeting, but Jay had detention, Alfie had Scouts, Babatunde had a movie date and Erin had a lesson with her voice coach. It was a quarter to ten when the five members of Jet finally got together for a group call on Skype.

'So they can all see me?' Len asked warily, as he dragged a chair up to the desk in Jay's bedroom, and waved at four faces in webcam boxes. 'Howdy everyone!'

Alfie spoke first, stripped down to his undershirt, because he knew everyone would take the piss if they saw his Venture Scout uniform. 'I've taken that Instagram post down. Sorry if I caused you any stress, Len.'

'My bad too, Uncle Len,' Erin added. 'Me and Tristan put him up to it.'

'Do I have to press a button to speak?' Len asked, setting off laughter from Salman, Alfie, Erin and Babatunde.

'Breaker one-nine, this here's the Rubber Duck,' Babatunde teased. 'It's not a CB radio, Len. You just talk.'

'Bloody technology,' Len huffed, as he leaned over and almost tilted off his chair into Jay. 'I don't know how you kids keep up with it.'

After regaining composure, Len reminded the five band members how important it was to not just post random crap online until he'd spoken to Wilton Music. Then he explained about his friend Sue volunteering to help with publicity until they – hopefully – signed with a new label.

'I also got an email from my legal guy,' Len continued. 'He's drafted a formal letter for me to send to Wilton Music, stating that we're going to sever all contractual ties with the organisation. But his opinion on the name isn't good. Wilton Music and Venus TV will almost certainly claim ownership to the name Jet. If they take us to court they'd *probably* lose, but a court case could take a year or more to resolve, and cost upwards of thirty grand.'

'How is that fair?' Alfie complained, shaking his head

vigorously. 'Can big companies just bully people by threatening to sue them?'

'Happens all the time,' Len said. 'And Harry Napier *will* sue if he can. He'll drop thirty thousand on a fancy watch without batting an eye and he's never much liked me.'

'Capitalism sucks,' Salman said, smirking. 'I demand a full communist revolution.'

'I can pay,' Jay said. 'I've got my royalties.'

'We'd chip in too,' Babatunde added. 'Even if we're not coining it like Mr Songwriter McMoneybags.'

Len looked at Jay sitting next to him. 'Jay, if I lost your royalty money in a court case, your mother would make me live in my van.'

'But it's *our* name,' Jay moaned.

'To be fair, Jet is hardly the greatest name,' Alfie said. 'It's just Jay's initials.'

Erin laughed. 'I'm still amazed Theo and Adam didn't beat you to a pulp when they found out you'd named the band after yourself.'

'Water under the bridge,' Jay said. 'All I'm saying is, Jet is the name *Rock War* fans know us by. Changing will make it even harder to establish ourselves.'

'True,' Len agreed. 'But Sue said the upside is that we can get publicity by portraying Wilton Music as evil bad guys forcing us to change names.'

'It's always bad *guys*,' Salman noted. 'It's like the most sexist thing ever.'

'And we sound different to the Jet that everyone saw on

Rock War anyway,' Erin said. 'It's kinda confusing.'

'Does it have to be a big change?' Babatunde asked. 'Like, can we call ourselves Jet Two, or Jet Engine, or something.'

'What kind of bogan name is Jet Engine?' Alfie moaned.

'It's an example,' Babatunde said irritably. 'I'm just asking, how big does the change have to be?'

'I'll check with our lawyer on that,' Len said. 'I know it's called *passing off*, if you give yourself a name that sounds a lot like something else. Like that bloke who got sued for setting up a kebab shop called McDoners.'

'What about, Not Jet,' Jay said. 'That way we've still got Jet in our name, but they can't possibly say we're trying to pass ourselves off.'

'Sounds like a pun for *not yet*,' Erin observed. 'Is that good or bad?'

'It's catchy,' Salman said. 'We can call our Grammy-winning first album "Not Jet You Don't".'

'I don't love Not Jet, but I could live with it,' Babatunde said.

'Same,' Alfie said.

'I'll check with my legal eagle,' Len said. 'But Not Jet should be OK, because you get tribute bands, like The Rolling Clones or Dread Zeppelin, and they never seem to get sued. And I've known enough bands who've torn themselves apart over what to call themselves to appreciate the fact you're all OK with this.'

'So we're all agreed?' Jay said.

'Not jet,' Salman joked, making everyone groan.

22. Black Phone

It was near midnight as Summer's phone erupted. Half asleep, she hooked her arm on the charging lead and knocked the phone off her bedside table as she tried to grasp it.

'Hello,' Summer said, imagining awful news about her nan as she put the phone up to her cheek.

'It's me,' Dylan said, his voice just above a whisper.

'Hey,' Summer said, as she sat up. 'Are you OK? I've been *so* worried about you.'

'You're incredible,' Dylan said. 'When I heard that you didn't pay the money I thought you'd abandoned me. But you're so smart, I never even *thought* about Heather Richardson.'

'Eh?' Summer said, recognising the name, but unable to place it while half asleep. 'I can still pay the money. Are you OK? Whose phone are you using?'

'I've got two feather pillows and I've borrowed a mobile,' Dylan explained brightly. 'JJ sorted it for me, just for tonight.

The guy who owns the phone said ten minutes maximum.'

'Who's JJ, Dylan? I just woke up and I'm not making much sense of what you're saying.'

Dylan told the whole story about getting battered, losing a tooth, and JJ stepping in to save his butt after Heather Richardson made some calls.

Summer was confused, because Theo just said that Dylan had to tough it out.

'I don't think I'm the brilliant one,' Summer said, after a few seconds' thought. 'It *must* have been Jay who told his mum.'

'Whoever it was sorted this, I owe them mega big time,' Dylan said happily, then his tone turned dark, almost tearful. 'I was so scared, Summer. I thought I was going to wind up getting stabbed. When I get out of here it's a new start. No drugs or smokes. Not even a beer. I had an induction at the gym earlier.'

Summer stifled a laugh.

'Why does everyone find the idea of me exercising so funny?'

'It's positive,' Summer said. 'Just, when we were at Rock War Manor, I always remember you as the chubby dude sneaking off for a smoke.'

'I screwed up and let you down,' Dylan said. 'Your nan is right to say I was a dickhead. Poor old girl with cops bursting into her house in the middle of the night . . . I could have given her a heart attack.'

'She'll come around,' Summer said. 'Everyone makes mistakes.'

Now Dylan laughed. 'But most kids get done for nicking six beers out of the Co-op. I steal two kilos of cocaine and get banged up for eight months for nearly killing someone.'

'Four if you behave,' Summer reminded him.

'I've got my phone privilege from tomorrow and you're on the list,' Dylan said. 'You gonna come up and visit me in school hols?'

'It's a trek, but I'll figure it out.'

'I'd give *anything* for a hug from you right now,' Dylan said. 'Or even just to see your face.'

'Same for you,' Summer said, feeling goose bumps down her back.

'And how's the guitar practice? Are you keeping your promise?'

'Not bad,' Summer said sheepishly.

'Did you practise today?'

Summer considered telling Dylan that she'd spent the night at the hospital, but she didn't want to wreck the mood by talking about ambulances and lung infections.

'I practised after dinner,' she lied. 'I might be slightly less terrible by the time you get out.'

'So this was just to let you know things are good,' Dylan said. 'But I'll be back in deep shit if the guards catch me with a phone, so I'll call you legit tomorrow.'

'Sounds good,' Summer said, as she smiled and tipped her head back. 'I can't wait till you get out of that awful place.'

'I was working up the courage to kiss you the evening before I got busted,' Dylan confessed.

Summer burst out laughing. 'How many days is four months?'

'Too many,' Dylan said, then after a pause, 'I kinda love you, Summer.'

Summer felt a big lump in her throat. 'I'm waiting for you,' she told him. 'I kinda love you too.'

*

Eileen was being looked after in hospital and Dylan seemed OK. Summer fell asleep, imagining a scene where Dylan stepped off a train at Sandwell and Dudley and gave her the best kiss ever . . .

She woke up relaxed, with her duvet on the floor and a crack of sunshine through the curtains making a warm line from ankle to shoulder. She smiled as she rubbed a gooey eye and decided on honey, toast and strong tea for breakfast. Then a long, hot shower to help relax before a two-hour history mock . . .

Then the clock sent reality crashing.

'Eight thirty-bloody-seven,' Summer yelled, as she shot out of bed.

She checked the alarm. It was on but she'd slept right through. If she gargled mouthwash and peed, put on school clothes, she could be out of the door in ten minutes. Grab a banana and a can of Pepsi, run to the bus stop. Hair and skin would look shit, but she wasn't that vain . . .

But even if her first bus was good and her second connected well, she'd be lucky to get to school for 9:35, five minutes after the exam started. If the traffic wasn't too bad a taxi would still get her there by 9:15.

She grabbed her phone. She used Sunny Cabs all the time. The controller even recognised Summer's panicked voice and said she could have a car there in three minutes.

Summer dressed, ignored the mound of scruffy hair on her head as she grabbed stuff from the kitchen, pocketed her keys, grabbed the school pack she'd mercifully sorted the night before. After a brain jolt she doubled back, snatching her Velcro wallet off the kitchen counter and anxiously checking that she had enough cash to pay her driver.

She bolted out the front door as a tatty Skoda taxi backed up the driveway. The driver was a woman who'd picked her up a few times before.

'Late for school?' she asked.

'Got it in one,' Summer said, throwing her bag across the back seat and slamming the door. 'Exam at half nine.'

'Traffic's not been too bad,' the driver said. 'I'll cut round the back to avoid the roadworks on Henry Street.'

23. The Magnificent Obernackle

The Rock War empire suffered another dent when Alfie Jopling posted an Instagram message stating that his group were ditching Wilton Music. The thirteen-year-old keyboardist from first season band Jet cited the company's inept handling of Summer Smith's solo album and branded former group director Sean Cox an 'arrogant dickhole'.

A spokeswoman at Wilton Music's Edinburgh headquarters stated that they were delighted with the success of Jet's track 'Strip' in the US singles charts and had had no contact with the group's management. However, Wilton Music's co-owner Harry Napier gave a starkly different message.

Speaking at a press conference, shortly after Napier and the band Terraplane touched down at Edinburgh airport, the notoriously fiery billionaire reacted angrily to questions about Jet and the lacklustre performance of the second season of Rock War.

Crash Landing

Slurring his words, and appearing tired after a thirteen-hour flight from Asia, Napier stated that, 'I've been in this business fifty years. Every artist signed to my companies will be expected to honour their contracts. No artist who broke one of my contracts has earned a dime for the rest of their careers.'

When pressed further, Napier said that the press conference had been called to 'celebrate Terraplane's return to their home city, with the biggest concerts Scotland has ever seen'. He then refused to answer further questions about Jet, or Rock War's ratings battle.

BizBuzz.com

Summer's phone said 09:23 as the taxi rolled up at her school's rear gates. She stuffed an empty Pepsi can and banana peel inside her backpack and told the driver to keep the change from a tenner as she hopped out.

This rear gate got locked just after school started, so Summer was chuffed to sneak through. You were supposed to go to the office and sign a late slip if you missed morning registration, but lining up behind a bunch of deadbeats waiting to fill in a late slip would cancel out the whole point of paying for a taxi and making it to the exam on time.

After a brisk walk across the school's ground floor, Summer made it to the assembly hall and joined a crowd of her fellow year elevens filtering through the main entrance. The school tried to make mock exams exactly like the real ones, partly so that kids took them seriously and partly so they were less freaked out when they started real GCSEs in less than a month.

She was about to sit at one of the fold-out exam desks when she saw Mr Obernackle strolling her way, with an iPad balanced in one palm.

'Summer Smith,' he announced, making it sound like he'd just discovered gravity.

Summer cringed. Obernackle was petty, pompous, and since a recent promotion to deputy head, he'd bought a couple of ill-fitting suits that gave him the air of a dodgy second-hand car salesman.

'Did you register this morning?' he asked.

The school was fanatical about its attendance stats, and Summer sighed, knowing she'd be on the list of pupils who hadn't registered on his screen.

'And I've had no response to the automated call we sent out regarding your absence.'

'My nan's in hospital,' Summer said, neglecting the fact that her first absence on Monday afternoon was to go to the bank to get Dylan's extortion money.

'Really,' Obernackle said, his eyes walking down Summer's legs as teens settled and chairs grated on all sides. 'Because you don't seem to have registered this morning. Did you pick up a late slip at the front desk?'

'I came straight here, because the exam was starting,' Summer said, a touch of desperation creeping into her voice.

'But that isn't school procedure, is it?' Obernackle snapped. 'And what about that footwear?'

The school rule was black shoes, or plain black pumps, but the rule only usually got enforced if you rocked up in something ridiculous, like stilettos, or neon basketball boots. Or if a dickhead like Mr Obernackle wanted to make your life miserable . . .

'Oh come on,' Summer said irritably, raising one dark-blue Nike off the floor. 'I bet there's ten other kids breaking the footwear rule in this room.'

'But I'm *not* talking to them,' Obernackle said. 'I'm talking to you. And while this school has made significant accommodations because of your role as a carer and your show business ambitions, you are not above the rules.'

Summer tutted. 'You've had it in for me since I gobbled your donuts in year nine.'

A couple of girls who'd settled nearby laughed, and Obernackle's shoulders went stiff. 'Your attitude is *not* acceptable. So, now you can follow the correct procedure by going to the front desk and getting a late slip. Then, you can sit outside my office, and when I get there we'll have a serious discussion about your attitude.'

'What about this exam?' Summer said, mourning her ten-pound taxi fare. 'I rushed here because my teacher says I need exam practice.'

'You can discuss taking the paper after school with your history teacher,' Obernackle yelled. 'Now do as I say.'

Summer shook her head and mouthed *wanker* as she headed out. There were a bunch of late arrivals by the door and she angrily shoved a desk out of the way as she pushed through them. She was in a foul mood as she went outside through a side door and crossed a paved courtyard, trying to calm herself with deep breaths as she headed for school reception.

Summer wished she'd gone by the book and got a late slip as she stood in line. The secretary was infuriatingly cheerful as she signed Summer in and gave her a slip to hand to the teacher of her first lesson.

She was tempted to walk back out of the front gate. Or go around to the car park and scrape her door key along the side of the Renault Megane in the deputy head's parking bay. But Summer was only a rebel in her thoughts.

She set off for the row of seats outside Mr Obernackle's office and just when it felt like her day couldn't get any more shit, she found Michelle Wei waiting there.

'Lookey, who it be!' Michelle squealed. 'It's the deserter.'

Summer slumped at the end of the row, as far from her former band mate as she could get.

Michelle had been a member of Industrial Scale Slaughter with Summer. When the band got voted off *Rock War*, Summer reluctantly agreed to sign a solo recording contract. This meant abandoning her mates, but guaranteeing enough money to buy the bungalow and make a decent home with her nan.

Summer tutted as Michelle bobbed up and moved to the seat next to her.

'What happened to your ritzy fee-paying school?' Summer asked.

Michelle smiled a little. 'Apparently, my standards of behaviour didn't meet their *ethos of academic achievement and passionate development of strong, independent young women.'*

'Right,' Summer said, as she noticed Michelle's polka dot tights and All Stars with The Hulk on them.

'The posh schools always kick you out before you get a chance to mess with their exam scores,' Michelle noted. 'Waited just long enough to cash Daddy's non-refundable cheque for winter term.'

'Waiting for Obernackle?'

'The butt wipe himself,' Michelle nodded. 'Though I'm simultaneously honing my plot to take over the world using a giant horseshoe magnet.'

'I hate him *so* much,' Summer sighed.

'They're making me go to anger management classes,' Michelle said.

Summer let this hang, because even Michelle's friendliest overtures could flip in a nanosecond.

Michelle glowered most of the time, but her face softened as she turned towards Summer. 'My therapist taught me this thing,' she began. 'When something makes me mad, I'm supposed to put myself in the other person's shoes and try to see things from their perspective.

'I told my therapist that you were a perfect example of how people are phoney assholes. Then he put me in your shoes and asked me a bunch of questions. And when he asked me if I'd quit the band, if I'd take money to live in a nicer place that was better for the health of the person who'd raised me . . .'

'It was the hardest choice I've ever made,' Summer said. 'You, Lucy and Coco were my only friends.'

'I haven't exactly forgiven you,' Michelle said, as she pulled her feet up to sit cross-legged on the chair. 'But I reckon there are people a lot worse than Summer Smith in this world.'

'I hope so,' Summer said.

'Your album was a gem,' Michelle teased. 'All those great tracks like, "All My Secrets", "Close My Eyes", "Defy the Stars".'

Summer cringed. 'So how's things? Is Industrial Scale Slaughter still playing?'

'We never *officially* broke up,' Michelle said. 'But Coco and Lucy are studying hard for A levels, and *Rock War* was intense. Nobody got their shit together to audition a singer to replace you.'

'Your dad was amazing, paying for my nan to stay in a home so I could go into *Rock War*,' Summer said. 'Which just piles on the guilt about abandoning you.'

'He walked out on our mum on New Year's Eve.'

'Sorry.'

'She crazy,' Michelle smiled. 'I wish *I* could walk out on our mum. She's drunk or in tears most of the time now. I want to live with Dad, but he won this big competition to design a university in Abu Dhabi, so I'm stuck with her drama while he earns the big dirhams.'

Summer smiled. 'Well, my nan's in hospital, my mum's in prison. Maybe we should break out the harmonica and start singing the blues.'

Michelle loved this line and was laughing noisily as Obernackle marched around the corner.

'Glad to see you both taking your situations so seriously,' he snapped.

Michelle stood up and screamed right in Obernackle's face, 'Aww, take the rod out of your ass, you pompous fanny.'

'Sit down,' Obernackle yelled, visibly shaking.

'Mr Obernackle takes it out on us cos his wife's sleeping with the postwoman!' Michelle shouted, as she backed up from the chairs, spinning around and flipping him off. 'And you can't do shit to me because I've got a statement. Special needs, baby!'

'If you walk out of here . . .' Obernackle warned.

'If I leave, you'll do what?' Michelle asked, as she started walking away. 'Are you coming with, Summer Smurf?'

Summer would have loved to defy Obernackle, but she wanted to get out of trouble, not dig herself deeper.

'Call me, Sums,' Michelle said, making a phone with her fingers. 'We should catch up properly. I'm a lonely bunny. I have absolutely no friends for *some* reason.'

'Good to see the anger management is working out,' Summer yelled, giving Michelle a thumbs-up, which earned a furious scowl from Obernackle.

'You!' he gasped furiously, as he unlocked his office. 'Let's get you inside and sort this out.'

24. Best Mum Ever

Jay walked into the kitchen, barefoot in boxers with his phone held up to his face. Hank and June were pictures of misery in front of their homework, while their mum, Heather, loomed over them.

'Ma, did you speak to Vinnie about Dylan?' Jay asked, as he lowered the phone.

'He always had a lot of associates up in Scotland,' Heather said, as Jay moved closer. 'It was a long shot, but I thought I'd mention it.'

'I'm speaking to Summer,' Jay explained. 'I guess your long shot paid off. Dylan's being looked after by some friends of Vinnie and she's *very* grateful.'

'That's a relief,' Heather smiled. 'Give Summer and her grandma my love.'

'Did you hear that?' Jay asked Summer, as he put the phone back to his cheek.

'Mystery solved,' Summer confirmed. 'Tell your mum

I owe her one.'

Jay swooped in and kissed his mum on the cheek. 'I might just have the coolest mum in the world,' he said cheerfully.

A big smile cracked on Heather's face as Jay turned to head out.

'Jay, you crawler!' Hank moaned, which made Heather tap furiously on his homework sheet.

'You'd have both been finished ten minutes ago if you concentrated,' Heather growled. 'I'm sick of this palaver every night.'

'So what happened after Michelle?' Jay asked Summer, passing his older brother Adam at the bottom of the stairs before starting up to his attic bedroom.

'Oh, the usual,' Summer sighed. 'Obernackle venting like it's the end of the world. But the only thing he could actually get me for was navy trainers and not getting a late slip.'

'But getting to an exam on time seems like a legit excuse to skip that,' Jay said.

'Not in Obernackle's petty little world,' Summer sighed. 'But I'm not letting myself get wound up about it. I've got two half-hour detentions, which have been deferred until my nan gets out of hospital, and a letter home.'

'I'd throw that in the bin,' Jay said, as he reached his room and threw his laptop out of the way before crashing on the bed.

'I will,' Summer said. 'I'm not getting my nan all stressed because of that dickhead.'

'And how is your nan?'

'She looks a lot better. The drip and the oxygen have helped. But she's still very weak, and the doctor explained that it's a delicate balance. They don't want to operate until my nan's temperature is more stable, but they have to take the infected clot out as soon as possible.'

'So what can they do?'

'The consultant wants to give it three to five days for the antibiotics to start working. So hopefully they can operate early next week. Then she'll need to stay in for at least another week after the operation.'

'And you're all alone?' Jay said. 'Though you might appreciate that somewhat if you lived in a madhouse with five other kids like I do.'

Summer laughed. 'I think Michelle's going to come round on Saturday. I've written a couple of songs, but my guitar-playing's awful. Plus, Michelle's parents are splitting up, so it's any excuse to get out of the house at her end.'

'Michelle's a whole bag of nuts, but you certainly won't be bored,' Jay said. 'I'm with my dad this weekend. Bailey's coming over and we'll see a movie or something.'

'How is your dad these days?'

'Better,' Jay said. 'He still misses being a cop, but he's got out of that awful security guard job. He's working as a private investigator. Like, workplace theft and stuff.'

'More interesting than sitting in a room watching CCTV screens.'

'Exactly,' Jay agreed.

'So Dylan can call me any time between seven and nine,' Summer said. 'I'd better go in a minute. And is it OK to give Dylan your number so he can add you to his permitted call list?'

Jay checked his bedside clock and saw that they still had three minutes. 'I'd love to speak to Dylan,' Jay said. 'One other thing before you go. You know Terraplane are playing Wembley? Not this coming weekend, the one after.'

'I heard something,' Summer said vaguely.

'Len got loads of free tickets out of Wilton Music. Luckily they were posted just before our big bust-up. I know there's a lot of stuff going on with your nan, but there's a ticket going spare if you want to come down for the day.'

'I'm not sure,' Summer said warily.

'Everyone's going,' Jay said encouragingly. 'And it's in the evening, so you could visit your nan on Saturday morning. You could see the concert Saturday evening, stay at my place overnight and get a train back Sunday morning. Bring a mate along too if you like.'

'The train fare's pretty expensive,' Summer said. 'It depends when my nan has her operation, but it *would* be awesome to come down and visit everyone.'

'Plus you get to see the biggest rock band in the world,' Jay added. 'I'll ask Len to set a ticket aside. And if you can't make it for any reason, I'm sure we'll have no problem finding someone else at short notice.'

'I'll look up the trains,' Summer said, sounding slightly more positive.

'So you give Dylan my best,' Jay said. 'And stay in touch, yeah?'

'Thanks,' Summer said. 'And I'll let you know about the gig.'

25. Kites In Cornfields

Unit B1 had four phones along one wall of the indoor courtyard. Each came with a stool bolted to the floor and a graffitied plastic privacy bubble. Calls were restricted to twenty minutes, though there was nothing to stop you calling straight back if nobody else was in line.

Dylan had just got off from speaking to Summer when one of the night staff rapped on the plastic. It was the badass who'd led the emergency response team after Stuart dragged him into the showers.

'You got a special,' she said, her voice badly muffled by the plastic.

Dylan stepped out of the bubble. 'What does that mean?'

'Santa Claus? How should I know?'

Dylan carried on looking baffled, until the guard put her hands on her hips. 'Special visitor,' she explained, scowling like he was dumb. 'Out of hours.'

'I'm supposed to know that?' Dylan muttered, shaking his head.

Lock-up was due in fifteen minutes. The TV was already off, the showers were busy and another guard was collecting up the ping-pong balls as Dylan got led off the unit via the locked doors by the guards' office.

Visitation was a single-storey block, separated from accommodation units by a pathway with five metres of wire mesh on each side.

Dylan's mouth was healing, but the cold air made it throb and drizzle pelted his face. They passed through a space where inmates got searched for contraband, complete with curtained cubicle for those needing special attention. Then they crossed the deserted main visiting room, with red hexagonal tables and a carpeted play area for little kids. A non-uniformed admin stood by the door of a private room, which was mainly used for trainees to consult with their lawyers.

Dylan's hardass escort altered her tone when she recognised the man inside. Long hair, leather waistcoat, skinny jeans and cowboy boots.

'Jake Blade,' she said, overawed. Then, smiling, 'Is Wilton your boy?'

'For my sins,' Jake said. 'Blade is a stage name.'

Dylan thought his dad looked tired. His hair seemed thinner. His posture was bad and his brow streamed sweat.

'Hey,' Dylan said, sounding bright, but feeling wary.

They made a stilted hug, during which Dylan got overpowered by a strong smell of cigarettes. Then the guard asked for an autograph, and Jake was all smiles as he scribbled his name on the back of a leaflet about sexually transmitted diseases.

'So you're a Bethany,' Jake told the guard, putting on an artificial charm that Dylan witnessed whenever his superstar dad got recognised. 'I always liked that name. Are you being good to my boy? Make sure he eats right? Read him a bedtime story?'

Bethany's laugh was chillingly identical to the one she'd cracked when she smashed Stuart in the ribs with her baton.

'So how's shit?' Jake asked warily, as he sat on a little two-seat sofa and spread his tattooed arms along the back. 'Looks like you've been scrapping.'

'It's no worse than Yellowcote once you get into the swing of things,' Dylan said dismissively. And it was almost true now that he had protection. 'When did you land?'

'Early this morning. I got the message from Mr Nash. Did you get the stuff the office sent?'

'Clothes and snacks,' Dylan nodded.

'Call Mairi whenever you need something,' Jake said.

There was an awkward silence, during which Dylan studied his father's skin. It was natural to lose weight when you were sixty years old and jumping around on stage for two hours a night, but Jake's skin was like old paper and the fingers on the back of the couch kept twitching.

'So you're keeping fit?' Dylan asked finally. 'Lost some weight . . .'

Jake Blade was a bad liar and Dylan saw right through, as

his dad flicked hair off his face and picked at a stain on the couch.

'Jet-lag gets worse as you get older . . .' Jake said, tailing off. 'I'm sorry I wasn't around more while you were in trouble. But tours are like trains, you know? Hundreds of people. Millions of dollaroos. Once you get rolling, the main man can't jump off.'

'I get it,' Dylan said, not really believing it. After all, Jake hadn't been on tour when he sent Dylan off to boarding school first chance he got, and ignored every plea to come home when he'd hated it.

'The lawyer Harry Napier sorted was a good lady,' Dylan said, searching for some common ground. 'She got the attempted murder charge down to aggravated assault. I'd have got a minimum two-year sentence if she hadn't.'

'Good,' Jake said. 'Has your mother been in touch?'

'Nothing,' Dylan sighed.

'She was on the news when I was in Melbourne,' Jake said. 'Over there with your brothers, launching some solo show at the Arts Centre.'

'Good for her,' Dylan said.

He didn't much like his mum, but it pissed him off that his two younger half-brothers got treated so differently. A change of subject seemed the best way not to have to think about it.

'I've stopped smoking and I want to start getting fit while I'm in here.'

'Sounds like a plan,' Jake said, then after yet another pause, 'You know I care about you. I'm just . . .'

Dylan didn't want to fight, but snorted without thinking.

'I didn't grow up in one of those sitcoms,' Jake said, putting his hands on his knees and leaning forward. 'Your grandad worked in the shipyards, got pissed up every night, battered my mum and whipped me with his belt. I'm not built for half-term week at Center Parcs and kite flying in cornfields. I just drift off into scoring a film, or fixing a car.'

'I'm an introvert too,' Dylan said, intrigued to hear his dad opening up. 'I didn't even like hiding behind a keyboard during *Rock War*. I'd never make it as a front man like you.'

'The way I've been hasn't helped you,' Jake said.

'Having ten grand's worth of gear in a bedroom across the hall probably didn't help,' Dylan said. 'But plenty of kids have it worse than me and don't screw up like I did.'

'Maybe Yellowcote was a mistake,' Jake said. 'Sensitive kid like you in a school full of jocks. If you don't want to go back there . . .'

Dylan was irritated that his dad was so out of touch and turned slightly sarcastic. 'Seeing as they caught me with cocaine in my room and *expelled* me, I don't think my return is an option . . .'

'I raised some hell in my day!' Jake said, making a laugh that turned into a retch, then standing suddenly and stumbling into a wall. 'Good times always just around the corner, buddy!'

'Dad, Jesus,' Dylan gasped. 'Are you high?'

Rather than answering, Jake stumbled out of the little room, mumbling about needing to get home because he had a gig to play.

'I'll see you again before the tour goes Stateside,' Jake said. 'Love you, son.'

'Dad, be careful,' Dylan said, watching his dad almost knock the admin flying, then turned back and noticed how the spot on the vinyl couch where his dad had been sitting glistened with sweat.

Dylan had watched documentaries about Jake Blade and skipped through a couple of badly written Terraplane biographies. The band's eighties and nineties tours were legendarily debauched, and Jake's faded appearance suggested that corporate sponsorship and middle-aged audiences for this first tour in twenty years had done nothing to stem the antics backstage.

'Your dad didn't look too well,' Bethany noted, as she escorted Dylan back to B1.

Heroin, Dylan thought to himself as his trainers sloshed through a puddle. *Just like when Mum left.*

Eight Days Later

26. Dave In Truro

. . . *The band known as Jet as named in paragraph XIV (above) have a valid and exclusive contract to release their recorded music through Wilton Music LLP whether under Jet, or any variation of said name.*

This notice demands cessation of all musical recording and performance activity in breach of contract by members of 'The band', as set out above. Failure to acknowledge in writing and comply with the terms of this notice, along with all other provisions of the attached recording contract (Supporting Document A) will result in claim for compensation being filed at the Edinburgh Sheriff Court.

Cease and desist notice, issued to Leonard Crouch and the seven past and present members of Jet by Bogle, O'Hare & Partners, solicitors acting on behalf of Wilton Music

'This is BBC Radio One Extra. I'm Mark Marker and this is

the show where you get to hear the hottest new tracks, the biggest music industry news and of course call in now or Tweet to have *your* say. We've already had a couple of callers talking about season two of *Rock War* on this show . . .'

The balding DJ kept talking as he gave a thumbs-up to a pair of teenagers moving stealthily into his live studio. They each sat at a desk in front of a microphone and an assistant gestured for them to put on headphones.

'. . . I'm sure my next guests will have great insight into the whole *Rock War* saga. Last year, Jay Thomas and Babatunde Okuma were contestants in *Rock War* season one, as members of the band Jet. Guys, a big welcome to my show.'

'Evening, Mark,' Jay told his giant sponge microphone, slightly anxious. Babatunde's *hi* was more confident.

'So what do you two insiders make of *Rock War* season two?'

'I think the musical standard is really high,' Babatunde said. 'With season one being such a hit, thousands of bands applied to get in and the competition is much more professional.'

Jay laughed. 'I doubt rabble like us would have got into season two.'

'So you're saying the standard of music is higher,' Mark said. 'But that doesn't seem to have translated into bigger ratings.'

'Season one was like a train wreck mixed up with a soap opera,' Babatunde said. 'Summer getting run over. Theo going nuts. Rage Cola pulling out and Karen Trim getting involved. That kind of craziness was always going to be a one-off.'

'So the 2017 bands are boring?' Mark asked.

'They're not boring,' Jay said, remembering how media training had taught him that publically criticising people always winds up making you look bad. 'But there seems to be a lack of standout characters.'

'Plus it's all filmed in a studio in Salford,' Babatunde added. 'That's saved Venus TV a lot of money, but we had a great atmosphere, going out to different towns every week. Driving limos cross country with drivers hooting horns at us. Meeting crazy fans and playing all those historic music venues.'

'Interesting stuff,' Mark said. 'But you guys have been in the news this week for other reasons.'

'We're getting our butts sued,' Jay said, making his words extra dramatic.

Mark made an empathetic ummm sound. 'As I understand it, Wilton Music, which is jointly owned by billionaire Harry Napier and the Terraplane front man Jake Blade – who I'm sure isn't short of a few quid either – are suing your band for breach of contract and trying to stop you using the name Jet.'

'That's it in a nutshell,' Jay agreed. 'We've spoken to our lawyers. They say Wilton Music's case is weak, because we're too young to have signed legally binding contracts with a record label. But our lawyers are charging us four hundred pounds an hour, and Wilton Music are sending warning letters to websites, TV and radio stations, trying to stop anyone playing our latest demo tracks.'

'If you take those notices to court, Wilton Music have nothing to stand on,' Babatunde explained. 'But if you're some executive at a radio station, or a kid with a YouTube channel who gets a scary legal letter, very few people will spend time and money getting legal advice. It's easier to just play someone else's music.'

'I see,' Mark said. 'So you're saying it's intimidation tactics.'

'Pure and simple,' Babatunde agreed. 'But we already defied the legal notice by putting a couple of Not Jet demo tracks on YouTube and we've got gigs lined up in Brighton and London.'

'No way we're giving in,' Jay said, as he remembered the message Sue the publicist had told him to hammer home for maximum publicity. 'We're five kids in a band who love music and some billionaire has had a hissy fit and decided to crush us.'

Mark's tone got slightly more serious. 'In the interests of balance, the BBC did ask representatives of Wilton Music to comment on this topic, but so far we've heard nothing back. Going back to you, Jay, I understand that Jet have had a hit in the US of A?'

'We had a spot of luck,' Jay admitted. 'Our track "Strip" got picked up as the theme tune for a new TV show called *Tenured*. The show's been a hit and "Strip" broke into the top ten download chart after we appeared on Jennifer Moon's chat show.'

'*Tenured* starts airing in the UK next month,' Babatunde added. 'So hopefully it'll get us a lot more exposure here too.'

'"Strip" *is* a wicked track,' Mark said energetically. 'I'll give our listeners a chance to hear it in a few moments. But first we're going to take our first call, from Carmine in Edinburgh.'

'One shout-out first if you don't mind,' Babatunde

interrupted. 'I'm sure a lot of *Rock War* fans remember Summer Smith and her grandmother, Eileen. Eileen had major surgery to remove part of her lung on Wednesday. She's recovering well, but I'd like to give my love to Summer and ask your listeners to keep her in your thoughts and prayers.'

'I'm sure they'll do that, and my sympathy to Summer and Eileen too,' Mark said warmly. 'Now Carmine, thank you for waiting, you're on the air.'

'Big fan of the show, Mark!' Carmine gushed, her Scottish accent made sharp by the telephone line. 'And big hugs to Summer and Eileen. I actually called, because I rented one of Harry Napier's Edinburgh apartments when I was first married and that man just did not give a *damn*. Our boiler broke when my oldest was three months old. We had snow on the ground. No heat or hot water and Napier's people never picked up the phone. So I want to wish you boys all the luck. But watch yourselves, because Harry Napier is not a nice man.'

'And did you have a question for the boys?' Mark asked.

'I loved every second of *Rock War* season one,' Carmine said. 'I wanted to ask the boys if they'd stayed friends with the other bands after it ended?'

'As much as we can,' Jay said, keeping the tone bright like his publicist wanted. 'Noah and Sadie are in touch all the time. Eve and Coco. Dead Cat Bounce even rocked up at one of our pub gigs in Camden. Everyone seems to be doing well.'

'Dylan Wilton has had better days,' Babatunde joked, before Jay continued.

'We all live pretty far apart, but we're hoping to organise

some kind of *Rock War* season one reunion during summer holidays.'

'The only band we never hear from are Half Term Haircut,' Babatunde added. 'But they had a snooty attitude even *before* they won the show and started selling out arenas.'

'So cool to hear that the show was a building block for so many friendships,' Mark said, as he leaned forward to cue a track. 'Thanks for your call, Carmine. Before we take our second call from Dave in Truro, let's have some music. This is Jay and Babatunde's band Not Jet, with their American top ten hit, "Strip".'

27. Wembley Way

'This is my dad, Chris,' Jay said, just after Summer and Michelle passed through the ticket gates at London's Marylebone station.

Jay was slightly embarrassed because his dad's ensemble of leather jacket, tie-dye T-shirt, drainpipe jeans and his old police boots was a crime against fashion.

'And I think you've both met Bailey.'

'Briefly,' Summer said, as Bailey faced down with embarrassment.

'I was such a fangirl when I saw you at the *Rock War* finals,' Bailey admitted. 'Sorry!'

'So how's being a private detective?' Michelle asked Jay's dad, as they set off past a flower stall towards the Tube platforms. 'Do you get to carry a big gun?'

'Not allowed to shoot bad guys for some reason,' Chris joked. 'It can be interesting, but it's certainly not glamorous. I spent the last three days in a freezing-cold office watching

CCTV footage of a stockroom. I eventually worked out that the lady they thought was stealing stuff was just reading dockets wrong. The stock they thought she'd stolen had just been put on the wrong shelves.'

'Another victory for the crime lab,' Michelle said in a daft American voice, as she tapped her Oyster card on the electronic entry barrier for the Tube.

'Did you see your nan this morning?' Jay asked, as they stepped on a down escalator.

'For a bit,' Summer said, sounding sad. 'She's still in a lot of pain from her operation. And she's not sleeping much, because the guy next to her in post-op is shouting and moaning the whole time.'

'Sounds like you deserve this break,' Chris told her. 'And if you kiddies are lucky I'll buy you all Half Term Haircut baseball caps.'

Jay laughed. 'Says the guy who was too mean to pay three fifty for ice cream when he took me to *Ben 10 Live*.'

The Metropolitan line was a pre-concert crush. At ninety-five quid for the cheapest tickets, Terraplane were beyond the budget of students and teenagers. This meant the bodies shuffling through tunnels at Wembley Park Tube station were more like an overly busy parents' evening than a monster rock party.

Michelle and Bailey teamed up to snipe at flabby women in leather skirts and gangs of balding men who'd drunk too much and spoke too loud. But Summer didn't join the fun and Jay was concerned.

'Feeling OK?'

'Just tired,' Summer admitted. 'I've got my GCSEs starting, so I've got heaps of revision, but I'm not getting home from the hospital until after seven most nights. And then Dylan calls for at least twenty minutes every night. By the time I've made dinner it's half nine.'

'Dylan seemed OK when I spoke to him on Tuesday,' Jay said.

'I'm so glad he's got protection,' Summer said, as she tapped her overnight bag. 'Does your mum like chocolates? I got her some fancy Thorntons ones as a thank you.'

'I'll scoff 'em if she doesn't,' Jay said, smiling.

Spring sunshine hit buildings as they stepped out of the station, with the giant stadium arch visible at the end of Wembley Way a kilometre away. After a lot of shuffling, the quintet pushed their way into an open-air bar where they met everyone else.

Jay's brothers Kai, Adam and Hank were there, along with both his sisters. Len shook Chris's hand. Jay's mum Heather was there, along with her best friend Mags, Adam's girlfriend, Jay's Auntie Rachel, three of his girl cousins, his four band mates in the newly named Not Jet, plus Babatunde's dad and Salman's big brother.

'Sorry for the hold-up,' Chris told everyone, as coos and hugs broke out. 'The girls' train was twenty minutes late.'

There was a speckling of kids amidst the grey hairs, almost all with their parents and plenty wearing Half Term Haircut T-shirts, or beanie hats. The walk down Wembley Way got interrupted as several groups stopped Summer for selfies. Some Half Term Haircut fans recognised Jet, giving good-natured jeers to stoke the old rivalry, and an older girl even cheekily got Salman, Alfie and Adam to sign her Half Term Haircut vest.

'They must be coining it from merchandise sales,' Jay noted, as the posse rode the escalator up to their seats on the stadium's fancy Club Wembley level.

'More likely that thief Napier is pocketing it,' Salman's brother noted. 'Paying them about two pence out of every pound he makes.'

Although they made jokes about booing Half Term Haircut, all five members of Not Jet were curious to see how Haircut's act had evolved, and more than a little jealous as Owen and his band mates took to the massive stage.

The stadium was three quarters full as a battle broke out between squealing, mostly female, Half Term Haircut fans and jeering rockers who thought having the winners of a TV talent show as Terraplane's support band was a sell-out.

Babatunde, Alfie and Salman made sarcastic comments, but Jay knew Bailey was a closet Haircut fan, so he put an arm around her back and kept his trap shut.

Always more of an indie band, Half Term Haircut had stopped pretending to be rockers after winning *Rock War*. And while Sean Cox's attempt to turn Summer into a pop diva had misfired, he'd done a better job partnering Half Term Haircut with a songwriting team that had given them a catalogue of workmanlike indie tracks, along with peppier numbers that had done well in the charts.

'Fries and hot dogs,' Len announced, as he got back to the seats laden with food. 'Pass 'em along.'

After some switching around so that the little kids could see, Jay's life felt good, with Bailey on his right, Summer on the left and curly fries in his lap. Although he'd spoken to Summer on the phone a lot since Dylan's sentencing, this was the first time they'd hung out since he'd cheated on her.

'Look at those ninnies dancing,' Alfie moaned, as Half Term Haircut boogied with four backing singers. 'I'd rather play proper music to fifty people in a basement than trash like this.'

But it was the kind of music a lot of people did like, and it was being played live by four talented teenagers, in the kind of groove that comes by honing your act night after night on tour. For Jay and his band mates, it was also an uncomfortable reminder that they'd turned down Wilton Music's offer, including the opportunity to support Terraplane on the US leg of their tour . . .

Although Half Term Haircut had released an album and two singles since *Rock War* ended, 'Puff' remained their best-known track and they used it to climax their fifty-minute set.

'Here, Jay,' Babatunde teased. 'This sounds like something *you* might have written.'

Adam was directly behind and jabbed Jay in the back. 'Yeah, bro, are you getting royalties for this?'

'Screw you guys,' Jay said, turning around and flipping

Adam off. 'Maybe Owen ripped off my riff, but I *still* make more than you plebs.'

'Oooh, listen to Big Bollocks,' Babatunde said, as he flicked a curly fry remnant at Jay's head.

'Watch that mouth in front of the kids,' Babatunde's dad snapped, as he pointed at Hank and June.

In best rock star tradition, Terraplane built suspense by making the audience wait forty-five minutes after Half Term Haircut left the stage. Every seat was sold and the sun was setting over the stadium's giant arch as flaming oil drums beckoned Jake Blade and his band mates on stage.

Jay had a girl's head on each shoulder and a tingle down his spine as Blade's face filled four huge video screens.

'Hello London!' Blade shouted, piling on a fake cockney accent. 'Nice weather, innit?'

Blade strummed his guitar and broke into Terraplane's early hit, 'Kitty Litter'.

The eighty-five thousand fans had paid an average two hundred pounds a ticket. Terraplane's three Wembley dates had sold out in minutes, contributing almost fifty million pounds to what the press were hyping as a tour that would beat U2 for the biggest tour ever, and make Terraplane the first band to sell a billion dollars' worth of tickets on a single tour.

The crowd cheered and stamped like people who wanted their money's worth, but doubts were creeping in before the first song ended. By the time the third track kicked off it was clear Terraplane were a long way from their late 1980s prime.

Reviews of the early shows in Asia said that Terraplane's playing was poor. To compensate, Harry Napier had brought in a guitarist to handle most of Blade's lead parts, leaving him to focus on vocals. But his voice was flat and he stooped dead-eyed over his microphone. The other two guitar players seemed embarrassed to share the stage with him, and drummer Dave Ingham struggled to keep time.

'He's worse than Tristan,' Alfie noted, cheerfully slagging off his absent big brother.

Other bands past their prime concealed their weaknesses with pyrotechnics, dancers, hydraulic platforms, video walls and costume changes. But while Harry Napier had set ticket prices sky high, he'd kept production costs down, leaving five guys in their sixties brutally exposed on the massive stage.

Jay yelled in Summer's ear. 'If they weren't making so much money I'd feel sorry for them.'

The cheapest seats in Club Wembley were five hundred quid, but people cut their losses and started trickling out after less than an hour. Up on stage, Jake Blade had a stool brought on to stay upright and one song broke down three times before it got abandoned.

After four more tracks, tradition dictated that Terraplane should return to stage for an encore and play their biggest hit, 'Grace', but the chants of *What a waste of money* were louder than claps or cheers. Jake Blade looked too wasted to care, but it antagonised the drummer, who stepped up to the edge of stage and gave the crowd a flash of his ass, before storming off and telling the stage manager to turn on the house lights.

Crash Landing

The atmosphere heading out was hostile. The merchandise stalls were deserted and the *waste of money* chants continued as thousands shuffled out of the stadium.

'At least we didn't pay for the tickets,' Len said, as he piggybacked a tired Hank through a mass of bodies heading for the Tube.

28. On The Barbie

'I've made beds up for you girls in Jay's room,' Heather explained, when the gang got home to High Barnet. 'He can bunk in with one of his brothers.'

Heather was keen to get her three youngest kids to bed, but Len was the worse for several whisky and Cokes at the stadium. She didn't look pleased when he asked who was hungry, before wheeling a gas barbecue out of the garage and ordering Adam and Jay to go to the nearby Sainsbury's and buy lots of meat.

By the time the brothers got back, to cheers of appreciation, there was a lively scene in the back garden. Tristan and his parents stuck around when they came out to collect Alfie, a couple of neighbours had been invited, and Bailey had called a couple of mates who lived nearby.

After her initial reluctance, Heather started fixing drinks, while her sister Rachel put sausage rolls and nuggets in the oven for the little kids. Jay chanced his arm going into their giant American-style fridge and grabbing a twelve-pack of Estrella lager.

'No more than one if you're under age,' Heather warned, then narrowed her eyes. 'I mean it!'

'Would I?' Jay said cheekily, as he backed out and earned a cheer when he reached the back garden.

His joy didn't last, because the twelve beers went in two seconds and he didn't get one himself.

'We have the wine and the women,' Len shouted cheerfully, as he stood at his barbecue turning sausages with tongs. 'Now where's the bloody song!'

'All our gear's in the cabin at Tristan and Alfie's place,' Salman noted.

'I don't think the neighbours would appreciate a rock band in the back garden,' Heather said stiffly, as she walked into the garden with sliced burger buns in one hand and a wooden salad bowl in the other.

'Who cares about the neighbours,' Jay's obnoxious younger brother Kai shouted at the top of his voice. 'They're all posh butt wipes anyway.'

More cheers went up as Adam came out of the garage with two twenty-four-can packs of Budweiser. Jay opened a can as his cousin Erin approached.

'You must have an acoustic guitar,' Erin said. 'My sisters say they'll sing if I play.'

'Your funeral,' Jay laughed, slugging his beer as Hank raced by. The eight-year-old had been asleep on the Tube home, but the excitement of the barbecue had given him a second wind.

Jay headed up to his room and knocked because he heard voices inside. 'Can I come in?'

'We're doing hot naked lesbian stuff,' Michelle shouted.

'Ignore her, come in,' Summer said.

'What you hiding up here for?' Jay asked, as he looked around his room and saw an unfamiliar lemon duvet cover on his bed and a mattress on the floor with Michelle's overnight bag on it.

'Nice Deadpool briefs,' Michelle said, as she held up a set of Jay's underwear.

'We'll be down in a minute,' Summer said, as Jay went on tiptoes and grabbed an acoustic guitar off the top of his wardrobe. 'There was no signal at the stadium, or on the Tube. Dylan left a long voice message and I wanted to call my nan's ward.'

'She OK?' Jay asked.

'No change,' Summer said. 'I should be there really . . .'

'I saw your nan this morning,' Michelle said, unusually serious. 'She told you to come here and have some fun. You can sing the songs you've been writing.'

'Nah-uh,' Summer said, rocking back on Jay's bed and shaking her head so fast her hair flailed. 'I should burn them, nobody is *ever* going to hear them.'

'They're good, Summer,' Michelle said firmly. 'I don't sugar-coat. If they sucked, I'd have told you.'

Summer continued shaking her head. 'Well, the experts at my record company certainly don't think I'm great. They were supposed to bring my Facebook back up and set a meeting, but they've not even bothered to call me back.'

'What experts?' Jay snorted. 'I'd love to hear your songs.'

'Where's this guitar, Jay?' Erin yelled up the stairs. 'If you don't hurry up, I'll show Bailey your naked baby pictures.'

'Kai already did that,' Jay shouted back.

After hopping downstairs and passing his guitar to Erin, Jay retrieved his beer off the garden wall and put teen boy hunger above his fear of E. coli as he slid one of the first burgers off the grill into a bun and slapped on mustard. He noticed his dad talking to Alfie's dad and Babatunde taking a long shot with the nineteen-year-old biology student from next door, as Erin started strumming guitar.

Erin's big sisters started with a duet of the Beatles' 'Yesterday', then there were some groans as they played Justin Bieber's 'Love Me'. Salman and Erin hammed up a couple of Jet tracks and got warm appreciation before Erin took a bow.

'More,' Salman's brother shouted.

'I can smell barbecue and my stomach is growling,' Erin said, as she leaned Jay's guitar against the garden wall. 'I'm not the only guitar player around here . . .'

As Erin headed off to kiss Tristan and grab a steak, Michelle took the guitar.

'Important announcement,' Michelle shouted. 'I've been helping to arrange two songs that Summer wrote, but she's a shy ickle babykins. Now who wants to hear them?'

Everyone urged Summer on, but she stayed over by the barbecue.

'I'm eating,' Summer slurred, pretending her mouth was full.

Adam was close by and craftily whipped the last sausage off her plastic picnic plate.

'No food left!' Adam shouted, then gave her a gentle shove in the back and began a chant of, 'Summer, Summer . . .'

Summer reluctantly arrived in the middle of the lawn. It was too dark to see her blush, but the night had turned chilly and her breath spiralled as she exhaled in the almost dark.

Michelle spent a couple of seconds adjusting Jay's guitar strap to her short frame, then started a simple intro. Erin's sisters could belt out a decent tune, but the difference between their voices and Summer's was like comparing a pointy stick with a lightsaber.

Summer's voice had been amazing when she'd first auditioned for *Rock War*. Now she was older and had proper singing lessons under her belt, it seemed to fill the whole sky. Hank and June stopped running around. Bailey was holding Jay's hand and squeezed it tight the instant Summer opened her mouth.

'You don't realise the power when she's on TV,' Bailey gawped.

Summer's two original songs drew decent applause, but this was a party. People wanted songs they knew, and she felt a surge of confidence and broke into 'Someone Like You', by Adele. There were chants for more as Summer walked back towards the food, but Len had passed his barbecue tongs to Babatunde's dad and took the guitar off Michelle.

Len preferred playing sitting down, and looked wobbly as he squeezed into a plastic garden chair.

'Might be a little rusty,' he said apologetically. 'And I've had a couple of drinks . . .'

Len showed why he'd once been a highly paid session musician by picking an elaborate piece of Spanish classical guitar music. He then flipped to an almost impossibly fast part of Rossini's *William Tell Overture*. When that broke down in tangled fingers and drunken laughter, Len stood and sang a barnstorming 'Knees Up Mother Brown' while occasionally urging his bemused audience to sing along.

Bailey and Jay had backed inside to stay warm.

'I love your crazy family,' Bailey told Jay, so close that her lower lip touched his earlobe and she turned the accident into a gentle kiss. 'But I wanna go make out.'

'Summer and Michelle have got my room,' Jay reminded her, as Bailey tugged gently on his arm.

'It's a big house,' she smiled. 'I'm sure we'll find somewhere.'

29. Hot Rashers

BLADE'S BANDITS

'RIPPED OFF' FANS VENT FURY AFTER
WEMBLEY GIG FIZZLES

. . . *Terraplane's success was built on three classic albums and the brilliance of their live performances of the late eighties and early nineties. But fans hoping that Terraplane's mediocre Japanese shows were just cobwebs being shaken off by a band that hadn't played together in over twenty years were sadly disappointed by last night's Wembley show.*

Front man Jake Blade appeared clammy and bored in a pre-concert press conference, which publicists ended abruptly when Blade was asked if he had a drug problem.

On stage, the legendary guitarist had been relieved of most playing duties, but struggled to sing, at times repeating verses and scrambling his own lyrics.

Crash Landing

While most of those leaving Wembley Stadium quietly resigned themselves to a poor return on their record-breaking ticket outlays, police say three arrests were made after toilets inside the stadium were vandalised, while in a separate incident a programme seller was bundled to the ground and several hundred £35 Souvenir Programmes were torn up and trampled by angry fans . . .

News on Sunday, 8 May 2017

Jay woke in a strange spot, shirtless, with no sign of Bailey, and a crochet cushion made by his late grandma as a pillow. He thumped his head on a shelf lined with fake spider plants as he sat up, swearing to himself as he realised he was in the walk-in wardrobe at the back of his mum's bedroom.

Len used the space as an office, so there was a small desk where clothes were supposed to hang and shelving populated with file boxes and photos. Most pics were of Hank, Patsy and June, but a few ancient ones showed Len in the studio with bluesmen and rock gods.

Jay's phone had dropped out of his pocket and died overnight. The walk-in had no window, so he had no concept of time as he nudged the sliding door, hoping it didn't squeak. It was a genius place to make out, but the only way out was by crossing Len and Heather's bedroom and he had no idea if they were asleep.

The light coming through the bedroom's wooden shutters indicated morning. Jay buttoned his shirt before sliding the wardrobe door a little further and peeking towards the bed.

The covers were all on the floor and he could see Len's bare bum rocking between his mum's legs. They were . . .

AAAAAARGH . . .

Jay wished his brain had an erase button as he lurched back inside the wardrobe. He'd always assumed that his mum and stepdad were sexually active, but he certainly didn't want to see the act in all of its flabby glory.

He might have waited it out, but one and a half beers had worked their way through his system. After briefly considering relieving himself in Len's shredder bucket, Jay pushed the wardrobe door back as quietly as he could, then did the fastest crawl of his life while his mum made sex noises.

Mercifully, they hadn't locked the door and Jay was out into the hallway before Len noticed the door moving and yelled, 'What have I told you kids about knocking?'

'Close the effing door!' his mum added frantically.

'Rank,' Jay told himself, as he realised he'd buttoned his shirt in the wrong holes.

He instinctively went for his own room. His hand was almost on the doorknob as he remembered that the girls were staying. After a mighty pee, Jay wandered downstairs, where Hank and June were in their pyjamas watching Disney Channel.

'Look at Mr Lipstick Face,' June said, cracking a gap-toothed grin.

'Dirty boy!' Hank added.

Jay looked in a mirror, wiping his face on his shirt cuff as his dad stepped through from the kitchen.

'Had a few drinks so I slept on the couch,' Chris explained.

'Is Bailey around?' Jay asked.

'Her dad picked her up at about two,' Chris said. 'She said you were sleeping and she didn't want to disturb you.'

'Have I got all the lipstick?' Jay asked.

Chris took a closer look before nodding. 'Hank and June want bacon sandwiches. Your mum won't mind, will she?'

Jay shook his head. 'I'll give you a hand with the bread.'

Chris wasn't familiar with the kitchen, so Jay found a frying pan and cooking oil. The bacon was sizzling and Jay was buttering as his dad sidled up.

'You and Bailey have been going out for a while,' Chris asked warily. 'Are you . . . you know, careful?'

Jay smiled awkwardly. 'Bailey won't give me a chance to be careful, so don't worry about being a granddaddy just yet . . .'

'It's just, when your son comes down pasted in lipstick . . .'

'Who's covered in lipstick?' Adam asked, as he wandered in, shirtless and with one hand buried down the front of Abercrombie jogging bottoms. 'Bacon smells good!'

'Hank and June have dibs on the first lot,' Chris said. 'But I can cook more.'

Bacon waft drew more souls to the kitchen. Kai brought the benefits of his deodorant-free lifestyle to the morning air and was followed closely by Michelle.

'Concert sucked, but the after party made up for it,' Michelle said cheerfully.

Heather was all smiles as she reached the kitchen. Dressed in a pink bathrobe, she gave Chris a kiss as Jay tried to blot out the horror he'd seen upstairs.

'Nice to come down and find someone else doing breakfast,' Heather said brightly, then seemed less cheerful as she peered out the back door at the mess in the garden. 'But you'd better not think muggins here is clearing up all of that lot.'

'Why not?' Kai asked tactlessly. 'You've not got a job since you sold the chip shop.'

Heather thumped Kai on the back. 'And look who just volunteered to collect all the empty bottles and put them in the recycling.'

'You wish,' Kai grunted.

Jay took a pile of bacon sandwiches through to the living room and set them down for Hank and June.

'Yours are the ones without ketchup, on this side of the plate,' Jay told his younger sister.

'What kind of idiot doesn't like ketchup?' Hank sneered.

'You're the idiot,' June snapped back as she flipped her brother off.

As Jay backed off from the bickering, he saw Summer standing in the living room doorway, bare-legged in his Florence and the Machine T-shirt.

'I hope you don't mind me borrowing it,' Summer said warily. 'I got HP sauce down my top last night.'

'It's a man's XL,' Jay said, smiling. 'Keep it, it hangs off me like a sack. Did you have fun last night?'

'Sure,' Summer nodded. 'Do you know much a taxi from here to Marylebone station would be?'

Jay sensed that she was upset. 'Quite pricy I'd have thought,' he said, making a big gap with his hands. 'Marylebone is central London, and we're in High Barnet, which is about as far north as London goes. But don't sweat it, you can pick up the Tube when you're ready to head home.'

'The ward just called,' Summer explained. 'My nan had a rough night. She's been coughing a lot of blood and ruptured her stitches. There's not much I can do, but I really want to be with her.'

'Of course,' Jay said, before yelling towards the kitchen, 'Mum!'

Summer told Heather that there was a train from Marylebone to Birmingham in fifty minutes, but that it would take almost three hours because there was maintenance work on the line. Then she'd have to get a bus or taxi to the hospital.

'Aren't the trains from Euston to Birmingham faster?' Jay asked.

'They are, but we're banned from using that line,' Summer explained. 'After our tussle with Tina the train guard . . .'

Summer's news filtered quickly into the kitchen and Chris stepped through, wiping greasy fingers on a kitchen towel.

'There'll be no traffic this early on a Sunday,' Chris said. 'I could have you there in a two and a bit hours.'

'But you'd have to drive all the way back,' Summer said.

'Don't sweat it,' Chris said. 'Car's outside and I'm off work till Tuesday. If someone takes over bacon duty, we can leave as soon as you're ready.'

30. No Pain No Gain

Dressed in shorts and a hoodie, Dylan sat astride a weight bench as Costco grabbed two hexagonal dumb-bells from the springy gym floor.

'Rest on your shoulders, then push up,' Costco said, as Dylan wiped sweat off his brow. 'Twelve and half kilos.'

JJ and a few other guys watched as Costco handed the weights over. Dylan's arms wobbled as he curled the two weights up to his shoulder.

'No jerky movements,' Costco warned. 'Keep it smooth. As many reps as you can.'

Dylan made a big huffing sound as he pushed both dumb-bells up above his head, turning his wrists so that the weights met with a gentle clank when he hit full stretch.

'Gently down,' Costco said. 'One.'

The next four reps weren't too bad. Dylan's arms started to shake on five and six and by seven he was fighting for air. But the gym instructor had explained how your muscles grow back stronger when you damage them. Hence the phrase, *no pain, no gain.*

'Three more,' Costco said.

'You've got it!' Wilfred added.

Dylan felt like he was putting his past behind him. He wanted to be strong enough to fight his own battles and look after Summer. The sweat beading on his face was clearing out nicotine, cocaine and the whole lazy mess that he'd made of his life.

'Nine.'

'Christ,' Dylan gasped, as he lowered the weight and started another rep.

Sweat trickled into his eye and his neck and shoulders hurt like hell as the weights clanked again.

'Ten,' Costco said. 'Go for two more.'

'Awwwww . . .'

'Come on, you soft shite,' JJ roared. 'We'll make a man of you yet.'

'Eleven,' Costco roared, shaking his fist.

Dylan tried for number twelve, but he could only push the weight level with the top of his head before his arms gave out. He let a weight drop on either side of the bench and raised a huge breath as he grabbed his water bottle off the floor.

'God that *hurts*,' Dylan gasped, as he stood up, clutching his stomach.

His thighs ached from squats, his back was sore and his arms could barely move. But it was a good, wholesome kind of pain.

'A week ago you could only do six,' JJ said, as he took Dylan's spot on the sweat-smeared weight bench. 'Gimme the thirties.'

Dylan's achievement seemed less impressive as he watched JJ's stocky arms pump twenty reps with over twice the weight. He drank more water as he sat against the back wall. A little guy called Connor, who was on B2, passed Dylan a crumpled copy of *News on Sunday*.

'See this one about your dad?' Connor asked.

With limited TV and no internet, newspapers were the main source of information in Whitburn Training Centre. The article headline was *Blade's Bandits*, but Dylan's eye was drawn to a little white-on-black timeline printed alongside the article and titled *Blade's Drug Scrapes*.

Connor irritatingly read aloud over Dylan's shoulder.

'Nineteen eighty-one arrested for possession of cocaine, Edinburgh. Eighty-five, Terraplane roadies arrested with heroin and marijuana at JFK airport. Eighty-nine, Blade and two band mates arrested. Nineteen ninety, twelve weeks' rehab in Barbados. Ninety-three, deported from Manila after found in possession of cocaine.'

Costco seemed impressed. 'Proper lad, your old man.'

'Bet he shagged about a thousand women on those crazy tours as well,' Connor added enviously. 'Open the stage doors and there's twenty tits flashing in your face!'

'My dad's a dick,' Dylan said sourly, as he tossed the paper. Mentally adding, *And I'm an even bigger dick for going down the same path . . .*

There was no school or workshops on Sunday, so JJ's crew stayed in the gym for another hour, during which Dylan did an ab workout and some more sets for his arms and chest. When the older lads went off to shower in unit A, Dylan washed with Connor on unit B, then ran his sweat-drenched kit under the showers so that it didn't stink up his cell.

Dylan had serious muscle ache as he sat on his bed, draping his wet gear from a shelf, before pulling on clean trackies and T-shirt and wandering over to the phones. Fat Man was coming out of a visit with his mum and nodded dopily as their paths crossed. Stuart had been moved north to Dingwall after getting out of hospital and his crew was nothing without him pulling the strings.

'You going up to lunch in a bit?' Fat Man asked. 'Best feed of the week Sunday lunch, I reckon.'

'Gotta call a pal first,' Dylan said.

Fat Man had smashed a new arrival's face into the vending machines the previous night and Dylan would have loved to tell him to piss off. But most of JJ's crew lived on unit A, so it was still safest not to make enemies.

'Maybe I'll see you up there,' Dylan said.

'Ma brought me a big Chocolate Orange if you want some,' Fat Man said.

Dylan shook his head at this pathetic attempt to make friends as he reached the phones. A lot of trainees got visits on Sundays and others had already headed up to lunch, so he had the pick of four phones.

He'd missed speaking to Summer the night before, but he

figured she'd be travelling home and had already decided to leave calling her until early evening. After tapping in his inmate ID and PIN, he selected Jay's mobile from his list of permitted callers.

'Dylan, my man,' Jay said warmly, as he grabbed his phone with the charging lead sticking out of the bottom.

'Was the gig as shite as the papers make out?' Dylan asked.

'Wasn't the best,' Jay said, reluctant to slag off Dylan's dad.

'Summer left a while back,' Jay said. 'My dad's driving her straight to the hospital in Dudley. Her nan had a bad night.'

'Really?' Dylan said. 'That sucks. Eileen's a good lady.'

'Summer doesn't get much luck,' Jay agreed. 'She enjoyed the day though. Had a little barbecue after the gig. She even sang a couple of the songs she's been working on with Michelle.'

'Aww,' Dylan said, looking up mournfully at blobs of gum and KILL ALL FAGS scratched into the plastic privacy dome around his head. 'I'd give *anything* to have been there with everyone.'

'You will, soon,' Jay said, feeling tactless for mentioning the good time they'd all had. 'Everything OK at your end?'

'Could be a lot worse,' Dylan said. 'I've been pumping weights every day. My whole body aches.'

'You?' Jay said, stifling a laugh.

'Why does everyone find it funny?' Dylan said indignantly. 'And don't mention the weights to Summer. I just told her I'm using the rowing machines to keep fit.'

'Why the secret?'

'I want to surprise her when I get out,' he explained.

Jay cracked up laughing. 'So she's expecting your usual chubby ass and you come out all ripped! That will be so many kinds of awesome.'

'If I keep at it . . .' Dylan said, laughing awkwardly. 'But there's something else I wanted to mention. Harry Napier is suing you guys, right? Claiming you can't call yourselves Jet or release any new music.'

'Don't worry about that,' Jay said. 'You've got your own problems.'

'Remember what I told you on the night of the *Rock War* final?' Dylan asked. 'Remember, about QStat? And Harry Napier and my dad fixing the voting?'

'Sure,' Jay said. 'But you threatened to go public and they put a stop to it.'

'Even so, if that information became public it would be dynamite. *Rock War* is running in ten countries now. It's making Napier and my dad millions and would be a major scandal if the media found out that they'd tried to rig the voting. I'd bet that every TV company they've sold the show to overseas would want to sue the shit out of them as well.'

'Sue, our new publicist, wants us to pitch ourselves as victims, because she says the media is looking for stories to knock *Rock War* down,' Jay explained.

'So put yourself in Harry Napier's shoes,' Dylan said keenly. 'What's a little scuffle with Sean Cox over Jet's recording contract, compared to the hundreds of millions that *Rock War* is generating?'

'So you're saying we should somehow try and blackmail Napier?'

'Napier is such a prick,' Dylan fumed. 'He's *supposed* to be my godfather. He supposedly has all kind of links to the Scottish underworld, but did he lift a finger to help me when I was about to get my head stomped in? You and Summer are the best friends I have, and it was your ma who stepped up and saved my sorry ass. I owe you guys, so I'm on your side in this.'

'How strong is your evidence?' Jay asked.

'I guess the word of a convicted teen coke head doesn't count for much,' Dylan admitted. 'But my dad's not a computer boffin. He's had the same password for years, and if I could get back into the Wilton Music offices, or access my dad's laptop, I bet I could find a ton of evidence . . .'

'I'll bet Napier has covered up since you found out last time,' Jay said. 'And you are *kind of* in prison for at least the next three and a half months. Can you even get online?'

'No chance,' Dylan said, slightly deflated. 'There's a couple of illicit phones around, but there's no mobile broadband out here in the middle of nowhere. But I was thinking, if I told you everything I found out back in 2016 and you showed it to your dad? He's a private detective now, right? Maybe he could get more evidence.'

'I suppose I could ask,' Jay said warily. 'But last year my dad spent two nights hiding in a skip trying to catch fly-tippers and wound up getting bitten by a rat. He's not exactly Sherlock Holmes . . .'

Dylan laughed. 'I'll write down all the details I can remember and post them, so you can show to your dad. No harm done if I'm wasting my time, cos there's no shortage of that in here.'

31. Break A Leg

Summer spent Wednesday doing revision lessons and headed straight to the hospital after school. Eileen was conscious, but her face was pained. Every breath brought the rattle of blood and mucus inside her lungs and she didn't sense Summer's presence until her granddaughter took her hand and squeezed gently.

She had a pack stuffed with revision guides, and exams starting in ten days, but her nan's tormented breathing was awful to listen to and tears welled in her eyes. There had been bad times before, but Summer had never seen her nan so completely out of it.

She'd got as far as resting a maths textbook on her lap when a young nurse came in, with a fresh drip bag and a packaged syringe filled with antibiotics.

'Eileen's very sedated,' the nurse explained politely. 'We've given her opiates for pain relief and to stop the cough reflex.'

'I still don't know why she's like this,' Summer explained

intently. 'I waited here till quarter to eleven last night. Dr Kendall was supposed to come and speak to me, but then I found the senior nurse and she said he'd already gone home for the night.'

'I'm really sorry about that,' the nurse said, as she rolled back Eileen's sheets. 'Did you leave your mobile number?'

'I had a missed call,' Summer explained. 'We're not allowed phones in school.'

The nurse looked slightly surprised. 'Even in situations like this?'

Summer shook her head. 'If there's an emergency you're supposed to hand your phone in at the admin desk and then one of the school secretaries will come and find you. But you have to queue up to hand your phone in, then queue up again to collect it at the end of the day. I just leave it on vibrate in my bag, but the deputy head has it in for me at the moment.'

'Did you return the call?'

'Hospital switchboard,' Summer explained. 'They just said Dr Kendall was busy and would call me back again later. I'd skip school, but my GCSEs are about to start.'

The nurse nodded sympathetically as she dropped the used syringe into a grey bin. 'You look exhausted.'

'How can I sleep?' Summer asked, shaking her head.

'I'll see if I can find someone familiar with your grandmother's case and ask them to come and speak to you,' the nurse said.

Summer stifled a sob as the nurse headed out. She grabbed

her phone to try and distract herself and saw a message from Jay:

Hope your nan is improving. Seen this? Not sure if Dylan knows yet.

The link at the end of the message sent Summer to the Channel Six News website. There were two pictures at the top. The first showed City of Manchester stadium. The second was a shot of Terraplane on stage in the nineties.

TERRAPLANE CRASH LANDS

'EXHAUSTED' FRONT MAN JAKE BLADE FALLS OFF STAGE IN MANCHESTER REHEARSAL
WRIST AND RIGHT LEG FRACTURE LEADS TO CANCELLATION OF REMAINING UK TOUR DATES
VIDEO FOOTAGE SHOWS BLADE LOOKING COMATOSE BEFORE FALL

Summer was about to start reading the article below the sub-headlines when her nan made a gargling noise and jolted upwards.

'Shit,' Summer gasped, diving across the bed as blood streamed out of Eileen's nose and an alarm sounded. 'Nurse!'

Summer raced out into the corridor, almost crashing into a white-coated duty doctor and the nurse she'd just spoken to.

'Honey, move clear of the bed,' the doctor ordered, as she raced across.

As the nurse cancelled the screaming alarm, the doctor yanked Eileen up in the bed and hit her gently on the back. Eileen made a slight cough and more bloody mucus streamed down her chin.

'Lungs are full of fluid,' the doctor shouted. 'She's drowning.'

Summer shook with fear as a second nurse ran into the room.

'O_2 is critical,' the first nurse said.

'We need a vacuum pump, fast,' the doctor shouted. 'Her lungs are full of fluid. She can't breathe.'

As one nurse rolled a machine in from the hallway, the doctor tilted Eileen's head back and the other nurse tore a long plastic tube out of sterile packaging.

'Mrs Smith, we need to suck out the blood and mucus that's built up in your lungs. You'll feel some discomfort as this tube passes down your throat.'

As Eileen gagged, Summer noticed fresh blood on her nan's hospital gown. Summer felt like she'd faint if her back wasn't up against the wall.

'Summer, you need to step outside,' a nurse said, as she wheeled the pump up to where Summer had been sitting and plugged it into a wall socket.

'Is the extractor working?' the doctor shouted anxiously, as Summer grabbed her schoolbag. 'Is this the one that keeps breaking?'

The nurse reached around and flipped a switch, setting off a bank of lights and a sigh from the electric pump.

'Thank you, Sarah,' the doctor said, as she started connecting the tube to a socket on the front of the machine.

Summer was in the doorway and glanced back as Eileen made an unbearable moan.

'I'm sorry, Mrs Smith. This will be painful but we *must* clear your lungs.'

As the door shut, Summer stumbled across the hallway, face first into a wall. She was shaking and thought she was going to be sick. Her legs were weak and she clutched her stomach and bent forward, sobbing uncontrollably.

'OK, we're drawing the fluid,' the doctor shouted from inside. 'This is looking good.'

'Try to hold still, Mrs Smith.'

The next thing Summer knew, she had an arm around her back. It was a woman she'd spoken to a couple of times, whose father was the patient in the next room.

'Calm down, pet,' she told Summer softly. 'I'll walk you up to the comfy seats at the end. They know what they're doing. I'm sure everything will be fine . . .'

32. In Car Urination

Chris Ellington's car had remains from a Burger King breakfast and a Subway lunch. His big flask of black coffee was almost drained, much of it into his Travel John in-car urinal. His instructions were to sit tight, waiting for a man named Jack Green to leave his flat, then call his office and let them know.

Since Chris wasn't running this case, he had no idea who Mr Green was, or why someone wanted to know when he left his apartment. When his mobile rang, Chris hoped it was his boss telling him to call it a day and head home, but he was surprised to see an international number.

'Hello?' he said suspiciously, half expecting a sales call, or a conman from Bangladesh telling him that he had a virus on his laptop . . .

'Beverley Cross-Holland,' a gruff smoker's voice announced. 'I got this weird call via my accountant's office, saying that you wanted to speak to me on an urgent matter.'

'It's a little complex,' Chris explained, as he sat up in his car seat. 'It's a matter relating to Dylan Wilton, and my son, Jay Thomas.'

It took Bev a couple of seconds to place the names. 'You're Jay Thomas' dad?' she said suspiciously. 'Why are you contacting my accountant?'

'I couldn't find you on the UK voters register,' Chris explained. 'But I tracked you down through a Companies House document, relating to the graphics company you set up with Glenn Horowitz a few years back.'

'That's a man I'd care not to be reminded of,' Bev said.

'And judging by the display on your phone, I'd say you've moved to work abroad.'

'I'm in Australia, working graphics on *Super Chef Down Under*. No offence, Mr Thomas – if that really is your name – but this all seems a mite dodgy.'

'Dylan Wilton told me that besides working graphics on *Rock War* season one, you were involved in setting up the voting systems for Venus TV.'

Bev laughed. 'Dylan was my little smoking buddy. I might, at one point, have shown him something I shouldn't have.'

'The QStat application on your mobile phone,' Chris said knowingly, as he kept one eye out for Mr Green leaving his apartment.

'Is this call being recorded?' Bev asked suspiciously.

'Absolutely not.'

'It's just weird that Jay Thomas' dad knows how to track me

down in Australia. That's more like something a journalist could do.'

'I was a police officer,' Chris explained. 'You may remember, there was a scandal during the series? I had to resign and I now work as a private investigator.'

'I don't remember,' Bev said. 'But there were three scandals a week on that series. It was hard to keep up.'

Chris could hear Bev tapping keys at the other end of the line.

'I just Googled your scandal,' Bev said, laughing. 'Naughty boy, letting a criminal off in return for sex. And Jay was the result . . .'

'I was only nineteen,' Chris said. 'My point is this. I received information from Dylan Wilton yesterday, outlining a lot of dodgy practices in the voting on *Rock War*. He gave me your name and said you almost certainly know more about it than he does.'

Bev huffed. 'What good would it do, dragging all this up now? The show's over.'

'You've got a computer in front of you. Google *Harry Napier sues Jet* and see what he's doing to my son's band. His case is weak, but he's crippling us with legal bills and we're looking to get some leverage over him.'

'Jay's a nice kid,' Bev admitted, as she Googled, then started reading a story from a British newspaper website.

'My boy just wants to play his music. If you were willing to make a written statement . . .'

Bev seemed uncomfortable. 'The only way I see this working

for you, is if you're trying to blackmail Harry Napier.'

'We prefer not to use that word,' Chris said, before coughing. 'If this worked out, you'd be looked after financially.'

'You don't understand TV, Mr Thomas,' Bev said firmly. 'Reality shows are a small world, where everyone knows everyone else. When Dylan found out about this *alleged* vote rigging I got called in by Karolina Kundt, who was running *Rock War* at that time.

'Karolina knows everyone, and she tore into me, making it clear that Harry Napier was insanely angry, and that if I ever opened my mouth, I would never get another job in the industry. So I'm sorry about Jay's predicament, but I'm not willing to throw my career away to help him.'

'That seems reasonable,' Chris admitted.

'Harry Napier is not a nice man,' Bev sighed. 'I really do wish you well with this.'

'I get it,' Chris said, as he made his detective brain work for a different angle. 'I'm sorry to have disturbed you. Is there any other snippet of information that might help us, *without* dragging you into this personally?'

Bev paused for several seconds before answering. Chris could hear her drumming fingers on something.

'There was an unpaid runner,' Bev said thoughtfully. 'A Spanish girl named Ines Terrazas. Probably twenty years old. She was studying TV production at York uni, or Leeds I think. She worked in Karolina's office for about ten weeks during Battle Zone. Ines got fired, because she was making a bunch of overseas calls, after she paid some con artist who said he could get her short film into Sundance.'

Chris sounded baffled as he jotted *Ines Terrazas* on his note-pad. 'Sundance?'

'It's a massive indie film festival, in Colorado,' Bev explained. 'It shouldn't be hard to track her down, Mr Investigator.'

'And Miss Terrazas knew what was going on?'

'She's your smoking gun. *If* you can persuade her to talk,' Bev said. 'And she was mightily pissed off when Karolina fired her, so the odds may be in your favour.'

Chris started to smile. 'I'm so grateful. If you ever need anything looked into . . .'

'Jay and his band mates are good kids,' Bev said firmly. 'But I've probably said more than is good for me, so the only help I need from you is to keep my name out of this.'

33. Great Expectations

Nash had helped Dylan stay sane when he first got sent down, and although there was always tension between guards and trainees, it was hard to find anyone on the unit with a bad word to say about him. But while the guard was well respected, his attitude to Dylan cooled after Freckles got badly beaten and JJ's crew had taken him under their wing.

'Wilton,' Nash said, as Dylan stood in the guards' office doorway. 'Or should I start addressing you as Mr Universe?'

Dylan held a crumpled copy of a newspaper, opened to an article about his dad falling off stage. Connor was looming behind, which made Nash wary, because inmates often caused some sort of distraction around the office while their friends were up to something.

'Sir,' Dylan began respectfully. 'Some of the guys were saying that if your parent is sick you can get compassionate leave and go visit them.'

Ignoring this, Nash stepped around Dylan, looked down

the hallway and then eyeballed Connor. 'And you're here because . . . ?'

'Just with my pal, Dylan here,' Connor said.

'Well I'm sure *Dylan 'ere* can speak for himself. So buzz off,'

Nash beckoned Dylan into the office as Connor skulked off.

'I'm assuming your falling under JJ's protection isn't purely a benevolent arrangement?' Nash asked, as he opened a small metal cabinet drawer and pulled out a *compassionate leave* form.

'They've been nice to me,' Dylan said, deliberately steering clear of any facts.

'If you're hanging with that crew, don't expect my assistance if you get yourself into trouble again,' Nash warned.

Dylan felt like reminding Nash that he'd almost got his head caved in in the showers while Nash had been *looking out for him.* But there seemed no point winding the guard up when he was fishing for a day out.

'I assume your father's condition isn't life-threatening?' Nash asked, as he put a form on a desk.

'Does it have to be?' Dylan asked.

'If your father was about to die, I'd take the form straight up to the governor's office for immediate consideration. Normal applications take a day or two to process.'

Dylan sat at a desk, pulled a scratchy biro out of a pen pot and wrote his name and inmate number on the form. After that came a ton of boxes with questions about who he wanted to visit, what prevented the person from visiting the prison, who would accompany Dylan during his release. At the end of the form, Dylan had to make a personal statement on why he wanted to see his dad and finally he had to tick to say that he understood that he faced a loss of remission if he didn't obey all conditions of a conditional release order, or if anything he'd written on the form wasn't true.

'Makes a bloody change having a kid who can write clearly,' Nash said, as he took the completed form.

'Do you think the governor will grant it?' Dylan asked.

Nash shrugged. 'A broken leg and drug rehab aren't much, but being your only family member might swing it your way if he's in a good mood.'

'Worth a shot then, sir,' Dylan said, as he stood up.

'Watch you don't get tangled in something with JJ's crew,' Nash warned, as Dylan headed out. 'I expect you'll have the governor's response by the time school kicks out tomorrow.'

*

The only thing Jay hated more than his Thursday afternoon games lesson was getting naked for a shower afterwards. But it was last lesson, so it wasn't hard to sneak off unwashed and he still wore trainers and had mud-splattered football socks tucked into trackie bottoms as he rode home to High Barnet on the Tube.

Jay's uniform was balled up at the top of his backpack and he rummaged around until he found his phone. After taking it off silent, he hoped to find a message from Summer on how her nan was doing, but there was nothing.

He pulled the copy of *Great Expectations* he was suffering

through for English lit as his train emerged from the underground part of the Northern line. His phone started ringing as they pulled out of Highgate and there was a woman with a Canadian accent on the other end.

'Jay Thomas?'

'Speaking,' he said cautiously. After being on *Rock War*, he always suspected that anyone calling out of the blue was a journalist digging for dirt.

'I'm Halley Roche, in Vancouver. I work with Purple Egg productions.'

Jay knew Purple Egg from somewhere. 'I'm sorry, I'm a bit confused.'

'I'm one of the producers on *Tenured*.'

'Oh,' Jay said, looking wary as some dodgy year nine kids came through from the next carriage and sat opposite. 'Purple Egg was the name on my royalty cheque.'

'I hope you don't mind me calling you directly,' Halley said. 'My assistant called Wilton Music four times, but nobody has returned our calls. I hope you don't mind, but I eventually wrangled your number out of a chum who works on the *Jennifer Moon* show.'

'Right,' Jay said. 'I'm actually on a train right now, so this might cut out if we go through a tunnel. I thought *Tenured* was American.'

'We film the show in Canada because taxes are lower here,' Halley explained.

'So are you just calling to say *hi*, or . . . ?'

'I have two reasons to be calling you. First off, me and some of the *Tenured* team are flying to the show's UK launch in a couple of weeks. We'd love to touch base with your publicity people, because we think having a theme tune written by a UK band is a great publicity angle for the show.'

The kids sitting opposite were glowering, and Jay had a horrible feeling that he was about to get hassled, or worse mugged.

'Secondly, everyone here on *Tenured* loved Jet's performance on *Jennifer Moon*. We feel that Jet's music is part of *Tenured*'s DNA, you know? We'd like to get a studio recording of the new version of "Strip". We were thinking we could use the version with Erin's softer vocal at the end of the show, when an episode has a more downbeat ending. And our music director was wondering if you guys would like to work with him on some pieces of incidental music, for when season two starts filming in the fall.'

As Halley explained, Jay was simultaneously excited, but increasingly unnerved by the meaty year nine trio sat opposite. Maybe he was being paranoid, but with a train every four minutes, Jay decided it was safest to jump off and switch to the train behind.

'Good to hear,' Jay told Halley, grabbing his backpack with his free hand as the Tube train slowed down for Woodside Park. 'We're having all sorts of problems with our record company at the moment. That's probably why they didn't pass your messages along.'

'We heard about your situation. I'd like to speak directly to your manager, but they only had your number on file.'

The train was slowing for the platform. Jay got no hassle from the first two kids, but just as the train halted, the smallest of the trio stuck his leg out and sent Jay flying.

'AHHHHHH! Skinny wanker!' the trip-up artist shouted, as his mates roared with approval.

With his school pack in one hand and his mobile held to his face, Jay couldn't save himself. He sprawled forwards, banging a knee and sending his phone spinning across the carriage floor. One of the other kids stood up and loomed.

'Your band's crap, Jay,' he carped. 'And your old lady's a fat pig's ass!'

The guys were in the year below Jay, but he was too skinny to pick a fight with three of them. He scrambled frantically over the train floor, grabbing his phone, finding his feet, then getting a filthy look off a businesswoman who'd started to board as he shoved past and jumped on to the platform, just as the door started to close. The three lads inside the carriage made wanking gestures and banged palms on glass as the train pulled away.

'Hello?' Jay said, putting the phone back to a face burning red with embarrassment. 'Halley, are you still there?'

She sounded alarmed. 'What was that? I heard a big crash. Are you OK?'

'Perils of teenage celebrity,' Jay said, as he took a deep breath. 'I'll be home in fifteen minutes. It's probably best if I call you back.'

34. Soft Toilet Tissue

Dylan ticked a bunch of boxes, signed his name and got handed an envelope with twenty-five pounds in cash. The governor had no problem granting twelve hours' compassionate leave, but Dylan wasn't allowed out without a responsible adult to accompany him at all times. Nash made some calls on Dylan's behalf, and it was Mairi from the Wilton Music Edinburgh office who stood waiting in the empty visitors' car park.

'Look at you all grown up,' the fifty-something secretary said fondly.

She'd been working as a model when Harry Napier employed her thirty years earlier. Mairi still cut a good figure in jeans and black leather boots, but she'd gained a few grey hairs since Dylan last saw her. There was an uncoordinated moment as Dylan reached out to shake hands, but Mairi lunged for a single kiss on the cheek. She followed with a hug that reminded Dylan of all his muscle aches.

'Thank you so much for coming out,' Dylan said, as they set off towards a white VW Golf.

'I was going to drop in on your dad anyway,' Mairi said. 'So it's just a detour.'

There were Roald Dahl story CDs in the door compartment and a child seat in the back.

'Got grandkids now?' Dylan asked.

The sun was coming up as they set off, through the dodgy housing on the prison outskirts before breaking on to the dual carriageway to Edinburgh. Mairi told Dylan at length about her two daughters, one who'd just qualified as a surgeon, and another who'd married some rich guy, had a four-year-old and volunteered for a homeless charity. It sounded like the kind of normal family that Dylan had craved for his entire childhood, and he liked hearing a woman's voice after the macho banter inside Whitburn.

'I'm sorry if I'm boring you,' Mairi said. 'Was the second batch of clothes and things I sent OK?'

'Excellent,' Dylan said. 'So many I gave some bits to guys who don't have much.'

To avoid morning rush hour, Mairi pulled in for breakfast at a picturesque hotel on the city outskirts. Inmates were only allowed out in tracksuits, hoodies and trainers and Dylan felt like a ned as he strolled into a dining room with white table linen, log fire and couples of a certain age.

Dylan's hormones kicked in as a waitress with cleavage served freshly squeezed orange juice. The weight training had increased his appetite, and while Mairi ate poached eggs on toast, Dylan went for a winter fruit platter, cereal, then a full Scottish breakfast with black pudding and potato farls.

'How's the food been?' Mairi asked.

'Cheap frozen stuff,' Dylan said, as he loaded his fork with mushroom and bacon. 'Haven't seen fresh veg since I got there, but no worse than you get boarding at Yellowcote.'

Mairi laughed. 'Well you're enjoying that for sure.'

'For sure,' Dylan agreed.

While Mairi got the bill, Dylan luxuriated in a marble-tiled toilet cubicle, with piped classical, quilted toilet paper and no slot for a guard to peer through the door. He took so long that Mairi anxiously put her head inside the bathroom as he was washing his hands.

'You're worse than my husband,' Mairi said. 'Thought you might have found a window and done a runner on me.'

'No fear of that,' Dylan said, as they headed through reception to the car. 'It's just over three months now.'

'If you behave yourself,' Mairi reminded him, sounding like the kind of mother he'd never had.

Dylan had imagined his dad in some fancy rehab place, not dissimilar to the hotel they'd just left. But Mairi fought for a spot in an NHS hospital car park and they walked ten minutes through squeaky-floored corridors before finding Saville Rehabilitation Centre.

This private wing of the hospital was indicated by a reception with bright green sofas and a water feature behind the desk. After a few minutes, a chunky nurse came out. He introduced himself as Ken and offered coffee, before explaining that Jake

Blade was currently seeing his doctor.

'Is he any better today?' Mairi asked.

'Heroin withdrawal is never easy,' the nurse said.

Dylan sat forward. 'So is it like you see in the movies: cold turkey, banging on the door and stuff?'

'The aim at Saville is to reduce drug dependency gradually,' Ken explained. 'We use a variety of techniques, based around gradual substitution of heroin with less addictive methadone.'

'Guy in my unit at Whitburn said methadone is just as bad,' Dylan said. 'Maybe even worse than heroin.'

Ken didn't know Dylan's story and looked a little shocked as he answered. 'Heroin is a powerfully addictive drug and there's no easy way to reduce dependency. Particularly as your father was using a variety of other medications that have withdrawal symptoms.'

'Like what?' Dylan asked.

'Cocaine,' the nurse began. 'Ecstasy, methamphetamine, plus prescription anti-depressant medication and marijuana.'

'The full set,' Dylan said, tutting and shaking his head, as a doctor stepped out of reception and told them they could go through. Ken apologised and explained that he had to look through Mairi's handbag and pat them down for drugs. While the reception was fairly swanky, Dylan was hit by sweat, vomit and strong disinfectant as the nurse opened the door on to the ward proper.

It was super-warm and the green hallway carpet was a mass of stains. They passed a little communal kitchen, where a rough-looking woman sat on a counter top scratching frantically at her ankle. There was a guy moaning in the first room and a nasty waft of shit as they passed a heavily built nurse carrying a bedpan.

Dylan tried not to retch as they passed more rooms, and a tattooed guy standing at his door in open dressing-gown and underpants.

'Ken, I cannae find my glasses,' he moaned.

'I'll come look in a minute,' Ken said warmly.

Mairi looked freaked out as they turned left. This annexe had better carpet, bigger windows and no obvious smell. It was where you did rehab if you had a few million in the bank.

35. Cold Turkey

Jake Blade's room was spacious, but clearly designed for people in a volatile state, with tiled floor, easy-wipe cabinetry and Plexiglas over the flatscreen, exactly like the one in the courtyard at Whitburn. The man himself wore a beige hospital gown and was tangled in sheets and cushions.

'Ken, I'm freezing my tits off,' Jake shouted. 'Why are my windows open?'

Dylan reckoned the temperature was at least twenty-five, as Ken started shutting the windows.

'We always let fresh air in when we can,' Ken said soothingly, as he wound a handle to shut the highest part of the window. 'Now let's sort that tangle of sheets.'

'Mind my busted leg!' Jake fumed, as Ken patiently took off the top sheet and Dylan approached his father's bed.

'He's trying to help, Dad,' Dylan said.

'What do you know?' Jake yelled, glowering at his son as he raised his broken wrist. 'I'm in absolute agony, and they won't give me a damned thing.'

'You've had pain-killers, Mr Blade,' Ken said. 'But as I explained, their effect is limited because your addiction has left you with a very high opiate tolerance.'

'I need something,' Jake moaned. 'I'm dying.'

Ken shook his head as he started plumping Jake's pillows. 'Do you want to be on heroin for the rest of your life?' he asked rhetorically. 'I'd love to flip a magic switch, Mr Blade, but withdrawal doesn't work like that.'

There was an armchair close to the bed, but Dylan was put off by his dad's aggression and stayed a couple of metres back.

'This place is the pits,' Jake shouted. 'I've been in better rehab than this. I've got a broken leg, ringing in my ears and I'm freezing cold. Two grand a night and I'm getting no help at all.'

Ken's passive expression suggested he was used to cranky patients. 'Shall I make you a hot drink?' he asked.

'I can't keep anything down,' Jake snapped.

'What about a cup of ice cream?'

'I'm freezing my tits off,' Jake shouted, as he sat up, knocking the pillows Ken had just fixed to the floor. 'Freezing. Freezing! Why the hell would I be wanting ice cream?'

Dylan picked one of the pillows off the floor and was horrified to find it sodden with his father's sweat.

'I'll leave you with your wife and son,' Ken said.

Dylan and Mairi smiled at the nurse's mistake, but it pushed Jake over the edge.

'You're a thick idiot,' Jake shouted. 'I've picked snot smarter than you.'

Mairi spoke angrily. 'That isn't necessary, the nurse is just doing his job.'

'You do your job and shut your hole,' Jake hissed, then he looked at Dylan. 'Are you just going to stand around like a stiff cock? Sit your ass down, for god's sake.'

Dylan almost wished he was back at Whitburn Training Centre as he settled warily into the armchair. Close to the bed and with the windows closed, there was a smell like bleach and old trainers coming off the bed. Mairi was having trouble stomaching it.

'Dylan, I'm gasping for a coffee after the drive,' she said. 'We passed a machine. Would anyone else like something?'

'Sure, coffee,' Dylan said, feeling slightly like Mairi was abandoning him. 'No sugar, dash of milk.'

'This is what heroin does to you, lad,' Jake told Dylan, wagging a finger as Mairi headed out. 'Swore I'd never wind up back in a place like this. Picked up all the old habits as soon as I went back on the road.'

Dylan didn't know how to answer, then his dad pulled his sheets over his head and started shuddering.

'Don't end up like this,' Jake said. 'Drugs will always come back and bite you on the ass.'

'I've no plans to do drugs again,' Dylan said firmly. 'I've even stopped smoking.'

Dylan thought his dad would approve, but Jake threw the sheet off his face and narrowed his eyes. 'You self-righteous little shit,' he grunted. 'Do you think you're better than me?'

'I didn't say I was better than you,' Dylan snapped. He knew his dad was moody because of the heroin withdrawal but the jabs still hurt. 'What a waste of time this was.'

'Make yourself useful,' Jake said, hunting around his bed. 'Where is it? Where the . . .'

'Where's what?' Dylan asked, just as Jake found an iPhone Plus amongst the pillows and threw it into his son's lap.

'Harry's deliberately ignoring my calls,' Jake said, as he started scratching his good leg. 'I can't use this thing because I'm seeing floaters. I need to contact Spiros Aviation. They'll get me out of here, and into the Cook Centre in Barbados where I did rehab before.'

'It'll be the same wherever you are,' Dylan said. 'Barbados is a ten-hour flight and you can't even walk.'

Jake shook his head and opened his mouth, but only a grunt came out.

'What's your login?' Dylan asked.

Jake reached out with his index finger and used a fingerprint to unlock the iPhone. Ken came back into the room as Dylan half-heartedly Googled *Spiros Aviation*.

'I've spoken to Dr Carter about your pain,' Ken said. 'I can't give you more opiate pain-killers because they're chemically identical to the heroin we're trying to wean you away from. I can give you a muscle relaxant, but it will make you very drowsy.'

'Do it,' Jake said. 'This busted wrist is killing me.'

'You have visitors at the moment.'

Jake held his broken wrist in the air. 'I don't care if Her Majesty is outside waiting to pin another MBE on me. I need *this* to stop hurting.'

'But your son might not be able to come and see you again.'

Dylan raised a palm and shook his head. 'Ken, just do whatever keeps him happy.'

Dylan still had his dad's unlocked iPhone in his hand as Ken headed out to get the muscle relaxant. His first thought was to call Summer, but she'd be in school, as would Jay.

Jay, Dylan thought, jolting in his seat before glancing at his dad, who'd gone back to shivering under the covers.

Dylan opened his dad's email app, and typed *Harry Napier* into the search box. There were no recent emails between Napier and his dad, probably because they'd been together on tour. But pre-tour emails started popping up on the phone's screen.

Harry Napier and Jake Blade jointly owned Wilton Music and Venus TV, and there seemed to be regular emails, discussing hotel bookings for the Terraplane tour, along with copies of contracts and other documents that both partners needed to sign.

Dylan scrolled as far as the previous summer, finding an email from when he'd been on the run. Jake had asked Harry if they should hire someone to look for him. Harry replied saying *leave it for the cops to find the little turd.*

'Nice one, Harry,' Dylan muttered to himself.

He kept scrolling back in time as Mairi came in with the coffees.

'Ken's gonna sedate him,' Dylan said, as he put the cardboard cup down between his feet.

'I'm still here,' Jake moaned, from beneath his mound of covers. 'I do exist, despite what everyone else thinks.'

Dylan shook his head, turning his dad's phone slightly away from Mairi, as Ken came back with a vial and syringe.

'You youngsters live online,' she noted. 'It must have been an adjustment going back to phone calls and letters.'

'Tell me about it,' Dylan sighed.

Ken told Jake to rest his bad wrist palm-up against the bed.

'Is that a hypodermic or a red-hot knitting needle?' Jake howled, as Ken injected the pain-killer. 'Get me to Barbados before these butchers kill me!'

The muscle relaxant had an immediate effect on the tension in Jake's face.

'You got more of that?' Jake said, before ripping into a giant fart.

'That's an unfortunate side effect,' Ken explained, as Dylan recoiled from the stench and almost kicked his coffee over.

As Jake drifted into a haze, Ken opened a crack in the top window and left the room. Dylan's email search had got back to July 2016. He noticed a header titled *Rock War £££ opportunity* and began reading a long email conversation, which kicked off with Harry Napier mentioning a conversation about the possibility of buying Venus TV.

During his first couple of replies, Jake seemed baffled as to why they'd buy a TV production company. In his third reply, Harry estimated that they could make at least twenty million *and* fix the show so that Dylan won.

Jake and Harry were clearly having phone conversations between emails, because there were points where Dylan struggled to follow the written thread. But there was still a ton of evidence about fixing *Rock War*.

After skimming his way to the end of the thread, Dylan started looking at emails from the rest of that month. There was another thread five weeks later, where Harry seemed less keen about the idea of making Dylan's unpopular band win *Rock War* and said that it might stretch *credibility* if the Pandas of Doom won.

Dylan was oddly touched by a line in his dad's reply to Harry. *You and me have got more than we'll ever spend. I'm not cut out for parenting. I've not always done the best by Dylan, but I can set him up with a career and he'll never need to know that we fixed it.*

'Not much point sitting here if your dad's zonked,' Mairi interrupted, as she drained her coffee. 'Do you want to go into town? Maybe you need some more clothes, maybe get a burger, or even see a film, if you fancy? You don't have to be back until seven p.m., so we can always pop back later and see if your dad comes round in a better mood.'

'Still stuffed from breakfast, but a movie sounds good,' Dylan said. 'Can I just have five minutes to finish what I'm reading?'

'Or course,' Mairi said. 'I'll pop out to the ladies' and meet you in reception.'

'Works for me,' Dylan agreed.

Crash Landing

There was no way Dylan could read every email, along with all the attached contracts and documents. So he opened his own email account in the iPhone's web browser and grabbed Jay's email address. Back in his dad's account, Dylan highlighted every email between Harry Napier and Jake Blade, from the first email where Harry suggested buying Venus TV, through to Christmas Eve when *Rock War* season one ended. Then he forwarded the whole lot to Jay.

'Are you upset?' Mairi asked soothingly, as Dylan met her in reception. 'It might seem like a waste of time, but your dad will appreciate that you made the effort once he feels better.'

Dylan smirked as he zipped up his hoodie. 'Not at all,' he said. 'I actually feel a *lot* better for having come here.'

36. Dry Cheerios

Summer was a wreck. She'd slept in school uniform and padded through to the kitchen in black-bottomed socks, with one hand inside a box of Cheerios. Dylan and the hospital always called her mobile, so she let the ringing landline go to answerphone as she dropped dry Os in her mouth.

'This is an automated message regarding pupil Summer Smith in form 11H. Please contact the school at your earliest convenience to discuss this absence.'

Obernackle's dumb face flashed through Summer's head and she imagined grabbing something heavy and using it to pulp his stupid bulbous nose. She was torn between wanting to go to the hospital to be close to her nan, and the fact that seeing her in such an awful state was torture.

It was wet out, but getting a cab to the hospital seemed a waste, so she put on jeans and a waterproof jacket and walked to the bus stop. Liking the snap of outdoor air and the rain hitting her face, Summer kept walking.

Crossing roundabouts and busy junctions, the squelch of grass under her Nikes as she crossed a park and envied the existence of the little guy in bright yellow wellies stamping in puddles.

Even when the bus stopped thirty metres ahead, Summer didn't run for it. She got to a Costa Coffee in town and her soggy jeans itched as she lined up for an extra-hot latte and an orange berry muffin. After the break she marched through town, thinking about history revision: Hitler's defiance of the Treaty of Versailles, Autobahns, rearmament and the Strength Through Joy movement.

The hospital's automatic doors felt like the gates of hell. She thought about buying flowers to cheer her nan's room up, but what was the point when she didn't even know you were there? When she got to her nan's room it was empty. Fearing the worst, she jogged to the nurses' station.

'My god, you're drenched!' the ward sister gasped.

'Where is she?'

The sister did a weird thing, where her head snapped backwards while her body stayed still. 'Eileen had a bad night. She's been moved down to intensive care on the second floor.'

The sister pulled a long strand of tissue out of a wall-mounted dispenser and passed it to Summer to dry her face. The route to the second floor reminded Summer that she went through a phase of wanting to be a nurse, but now she loathed hospitals.

The signs on two were confusing and she walked a big circle before finding intensive care a few metres from where she'd first stepped off the staircase. The critical care ward had signs on its locked door. *Visitors Must Report to the Office before Entry, Breathing Masks & Shoe Protectors to be Worn at ALL times.'*

'Summer,' a buxom Irish nurse said, as she leaned out of a glass office. 'I just called you five minutes ago.'

Summer looked a state, with soggy coat and trainers and the balled-up tissue in her hand.

'I'm Assumpta,' the nurse said. 'I looked after your nan on the respiratory ward a few years back. You were doing a school project on The Fire Service.'

'Well remembered,' Summer smiled, as she unzipped and saw the message on her phone *CALL HOSPITAL WELFARE DEPARTMENT ASAP* . . . 'I guess I didn't hear with the rain pelting my coat.'

The thought of hospital welfare always filled Summer with dread. They were the ones who asked lots of questions, and would snitch to social services at the slightest hint that Summer was home alone.

'How's my nan doing?' Summer asked. 'Has she regained consciousness since she's been down here?'

'I came on duty about an hour ago,' Assumpta explained. 'She's stable, but extremely poorly. I think the consultant is keen to speak with you as well.'

There was a changing area next to the office. Summer hung her jacket on a hook, slid damp socks into disposable slippers, put on polythene gloves and cap, then hooked a face mask behind her ears. Assumpta swiped a card to open the door and Summer stepped inside.

Four of the six beds were occupied. A nurse wearing a face mask changed the sheets on one that wasn't and it made Summer wonder if someone had just died. Every patient had some kind of breathing assistance, and the hissing tubes, digital readouts and sighing ventilators made Summer feel like she was on the set of a sci-fi movie.

The sight of Eileen made Summer shudder. She was unconscious, but propped upright to stop fluid settling on her lungs. Below the oxygen mask, a plastic valve had been cut into her throat, which meant her lungs could now be vacuumed without the discomfort of the tube going through her mouth.

'Hey you,' Summer said affectionately, as she settled into a hard office-style chair, designed to be easily disinfected, and to wheel away giving medical staff space to work. 'It's pouring out there today.'

Summer rubbed her hands together and wondered what to do. A masked nurse gave a thumbs-up as he came past, wheeling some contraption that he started connecting to a hugely overweight man in the bed opposite. She thought about reading aloud, or telling Eileen about the A grade she'd got in a mock maths paper.

But Eileen's expressionless face and the machine inflating her chest were creepy and Summer was relieved when Assumpta called her out after barely ten minutes. There was another lady waiting, a slender Asian in a purple business suit.

'I'm Ali from hospital welfare,' she explained, as she shook Summer's polythene-gloved hand. 'Can I have a moment with you in the conference room?'

The space had a big meeting table and a pin board up back, covered in shift rotas and staff memos. Dr Kendall sat on the far side, with a pile of notes and an almond milk smoothie from the hospital café. Summer had spent enough of her life trying to pin down busy healthcare workers to know it was a big deal when two of them called you into a private room.

'Have a seat,' Ali said, as she pulled out a chair opposite the doctor.

Dr Kendall looked old-skool, with a tweedy brown suit, a battered leather briefcase and white caterpillar eyebrows.

'My granddaughter loved watching you on TV,' Kendall began. 'I even looked up your "Fairytale of New York" on YouTube.'

'Ahh, that's sweet,' Summer said, as her hands clenched. 'So, how's my nan doing?'

'I've been a physician for over forty years and bad news gets no easier,' Kendall began. 'Over the past few days, your grandmother has had increasing levels of fluid on her lungs and it's become increasingly difficult to keep the level of oxygen in her blood at a satisfactory level.

'Whenever oxygen is depleted, there is a risk of damage to the brain. I've been concerned about this since last Saturday. A couple of the incidents over the past week might have been serious enough to cause brain damage, but in the early hours of this morning your grandmother began coughing up large amounts of blood. This has not only caused further clotting in her left lung, but for several minutes her oxygen levels were below the level required to sustain brain activity.'

Summer gripped the arm of her chair. 'I thought the machine was breathing for her.'

Kendall tilted his head to one side. 'There are two aspects to breathing. The first is the mechanical action of inhaling and exhaling, which is replicated by the machine. But even when a patient is on a ventilator the lungs must have airways open to absorb enough oxygen for the body to survive. The blood clots, combined with the mucus your grandmother is producing to flush out her infection, are blocking the tubes that bring in oxygen, even with regular vacuum procedures.'

'So what happens now?' Summer asked. 'Is there another operation, or . . .'

'We gave your grandmother an electroencephalogram test earlier this morning. Her brain stem is still actively maintaining basic functions, such as the electrical signal that triggers a heartbeat, but there is no activity in the higher brain. This is the part that contains our thoughts and memories. I also had a very experienced colleague from the neurological department repeat the test and she confirmed these negative findings.'

'So that's like a deep coma?' Summer asked, close to tears again.

'A coma is a vegetative state,' Kendall explained. 'Rather like a car engine running at idle that might spark back to life. In your grandmother's case there is no activity at all. She is brain-dead and her condition will not improve.'

Summer had a tennis ball in her throat as tears flooded her eyes.

'But I thought the operation was supposed to cut out

the infection,' she said desperately. 'How can this happen . . . ? And I just saw her. Her heart is beating, she even twitched her fingers.'

'She's no longer suffering,' Ali soothed, as she wheeled her chair closer to Summer and slid a tissue box across the desk.

'I can't believe this . . .' Summer said, struggling to find words that matched the bombs going off in her head. 'So what now? Do you just . . . just, switch her off?'

'Only the flesh remains,' Dr Kendall said, as he reached across and held Summer's hand. Her vision blurred as she looked at the wiry hairs sprouting from his knuckles.

'Your mother is Eileen's next of kin,' Ali said. 'Is there any means to get in touch with her?'

'She's the last person I'd want to see right now,' Summer blurted. 'I've not seen Mum since I was eleven.'

'We need authorisation from next of kin before we can switch off the breathing apparatus,' Dr Kendall explained. 'Since you are a minor and if we can't contact your mother, a unanimous decision by three doctors will be needed to make the decision on when to stop the artificial respiration.'

'We can arrange for you to say goodbye in a private space,' Ali soothed. 'You can invite friends, or a spiritual companion from a local church.'

'Others don't want to make such a fuss,' Dr Kendall said, as he saw Summer recoil.

'She's Catholic,' Summer said, as she grabbed a bunch of tissues. 'I don't want to see her again like that, but she'd want that thing they do. You know?'

'The last rites,' Ali said. 'I can certainly arrange for a priest to be present.'

Summer stood up abruptly. Her head went funny and she grabbed the back of her chair.

'I need air,' Summer said, as she clutched her chest. 'I just feel really, really sick.'

'It's better to sit still and take a few deep breaths,' Dr Kendall said. 'No point running off and hurting yourself.'

'Dr Kendall has to get back to his other patients,' Ali said. 'But I can stay with you for as long as you need.'

'I'm really sorry,' Summer said, as she moved quickly towards the door.

She stumbled out, seeing the ward door on the other side of which her nan was alive, but not alive. She went into the changing room, swapped hospital slippers for her Nikes and snatched the soggy raincoat off a hook. Assumpta, Ali and Dr Kendall all stood outside.

'Sit and have a cuppa in my office, love,' Assumpta suggested.

Summer felt like she had bugs crawling inside her clothes as she pushed the nurse aside and made a charge for the stairs.

37. Seaside Special

Jay and his band mates finished school Friday, Ubered it to Victoria station and caught the 16:18 fast service to Brighton. Len met them at the other end and they stopped for fish and chips on their way to Garage Door.

The venue was a warren of low-ceilinged archways, right on Brighton seafront. Not Jet would be playing their first proper gig as co-headliners with Bongo Bongo Land, a Brighton-based band who'd been knocked out in the fifth week of *Rock War* season two. Like many of Jet's London gigs, it was an alcohol-free nappy night, for thirteen- to seventeen-year-olds.

Sue the publicist had driven down earlier in the day, while Len drove the band's gear in his van. Sue wanted to keep pressure on Wilton Music by making them look like evil corporate oppressors. She planned to take gig photos for a press release about the newly renamed Not Jet's first gig, and had also printed up badges and triangular plastic flags with a new logo. This emphasised the censorship angle by having the band name drawn behind prison bars.

The two bands hit it off, swapping stories about their time on the TV show. Alfie often felt left out amidst older band mates, so he immediately took to Bongo Bongo Land's spiky-haired thirteen-year-old drummer. He dressed like a skateboarder and liked to be called Dog, but the rest of his band mercilessly used his real name, Gideon, in a variety of faux-posh accents.

The Bongos had built a lively local following and the publicity around Not Jet brought in a fair few curious fans. Doors opened at seven thirty and by quarter past eight the place was rammed. Kids who wanted to arrive fashionably late wound up getting turned away and there were scuffles at the door and people out on the seafront calling parents for an earlier-than-planned pick-up.

Co-headlining a gig can cause friction, but the two bands seemed to get along and Len settled the issue of who got the more prestigious second slot with a coin flip, and a consolation prize of coming back on for an encore at the end of the night.

Not Jet lost and went on first. Starting off with 'Strip', the quintet blasted through a mix of originals they'd played on *Rock War*, covers of tracks by AC/DC, Black Sabbath, Ween and the Red Hot Chili Peppers, plus more recent stuff that Jay had worked on with Erin and Babatunde.

Sue balanced on a table at the back of the audience, shooting pics and some video clips of the youthful crowd waving their Not Jet flags. The response was great and the low brick archways and gloomy lighting made the sell-out crowd seem bigger than the actual three hundred and fifty.

Man hugs abounded as the bands traded places. Not Jet found themselves getting plenty of attention from the opposite sex as they settled in at a VIP booth, with Babatunde sneakily topping up their Pepsis from a giant duty-free vodka bottle he'd smuggled in inside his bass drum.

Like all the bands in *Rock War* season two, Bongo Bongo Land were great musicians. They were the only band ever to play in *Rock War* with two drummers and the percussion-heavy sound had furniture vibrating and the teenaged crowd bouncing.

Jay sought quiet when he saw that he had a pair of voice messages. He wound up at the end of a long hallway backstage, with his playback volume turned up to ten and a finger plugged in one ear. The first message was from his dad.

'*Good luck with the gig tonight, son. My boss has given me tomorrow off, so tell Len I can make the meeting tomorrow as planned.*'

Harry Napier was in London for the weekend and Len had set up a Saturday afternoon meet with the Wilton Music boss and his legal team. The concert had put Jay in a buzzy mood, but the thought of the ongoing legal hassle brought him down.

The second message was from Dylan. '*Jay, buddy. I was hoping to catch you before your gig and wish you the best. I know you'll blow the doors off the joint! . . . Also, I was hoping you'd heard from Summer. She seemed really down about her nan last night. Now I'm even more worried, because I've called four times and she's not answering. So, yeah, hopefully I'll hear from both of you soon. Night.*'

There was no way to call Dylan back inside the training centre, but Jay knew Summer had been suffering. He gave her mobile a try, but it just cut to voice mail.

'Hi Summer, I'm at the gig,' Jay shouted, as the Bongos went extra loud on stage. 'Hope you're doing good. Just a bit worried, cos Dylan said you didn't call him. We're all keeping fingers crossed for your nan down here. Call anytime, cheers.'

Back in the VIP booth, Babatunde had his arm around a girl with lavender lipstick, while Salman was getting face time with a chunky chick.

'You guys killed it,' Len shouted, approaching the table with Sue in tow. 'Looks like about twenty minutes till you're called back for your encore.'

Jay, Erin and Alfie gave thumbs-up signs, rather than shout over the noise.

'Salman's having a good night,' Sue added sarcastically, as she straddled a velvet rope. She settled with Len in the empty booth next door, and started drafting a press release on her Galaxy Note.

Jay grabbed Sue's DSLR and flipped through the gig photos, with Erin and Alfie looking on.

'I'm worried about Summer,' Jay told them. 'She's all on her own up there.'

Bongo Bongo Land took their bows and there was a tangle of guitar leads as the bands swapped gear. They played 'Strip' again, before Erin duetted on 'Fairytale of New York' with Salman. A few shouts of *Where's Theo?* came out of the crowd during the quieter parts, but they were way outnumbered by the swaying couples, who were themselves outnumbered by the pairings getting even more familiar in the venue's darker recesses.

'You don't have to go home but you can't stay here,' Erin announced, as the little hand passed eleven. 'Sleep tight, god bless and use a condom if you're planning anything your parents wouldn't approve of.'

'Don't let the bed bugs bite!' Salman added.

A blast of sea air swept away heat as the venue's louvred doors swung open and teenagers headed towards waiting parents, or crunched over the pebble beach towards the sea. On stage, Jay joined his band mates, untangling leads and equipment and almost stealing an effects box that belonged to the Bongos.

'Great night,' the club's long-haired owner announced as he passed Len a fat envelope. 'Three hundred and fifty heads at fifteen pounds a ticket. Your twenty per cent cut comes to a thousand and fifty. Cash as agreed. Hope to have you back in two or three months.'

With Len taking twenty per cent off the top for his manager's fee and petrol, that left each band member with a hundred and sixty-eight quid, minus their Uber fare and train tickets. It was way more than any of Jay's mates earned leafleting, or doing an eight-hour Saturday shift in a shop, but even with two bands to pay, Len knew that it was the club owner who'd really done well. He'd kept sixty per cent of the door money, plus the profit he'd made selling half pints of Coke for £2.80 and booze-free cocktails for a fiver. Even after paying security, bar staff and cleaners, Len reckoned he'd made a bundle.

Len had to get his van out of a car park, and drive it down a ramp on to the seafront to load up all the gear. The plan was for Jay and Erin to ride home in the van, while Alfie, Babatunde and Salman would get dropped off by Sue.

Jay checked his phone, but there was no message from Summer and since it was half eleven he decided not to risk waking her up. The drive home was a couple of hours, so he headed to the toilet while Len and Babatunde finished packing the drum kit.

He went into the gents' first, but one of the toilets had flooded and there were turds in a puddle, plus plastic cups and toilet paper strewn everywhere. Jay decided it was worth the effort of trekking backstage and using the staff toilet.

There was a smell of damp in a gloomy backstage area, filled with bar stock and cleaning gear. At one point, the narrow stockroom opened out under an adjoining arch and Jay saw Alfie kissing up against a set of beer barrels. He couldn't resist stopping for a peek, but almost inhaled his tongue when he realised that it was Gideon – AKA Dog – from the Bongos.

Jay had no problem with Alfie being gay, or more likely bi since he'd seen him with girls as well. But it was still a surprise and combined with Babatunde's illicit vodka and the fact it was nearly midnight, Jay felt slightly spaced-out as he reached the staff toilet, and almost walked into Erin coming the other way.

She'd changed a sweaty tank top for baggy T-shirt, and done a crude wipe-up job on her stage make-up.

'Did you see what I just saw?' Erin said quietly, cracking a mischievous grin as she wiped wet hands on her jeans.

'The err . . . Alfie and Dog?'

'What else, cuz?'

'I did,' Jay admitted. 'Fine with me, I guess . . .'

'Fine with me,' Erin agreed, as she stifled a laugh. 'But I'd give my left tit to see the expression on Mrs Jopling's intolerant mug when she finds out that her little Alfie-kins swings both ways . . .'

Jay nodded and covered his mouth. 'He just needs to bring home a black refugee boyfriend on benefits to make it perfect.'

'She'll explode,' Erin giggled, as she squeezed past Jay. 'Poor Alfie.'

'Great gig too,' Jay said, as he pushed the toilet door. 'I reckon we could have got five hundred in if there'd been space. Anyhow, I'm busting.'

'Enjoy,' Erin said, trying not to make eye contact, because she knew they'd start laughing again.

Jay locked the toilet door and unzipped his trousers. He tried not to think about Mrs Jopling, but wound up laughing so hard that he couldn't pee straight.

38. Wonderful World Of Disney

It was a quarter past two by the time Len's van dropped Erin off. Then they drove a final half mile and parked on the driveway in High Barnet. Jay slept through the usual Saturday morning family chaos and sauntered down from his attic bedroom at a quarter to eleven, when he heard his dad in the downstairs hallway. Jay was too wiped to shower when he got home and his hair was a disaster.

'Booze breath and hormones,' Chris said, wafting a hand in front of his face. 'Morning, son.'

'Nice suit, Dad,' Jay said, as his mum came out of the kitchen and gently pinched his cheek.

'A bit too much boozing going on for a fifteen-year-old,' Heather said disapprovingly, before kissing her son. 'I hear the gig went well.'

'Biggest one since *Rock War* ended,' Jay agreed.

Len joined Chris in the hallway. He also wore a suit, but in Len's case it looked like the chest buttons were set to pop.

'Usually someone has to die to get you two looking this smart,' Heather said, as she pulled her phone out of her jeans. 'Let's have a pic.'

'Are you nervous about the meeting?' Jay asked.

Len cracked a cheeky smile. 'Nah. It's your future on the line, not mine.'

Jay covered his face as his mum snapped a picture of his mangled hair.

'*Don't* put that online,' Jay said. 'These pyjama legs make me look so skinny.'

'You are skinny,' Heather pointed out. 'Enjoy it while it lasts.'

'All right,' Len said, as he grabbed a briefcase. 'Meeting's at high noon, so we'd better skedaddle.'

'Good luck,' Jay said. 'Maybe take the TK Maxx price tag off your briefcase if you're trying to look like a serious businessman.'

Heather ran into the kitchen and grabbed scissors, as Jay smiled. It was great having a mum, dad and stepdad who got along so well, even if it did mean you couldn't play them off against each other.

'And what are you up to today?' Heather asked Jay, as Len and Chris set off down the driveway.

'Meeting up with Bailey later,' Jay said.

'Homework?'

'All under control,' Jay said, not entirely truthfully.

'When you've had your shower, strip your bed and put your sheets in the wash.'

Jay tutted. 'I only did them, like . . . not that long ago.'

'They'll walk off the bed by themselves if they're on any longer,' Heather insisted. 'Now stop stinking up my hallway and shower. I've got your favourites when you come back down.'

'Potato cakes and bacon?' Jay grinned.

'Ready in fifteen minutes,' Heather warned, as Jay started up the stairs. 'And if those sheets aren't in the wash Kai can have it as seconds.'

*

Sweat poured off Dylan's head as he sat on a leg press machine.

'Four,' JJ shouted. 'What's the matter with you? Push, bitch!'

Dylan got to eight reps, but he'd managed twelve a couple of days earlier. Worrying about Summer was sapping his strength.

'I'll put the weight down to eighty kilos,' JJ said, but Dylan stepped off the machine, shaking his head as he grabbed a hand towel off the floor.

'Sorry,' Dylan said, as he mopped his brow. 'My legs are stiff and my head's not in the game.'

Costco and Wilfred were strolling over from the free weights.

'Told you not to get upset over any girl,' Costco said. 'Not calling for one night means squat.'

Dylan shook his head and sighed. 'Something's wrong. Her nan's in the hospital. I'm gonna go try calling her again.'

JJ laughed. 'You called two minutes before you came here.'

'You'll get yourself in a dark place if you spend all your time here worrying about what's happening on the out,' Costco warned.

But Dylan couldn't get Summer off his mind. 'Maybe she was at the hospital until late. She *must* be awake by now.'

'Bitches always be losing phones,' JJ noted, as Dylan headed out of the gym.

'It'll only take a minute to call her,' Dylan said.

But Summer didn't pick up. Again.

*

Len had lied when he told Jay that he wasn't nervous. His foot jiggled as he sat on a leather reception sofa and his heart pumped as a woman led him into a meeting room with a sixteen-seat conference table. One long wall was lined with law books, while the other had floor-to-ceiling windows and a downwards view over the dome of St Paul's Cathedral.

A white-haired senior lawyer named Isaac Disney sat in the middle on the window side. Harry Napier was to his left, there was another lawyer to Disney's right and the Wilton Music legal team was rounded out with two legal assistants and a legal secretary to take notes.

Napier had folded arms and a bulldog expression. The lawyer looked surprised as he reached across the table and shook Len and Chris's hands.

'Isaac Disney, senior partner,' the lawyer said, raising one eyebrow curiously. 'Are we still awaiting your legal counsel?'

Len smiled as he sat in a chair. 'Legal counsel charges double to meet on a Saturday, out of hours,' he explained. 'Eight hundred an hour, plus a clerk to take notes, was a little expensive for a man who earns a living running sing-alongs in old folks' homes.'

'Perhaps you knew it would cost us extra, when you suggested that Mr Napier could only meet us on a Saturday or Sunday?' Chris suggested.

As an ex-cop, Chris got the same buzz he felt when he'd interrogated a suspect.

'My client has a busy schedule,' Disney purred, as Chris noted the way that Big Len and Harry Napier were scowling at one another. 'I can't impress upon you enough how seriously we take these breaches of contract. Jet's performance in Brighton last night was a further breach of contract and we'll be issuing further action in relation to this matter through the courts on Monday.'

Len grunted. 'Another injunction, so the judge sets a hearing in a month, and another bunch of paperwork. And by the time the judge throws your baseless action out, I've lost two days' pay, and racked up another three grand in legal costs.'

'It would be in everyone's best interests to settle this matter quickly and amicably,' Mr Disney said. 'But the absence of your legal counsel makes it very difficult to discuss a detailed proposal.'

Len laughed. 'Oh dear, I'd hate to think we'd wasted *your* time and money.'

Harry Napier didn't share the joke and slowly shook his head. 'Big Len,' Napier said quietly. 'Still a total cock.'

Disney didn't seem too happy with his client's comment,

but Len didn't take the bait. Instead, he opened up his briefcase and spoke sharply.

'I actually have my own proposal document,' Len said. 'I've printed out copies of my clients' requirements, including a new recording contract based on Venus TV and Wilton Music's standard template.

'The key terms are as follows. A one hundred and fifty thousand pound advance against future royalties for each of the five members of Jet. Clear legal title to the name Jet. A salaried chaperone for each band member until they reach the age of eighteen, with a salary of fifty thousand pounds per year. As you'll see, my proposal includes some modifications of your measly standard royalties in favour of my artists. There is also provision for guaranteed marketing spend, and for Jet to have full control over the material they produce and the release schedule. Wilton Music will also provide financial support for touring.

'Additionally, the contract you awarded to Summer Smith will be adjusted to match these royalty terms and she will receive an additional one hundred and fifty thousand pound advance and the right to produce another album of material that *she* wants to record with a production team of her choice.

'Finally, in respect of the 1987 recording of the song "Grace" by Terraplane, I would like to be acknowledged as the song's co-creator. I will not seek any royalties, but I will ask for a one-off payment of two hundred thousand pounds. This will be made as a charity donation to North London Children's Hospital, who looked after my youngest daughter when she was born nine weeks premature.'

There was a brief pause as Napier and his legal team looked aghast.

'Anything else?' Napier added sarcastically. 'Maybe five golden rings and a partridge in a pear tree?'

'You're all talk, Harry,' Len sneered. 'You made your money ripping off musicians and renting out slums. And you act all tough with your gangster past, but you don't even check in on your own godson when he's getting the shit kicked out of him behind bars.'

Napier stood up and growled back. 'There's a reason I'm worth eight hundred million and you're a washed-up session musician: you're the dumbest meathead I—'

'Gentlemen,' Mr Disney said, part standing up. 'You both need to calm down.'

Chris grabbed Len's suit cuff and got him to sit down, before clearing his throat. 'Perhaps I could interject here.'

Napier cracked a high-pitched laugh. 'Why not? You muppets are comedy gold.'

Chris put on his sturdiest police-giving-evidence-in-court voice as he took a plastic folder out of Len's briefcase. 'In the spirit of cooperation,' he began, 'I would also like to deliver some information that I'm sure will be of interest and concern to everyone in this room.'

'I know who you are,' Napier carped. 'Chris Ellington, the bent copper who knocked up Len's slag of a wife.'

Len flinched, but thought better of taking the bait and let Chris keep speaking.

'In my work as a private investigator, information has recently come to light regarding vote rigging on the popular television show, *Rock War*. This folder includes several interesting documents. They include a letter, written by Mr Napier's godson Dylan Wilton, on how he uncovered vote rigging during season one of *Rock War*. I have signed statements from two interns who worked on the show, testifying that they witnessed the vote rigging in progress. In one case, this has been backed up by an email the intern received from Karolina Kundt at Venus TV.

'Finally, the dossier contains printouts of one hundred and sixteen emails, sent between Harry Napier and Jake Blade. These outline a detailed conspiracy, in which the two men plot to purchase Venus TV and fix *Rock War* so that Dylan Wilton's band the Pandas of Doom win the show.'

Napier's lips got very thin as he rolled his chair back slightly.

'Blackmail is a criminal offence,' Napier said. 'You're on dangerous turf.'

Chris smiled. 'Gentlemen,' he said warmly. 'As an ex-police officer I am very familiar with the laws on blackmail. Len has presented a set of very reasonable contractual demands for the band he manages and in which my son plays.

'I have presented some troubling evidence that has come to light. Obviously if this information became public the reputational damage to the credibility of *Rock War* would run into many millions of pounds. But I can assure you that there is no link between these matters.'

'I saw in *Music Week* that you're negotiating to sell *Rock War* to Chinese TV for thirty million,' Len noted. 'Not a great time for a shit storm of bad publicity . . .'

'You think you're being clever . . .' Napier snarled. 'I'll spend every penny I have suing you before I sign that contract.'

Mr Disney looked at his client, using hand gestures to calm him down.

'The contract I've had drawn up is in line with Musicians Union's Fair Play terms for artists,' Len said. 'I'll require the signed contract by five p.m. tomorrow. Sorry if that means you have to work over the weekend . . .'

Chris rattled the other folder. 'I'll leave you one copy of this,' he said. 'I'm actually taking the rest of the weekend off, so we can decide how best to handle this information when I return to my office on Monday. And with luck, we can raise a toast to my son's revised contract with Wilton Music and my new role, employed by Wilton Music as my son's fifty-thousand-pounds-a-year chaperone . . .'

It was Len's turn to carp as he headed out of the room. 'Always a pleasure to see you, Harry.'

Chris and Len both hurried through reception. Paranoid about being overheard, they said nothing until they'd gone down thirty-two floors and on to the street through a revolving door.

'Harry sounded pissed off,' Chris said anxiously. 'Are you sure he'll go for this?'

'I've known Harry for more than thirty years,' Len said, as they walked back towards the Tube. 'He acts like a tough guy, but he's also a pragmatist. You don't reach Napier's level of success without being able to swallow your pride once in a while. And the whole package only comes to a couple of million, which is peanuts to him.'

'Hope you're right,' Chris said. 'Think I need a whisky or three to calm my nerves.'

'Hope I'm right too,' Len said, smiling slightly. 'Heather's already told me I'm sleeping on the couch for six months if I screw up Jay's career.'

39. China Cottages

Patsy had reached the final in her U11 soccer cup, and Jay spent Sunday morning cheering her on with Len and Hank. Len was the loudest voice on the touchline and almost blew a blood vessel when his daughter got clean through on goal, only for her to toe punt and send the ball miles over the bar.

Heather had stayed home, cooking a big Sunday spread with her sister Rachel, and Bailey had arrived just after Jay got home.

'Did you win the match?' Bailey asked brightly.

Patsy liked Jay's girlfriend, but she was a sore loser, and stamped upstairs without answering.

'Went down six-five on penalties,' Jay explained, before giving Bailey a kiss.

Jay helped Adam and Erin put all three extra leaves in the dining table. Everyone was pretty cheerful as the traditional roast got scoffed. Talk centred on Erin's oldest sister, who'd just announced that she was expecting a second kid, and Theo, who'd called the night before and announced that he was coming to London for a few days with Nessa.

'I hope they stay at a hotel,' Jay said. 'I hate bunking in with Kai and I'll never sleep in my bed again if I know Theo's shagged in it.'

After marmalade pudding and custard, Jay and Bailey helped stack the dishwasher, then went up to Adam's room and cuddled up watching *Suicide Squad* with Adam and his girl, plus Erin, and Tristan. Hank sneaked in too, and they let him stay even though the film was a fifteen and Heather would go nuts if she found out.

As the Sunday progressed, nobody spoke about Harry Napier's deadline. But it was on everyone's mind.

Jay couldn't get into the movie and tensed up when Bailey started kissing his neck. He kept wondering what Harry Napier was doing. Maybe Napier's lawyers were sat in a room sweating over paperwork. Maybe the notorious hard man was up for a fight. Or maybe a two-million-pound contract wasn't that big a deal to a billionaire and Harry had signed the papers and was spending a relaxing Sunday afternoon on the golf course, having left his lawyers instructions to make Len suffer until the last possible moment.

When the house phone rang, Jay darted up excitedly. But it was just his dad, Chris, calling to ask if they'd heard anything.

'Nowt,' Len said.

When *Suicide Squad* ended they started playing FIFA on Adam's PS4. Two years earlier you had to let Hank win or he'd throw a huge tantrum, but the eight-year-old had suddenly become awesome, beating Tristan 7-2, Jay 4-1 and Adam 4-3, much to the amusement of their respective girlfriends.

'We are so screwed,' Erin told Jay, as she held up her phone, showing 16:44 on the clock. 'I don't think Harry's going for it.'

'It's just a stupid band,' Adam said unhelpfully. 'Now if you don't mind clearing my crib, me and my lady have French Revolutionary history to study.'

Jay enviously suspected this was code for something more fun. He was helping Adam tidy, and held four empty coffee mugs as he heard a moped come up the drive and stop beside Heather's Volvo.

'Are we having pizza?' Hank asked excitedly.

'You ate a massive dinner two hours ago,' Jay pointed out.

The moped had a logoed box on the back just like a pizza bike and the driver was walking around the back to get something out.

'GoPhar Couriers,' Hank said, looking baffled as everyone else piled out of Adam's room. 'Wait! What is it?'

The helmeted courier looked surprised as he opened the door to Len and a dozen eager faces poised in the entrance hall behind him. After signing for a breezeblock-sized document box, the bodies made space as Len crossed to the dining room.

'Could be a bomb,' Len joked, as he opened the box by stripping out a red tab.

There was a stack of paperwork inside.

'Contracts,' Len said, as he tipped the papers across the

dining table and flicked through the one on top. 'Looks like the lawyers have made a few changes. But the key stuff seems to be here. The advance, the royalties, the chaperones . . .'

'Looks like two signed copies of a contract for each band member, plus one for Len,' Jay explained. 'One to keep, and one to sign and return to Wilton Music.'

'Why's that one different?' Erin asked, as she pushed her way to the table.

'Summer Louise Smith,' Jay said, tapping the name on the cover page.

Len found a letter paper clipped on the front of his management contract, which he read aloud. '*Contracts signed by Karolina Kundt on behalf of Venus TV and Mairi Cross on behalf of Wilton Music. Please sign where indicated and return ASAP. All parties to act in good faith, and please be aware of non-disclosure provisions related to all activities taking place before signature of contract (additional stipulations in paragraph 22.1 through 22.21). Yours faithfully, Isaac Disney, Senior Partner.*'

Erin grinned at Len. 'This means we won?'

'I'll run it by my lawyer first thing tomorrow to be totally sure, but yes, I think old Harry took the sensible option.'

'A hundred and fifty grand!' Jay shouted, as he raced back out into the hall and pressed the memory button to call his dad. 'Dad, it just came by courier. All the contracts have been signed. Len wants the lawyer to check, but it all looks good.'

'Nice one,' Chris said. 'That Napier's a shifty one. I didn't sleep a wink last night.'

'I've slept better,' Jay admitted, as more cheers and shouts came out from around the dining table.

'Five quid fizz,' Heather announced, as she popped the top off a bottle of Prosecco.

As Jay stepped back into the action, Erin led an all-girl conga line through the archway into the kitchen.

'So what present am I getting?' Bailey asked, as she gave Jay a kiss.

'Anything you like, maximum twenty-five quid,' Jay teased.

He was about to close in for a proper kiss when he felt his phone vibrate in his pocket. He'd have ignored if the display had said anything other than . . .

'Summer,' Jay gasped, going up to the first-floor landing because of the noise. 'Everyone's been going spare trying to get in touch. Are you OK?'

'Not really,' Summer said, breaking into a round of sobs. 'I couldn't face anyone. I've just come from the hospital. The priest came. I held his hand and my nan's hand, making a circle. We said a prayer, then the doctor came in and switched off her ventilator.'

'Oh shit,' Jay said, feeling weak from the shock and sitting on the top step. 'I'm so sorry. I don't know . . .'

Bailey had followed Jay up the stairs and he mouthed, 'Get my mum,' as Summer started speaking again.

'Hospital welfare got social services involved,' Summer explained. 'They want me to go to this foster care place tonight. I told them to stick it and ran all the way home. But the bungalow is full of nan's stuff. Like her chair and her oxygen. Her *TV Times* and her china cottages.'

'Where are you now?' Jay asked.

Bailey had passed the news to Heather, who arrived at the bottom of the stairs, with a concerned face and a flute of fizzy Prosecco.

'Sat on a swing in the park near my house,' Summer said. 'It's starting to get dark. I don't want to be in the bungalow on my own. I thought about walking to Michelle's, but her parents are splitting up. Her mum's so weird and Lucy still can't stand me after I betrayed the band.'

'Lucy will forgive you,' Jay said. 'I *definitely* don't think you should be on your own.'

Heather mouthed up the stairs, 'Tell her she can come here.'

'Do you want to come here?' Jay said. 'It's not a problem.'

Heather didn't like the way Jay phrased it as a question. She charged up the stairs and snatched Jay's phone.

'Summer, this is Heather,' she said, using her firm-but-fair mum voice. 'I'm really sorry to hear about Eileen. She was a fantastic lady, but you can't be on your own tonight, can you, love?'

'I guess not,' Summer said.

'You're welcome to come here and stay as long as you like,' Heather said. 'I know it's a madhouse, but you've got friends here. And that's what matters right now.'

'My exams . . .' Summer snorted.

'Don't overthink,' Heather said firmly. 'One step at a time. The funeral, social services, school, the house, can all be sorted out in time and with our help. But right now, all that matters is you're not on your own. So, I can jump in the car and pick you up, or if you feel up to it, get on a train and we'll meet you here in London?'

'I'll get a train,' Summer said, her voice barely above a croak. 'I'd rather be on the move than sat in this dodgy park after dark.'

'Sounds sensible,' Heather said. 'Can you sort your ticket and things out?'

'I've got my debit card,' Summer said. 'I can pop back to the house and pack a little bag. Then I'll book a taxi to the station.'

'Good girl,' Heather said. 'Text or call Jay as soon as you know what train you're getting and there'll be hugs waiting for you at the ticket barrier.'

'I could do with a hug,' Summer admitted, as she continued to sob. 'I'm sorry to be a bother.'

'Don't be bloody daft,' Heather said. 'Now wash that face, pack your bag and jump on the first train you can.'

Three Months Later

40. Scot Free

The Sunday Post, Arts & TV section, 6 August 2017

ROCK GODS RESUME FLIGHT

Terraplane, Wembley Arena

. . . Back in May, Terraplane stunk up Wembley Stadium so badly their angry fans smashed the toilets and left an unfortunate merchandise seller with a broken nose. When a drugged Jake Blade crashed off stage in sound check three days later, shattering his leg and wrist, many assumed that the legendary rockers' comeback tour was over.

Those who know the band's hard-headed manager Harry Napier say he's the one man who could have got this train wreck back on the rails. And he had plenty of financial motivation, with over $600 million contractually guaranteed by the tour's US promoter.

Crash Landing

Last night, Terraplane returned to Wembley, albeit to the 15,000-capacity indoor Arena, not the iconic stadium itself. The show was given a low-key billing as a warm-up for the US tour, with ticket money donated to an Edinburgh-based drug rehabilitation charity.

While the gigs this spring looked dated, theatrical producer Heinz de Mol has been brought aboard to reinvent Terraplane's act. A $14 million hydraulic stage won't see the light of day until the band plays Chicago's Wrigley Field in ten days' time, but fans were delighted, particularly in the first act when Terraplane resurrected the spartan sound of their first two albums.

Lead man Jake Blade and bassist Max McTavish have both spent much of the past three months in rehab. It would be an exaggeration to say that this was Terraplane back to their best, but there was a definite sense that the band was in this for more than a fat pay cheque.

Heinz de Mol made his name sustaining the Las Vegas careers of crooners and musicians well past their best and his bag of tricks rescued the artfully produced show whenever the middle-aged rockers started to flag.

Some of the duets and a lengthy drum solo may have appeared like padding, but the crowd seemed delighted and there was genuine emotion at the end, when studio musician Leonard 'Big Len' Crouch appeared on stage with the band for the first time, playing the guitar part he wrote for the band's biggest hit, 'Grace'.

Verdict: 7.5/10. We will probably never see Terraplane

back at their absolute best, but this was closer than most
fans dared to imagine.

The windows didn't open in Whitburn's reception area and Dylan was sweating as he pulled his tracksuit leg up to his knee.

'Foot up on the chair,' a skinny guard said.

As Dylan raised one leg, he recognised Salman's quirky voice, wafting from the radio back in the inmate storage area. But the song was new to him.

'Really important to fit this right, because you can't take it off,' the guard said, as she took a chunky plastic bracelet out of a box. 'You obviously don't want it so tight that it hurts, but if it's loose it'll chafe.'

The bracelet made a beep as the guard locked the clasp around Dylan's ankle, then she made a fine adjustment with a screwdriver.

'How's that feel?'

'OK, I think,' Dylan said.

'Take a few steps while I sort Niall out.'

Dylan felt emotional as he walked a few paces towards the exit, then back towards the storage cage.

Wilfred and Connor had beaten him out the door, but he felt sad for the years JJ and Costco still had to serve. He'd never have made friends with someone like Wilfred on the outside, but they'd bonded over dumb-bells and the street thug had warned Dylan that he'd batter him if he'd reverted to fat and flabby when they met up on the outside.

'That lazy little anthem was "Lavender Lady" from Jet's newly released EP,' the distant radio announced. *'Eagerly awaited follow-up to "Strip". I was at their going-away gig at The Old Beaumont in Camden last week and the place was blowing up.'*

'Comfortable?' the guard asked, as Niall took his turn to walk up and down with his bracelet.

'Seems fine,' Dylan said.

'It's waterproof, so you're good in the bath or shower,' the guard explained. 'But the signal can't penetrate deep water, so stick to the shallow end in swimming pools and no paddling in the sea above your knees. If you release the silver clasps, you'll get about a centimetre extra room so you can wash behind. But if the clasp is released for more than two minutes, the bracelet will start beeping and send a signal to the monitoring centre.'

'How often are the random bleeps?' Niall asked, as Dylan stretched his tracksuit cuff over the bulky bracelet.

'At least twice per day you'll get a bleep and you'll have to state your location to the call centre. The system adjusts automatically based on compliance, so you'll get more bleeps if you don't respond or you violate curfew. Speaking of curfew, the bracelet has GPS so it will report you automatically if you leave home after curfew time. If you're spending the night away from home for any reason, you must get permission from your parole officer and notify the monitoring centre.'

'What if there's no signal or something?' Dylan asked. 'My dad's place is way out in the country and there's never any mobile signal.'

'The bracelet records your position in memory and uploads when you get back to a signal area. If the bracelet is out of contact for more than four hours, it will start beeping and you'll have to call in and explain what you're up to.

'Also note, I've seen all kinds of attempts to tamper, whether it's heating up the strap and trying to stretch the bracelet over your foot, or wrapping it in tinfoil to block the signal. Nothing works, and if you get caught, you'll be sent back here. So you'll answer your bleeps and you won't tamper, will you?'

'No, Miss,' Dylan and Niall said, both smirking slightly because they were excited about getting out.

'So let's hope I'll never see you two again, eh? Off you go.'

The redhead unlocked a door as the boys grabbed bin liners with their stuff inside off the floor. Dylan knew his dad had flown up after the Wembley gig to pick him up. They'd spoken regularly once Jake got over the worst phase of heroin withdrawal and flew out to Barbados, but it was never going to be a regular father-son relationship. Dylan felt anxious as he stepped into a cracking August day and took a big breath of freedom.

Visiting didn't start until twelve, so there were only two cars in the visitors' parking lot. Niall shook Dylan's hand and wished him luck before jogging off towards a tatty Hyundai people carrier. The other car was an ostentatious Rolls-Royce Phantom with blacked-out windows.

Jake Blade sat on the bonnet, wearing a corduroy jacket and aviator sunglasses. He still had a lightweight cast on his wrist, but his skin looked tanned and he'd swapped the haggard junkie look for a slight paunch.

'You look great,' Dylan said, as he hugged his dad.

'Do I need to go in and sign shit?' Jake asked.

'I'm free,' Dylan said, shaking his head cheerfully. 'Lawyers sorted the paperwork yesterday. Subtle car. Is it new?'

'Napier's,' Jake explained. 'Chopper's parked up, waiting to take us down to London. I'm going to nip inside for a slash, but there's a gift for you on the back seat.'

'Is it the clothes I asked for? I'm gonna burn these bloody tracksuits . . .'

But it wasn't clothes and Dylan got a lump in his throat as he opened the tinted door.

'Summer!' he gasped, as she scrambled off the back seat, with her hair cut short and a lemon mini-dress. 'You look *incredible*.'

'Not so bad yourself,' Summer said, admiring Dylan's flat stomach and bulging arms. 'You kept that quiet.'

'Not much else to do but pump weights,' Dylan said modestly.

'The muscles are nice, but not smelling of cigarettes is even better.'

Dylan and Summer stood face to face. His chin was level with her nose and she'd been out in the sun, so her cheeks were freckled.

'I'm sorry about your nan,' Dylan said, as he pulled her into a hug.

'Gold tooth,' Summer said, smirking. 'Very gangsta.'

'Dad paid for an implant. Dentist can screw in a porcelain

one if I get sick of the bling.'

'Jay and his family have been so great.'

'Sorry I wasn't there for the funeral.'

'You're here now,' Summer said, as she went slightly on tiptoes and tilted her head.

And finally, they had their first kiss.

41. Season Three

During *Rock War* season one, Lorrie had been an unpaid intern, plucked from obscurity to become the show's presenter. Now she was dating a Premier League player and had just inked a three-year deal which made her Channel Six's highest-paid presenter.

'Welcome back to *Rock War Extra*,' Lorrie said to camera, before coughing. 'AAAARGH . . . Got it . . . Got it, keep rolling . . . Welcome back to *Rock War Extra*. Now, you'd be amazed at who you can bump into walking around Rock War Manor!'

The camera operator zoomed out, bringing Jay and Erin into the shot.

'It's Jay and Erin, both now members of season one band Jet. What brings you both back to the manor?'

'Interview for Channel Six News,' Jay said. 'We met a couple of the season three bands and spoke about how *Rock War* has affected our lives.'

'The manor's looking so swanky,' Erin added. 'Loving the new pool. And they threw out those cheap sponge mattresses.'

'They were the worst,' Lorrie agreed, before cracking a fake laugh. 'Now Jet only finished fourth in *Rock War*, but everything seems to be going amazingly for you at the moment.'

'We're having a blast,' Erin agreed. '"Strip" has done really well in the charts here in the UK and we played our biggest gig ever in Camden last weekend. Plus, we recorded a new version of Jay's old song "Christine" and that's been our second top ten hit in the States.'

'Awesome,' Lorrie purred. 'And I hear Jet are about to zoom off to the States on tour.'

'Packed my bag!' Erin said. 'We're flying off for rehearsals on Friday. Supporting Terraplane on the US leg of their tour.'

'Thirty-six stadiums over two and a half months,' Jay said.

'So, do you think Jet has a bigger following in the US, or here in the UK?' Lorrie asked.

'Probably the USA,' Erin answered. 'At least, we've sold more records there.'

'But we've never played a gig across the pond,' Jay added. 'The fans at our British gigs have been amazing.'

'Now I hear there's a chart battle brewing,' Lorrie said, cracking a big smile. 'Your new track "Lavender Lady" has just been released. Half Term Haircut have also just released the first track from their upcoming second album. Do you think you have a chance of beating them to number one?'

'I wouldn't bet my money on that,' Jay said, shaking his

head. 'The Haircuts are light years ahead of us. They've sold out arenas, they played Glastonbury last month and you can even buy action figures. Jet hasn't even released an album yet.'

'Is the album in the can?' Lorrie asked.

'Just a few finishing touches,' Erin said. 'It'll be out in November.'

'Maybe you can come back one Saturday and guest on *Rock War*,' Lorrie said.

'We'd be honoured to,' Jay said.

'So good catching up with you guys,' Lorrie said, before introducing the next item. 'Earlier today we had another special guest working with our drummers over in the rehearsal rooms. Here's Jake Fish with an update . . .'

*

The chopper touched down at Battersea heliport at noon and a waiting Maybach took Jake Blade, Dylan and Summer on a short ride across the river to the ultra-exclusive Icon Hotel in Chelsea Harbour. While Jake headed to Harley Street for a session with his addiction counsellor, Dylan and Summer rode the elevator to a twelfth-floor penthouse with a balcony overlooking the River Thames.

'It's such an amazing day,' Summer said, as she slid the balcony doors and looked out at a pair of tourist boats on the twinkling water.

'I've not seen a bathtub in four months,' Dylan said, his voice echoing around trendy slate tiles as he picked a pot of orange and bergamot bath salts off the edge of a huge circular jet tub. 'This is *very* tempting.'

'Are you hungry?' Summer asked. 'All I've had was some breakfast at six.'

'I could eat,' Dylan agreed, as he sprinkled bath salts and watched water swirl and turn orange as he turned on a tap.

He kissed the back of Summer's neck as he found her in the bedroom, studying a room service menu.

'Thirty-two quid for lemon sole,' Summer gawped. 'That was more than a week's food budget when I lived with Nan.'

'Have whatever you want,' Dylan said, as Summer turned and started kissing him.

'I can't believe you're all buff,' she said, grinning helplessly as she grabbed the back of his T-shirt. 'I wanna see the full effect.'

Dylan proudly pulled his T-shirt over his head.

'My little gym rat,' Summer said, as she turned her back to him. 'Want to unzip my dress?'

Dylan shivered as the dress fell around her feet. He kissed her neck and his breath shuddered as he studied her in bra and knickers.

'It went too fast with Eve,' Dylan said warily. 'And then everything got weird.'

'I've never . . .' Summer said, facing Dylan again, putting a nervous hand on his bum and backing up towards the bed. 'But if it's weird you'll be the first to know.'

'Right . . . Dylan said, as they closed up for another kiss. 'So, I'll take my trackie bottoms off?'

'I'm no expert, but it would probably make things easier,' Summer teased, undoing her bra as she climbed on the bed.

'I'm going to wake up,' Dylan said, throwing a balled-up sock and crazy turned on by Summer's breasts. 'This has to be a dream. You're too good for me.'

Then he was next to her naked, sliding an arm behind her back. Their weights pressed against each other, and they smiled and caught each other's smell. As the guy, Dylan worried that he might be responsible for the next move. But as he craned his neck to kiss, Summer sat up and almost butted him.

'Is that water running over the side of the bath?' Summer asked.

Dylan cursed as he scrambled towards the bathroom, naked but for his chunky ankle bracelet. The slate floor was slippy and he skidded and thumped his knee on the edge of the tub.

'OWW!'

Summer moved more cautiously, and was relieved to see all the water was running into a drain under the vanity unit. She watched Dylan stretch over the tub of peach-tinted water, reaching to shut off the taps. He had a cute bum and his back was all muscly and it just seemed wrong not to push him in.

42. Lavender Lady

They chased, kissed, threw cushions, had sex, ate room service in the bath and wound up cuddled up on the balcony, wearing thick hotel robes and watching boats on the river. Real life would intervene. Where would they go to school? Where would they live? How would feelings evolve when they were together all the time?

But none of that mattered as they sat on the balcony, hearing each other breathe.

'I'm not being seen in a tracksuit tonight,' Dylan said. 'I might actually buy lighter fluid and burn all those clothes in the bathtub.'

They took a taxi to King's Road, holding hands as Dylan bought trousers, shirts and shoes, then blagged a walk-in appointment in a traditional gents' barber shop. Summer read *Esquire* in the waiting area and signed an autograph for a customer's daughter.

'Are you doing more songs?' the dad asked.

'Hopefully,' Summer said. 'I've written a bunch, but I've been waiting for my boyfriend to be available to arrange and produce.'

She liked the way *my boyfriend* sounded, and she mouthed it over and over as she watched Dylan getting his neck stubble finished with a cut-throat razor.

'And your largest box of condoms,' Dylan said loudly, as he paid at the till.

Summer covered her face and went bright red as they headed back on to the street.

'That's for pushing me in the bath earlier,' Dylan explained, putting an arm around Summer's back as they looked along the street for a taxi.

It was almost seven as a bell-boy took charge of their shopping bags. Jay and his family were waiting in the lobby, dressed in their finest.

'Amazing to see you,' Jay said, pulling Dylan into a hug and mildly irritated by how muscly he'd got.

Dylan shook Len's hand, hugged Adam and Erin but got properly emotional when he got to Heather, who he'd only met very briefly while she'd served in a busy fish and chip shop.

'You saved my life in there,' Dylan told her, as he smudged a tear with his little finger. 'And you were amazing to Summer after Eileen died, so I can't thank you enough.'

'I just did what any decent mum would,' Heather said, as she rubbed Dylan's back.

'And thanks for letting me stay while my dad's away on tour.'

'You won't say that when you have to eat her cooking every night,' Jay joked. 'Or listen to Hank and Patsy scream at one another for three hours every Saturday morning.'

Dylan headed upstairs to swap his tracksuit for some of his new clothes. When he came downstairs, everyone had moved into a private alcove at the back of the hotel restaurant. Jake had ordered a huge cake shaped like an old-fashioned prison, complete with watch towers and barbed wire made from spun sugar.

Besides Jay and his family, the other members of Jet were there, along with Michelle, a bunch of Jake's friends and Mairi Cross from Wilton Music. The restaurant had been voted best in Britain two years earlier and the food comprised a super-fancy ten-course tasting menu. Out of respect for Jake's rehab, and Dylan's parole conditions, no booze was allowed.

To be sociable, people swapped seats between courses. Dylan found himself between Len and Babatunde for the sea urchin with anchovies.

'What do you reckon on the food?' Dylan asked, as Babatunde squeezed his bicep.

'I'm more of a meat and two veg man,' Len admitted, as he suspiciously eyed the slime on the end of his fork.

'Lamb ragu was sensational,' Babatunde said. 'This one's too weird.'

'I'm hearing "Lavender Lady" everywhere today,' Dylan said. 'On the radio when I was getting my bracelet fitted, then in the fitting room when I was trying on shirts. It's such a great track.'

'You should hear the whole album,' Babatunde said.

Len nodded. 'I've got a near-final cut back at the house. We even dragged Summer into the studio for backup vocals on two tracks.'

'I've missed *everything*,' Dylan moaned. 'And it's a shame Terraplane and Jet are off on tour just as I get out.'

'Summer's the one that matters,' Babatunde noted. 'She's sticking around for you.'

'I reckon you'll knock it out of the park, working in the studio with Summer,' Len said. 'And of course, if you need a bit of help from someone who knows his way around a recording studio . . .'

'That would be awesome,' Dylan said. 'You're Summer's manager now, anyway.'

Babatunde reached behind and thumped Len on the back. 'You're gonna be richer than any of us with your fifteen per cent cut of everyone.'

'That's the plan,' Len said, laughing. 'Milk you spotty teenagers for every penny! I've been poor for long enough.'

'Dad said you played "Grace" with Terraplane at Wembley Arena last night,' Dylan said. 'Are things all smoothed over with Wilton Music?'

'Day to day is OK,' Len said, smiling. 'They couldn't recruit anyone who wanted to run the label up in Edinburgh, so Mairi's officially the boss now and she's a good lass. But Napier still hates my guts, and I wouldn't bank on any birthday gifts from your godfather in the near future, either.'

'Screw him, I hate his guts,' Dylan said, as he spat something that tasted weird into his napkin. 'Wouldn't piss on Napier if he was on fire.'

'Napier can hardly complain, when Jet are doing well and making his label money,' Babatunde noted.

'So "Lavender Lady" will be number one download this week?' Dylan asked.

Len cracked a wry smile and spoke quietly. 'The publicity people have told us to play it down and act cool. But Mairi has a contact with someone inside the company that produces the chart. She reckons "Lavender Lady" is outselling Half Term Haircut's track by five to one.'

'Five to one!' Babatunde blurted, almost swallowing his tongue. 'It's not one of the Haircut's best, but that's still amazing!'

'Keep it under your hats,' Len said, as he glanced anxiously to see who else might have heard. 'Do not tell Jay. He's got two radio interviews tomorrow morning and he can't accidentally blurt what he doesn't know, can he?'

Dylan and Babatunde eyed Jay at the opposite end of the table as they laughed.

'"Lavender Lady" is just a great mellow track,' Dylan said. 'It could become a classic. Like "Bittersweet Symphony", or "Black Hole Sun".'

'The chart comes out on Friday night,' Babatunde explained. 'So we won't officially know if we're number one until we land in Chicago.'

A waitress was coming around the table, swapping the little sea urchin plates for bowls with orange stuff in the bottom and flakes of gold leaf. At the same time, Summer walked up.

'Can I sit with my man?' Summer asked, and Babatunde obliged by heading around the table to talk drums with Terraplane's Dave Ingham.

'Carrot bleeding porridge with saffron and gold leaf,' Len said, shaking his head as he read from the menu. Then he smiled at Summer. 'I'd have loved to see what the Lavender Lady herself would make of this menu.'

Summer laughed as she rested her head on Dylan's shoulder. 'Nan definitely would have preferred poached eggs on toast and a nice mug of tea.'

43. Departing Jet

'I finally got the email,' Summer shouted. 'They're here.'

She was at the desk in Jay's bedroom – which would become Dylan's temporary bedroom when Jay left for America in three and a half hours. Summer was disappointed that nobody had burst into the room to share her news and her heart thudded as the message opened up on screen.

Dear Summer,

I am delighted to say we have now received the results for the GCSE subjects you have been studying at the academy. I trust that they are a just reward for the efforts I know you put into achieving them.

Mathematics	B
English Language	A
English Literature	A*
Chemistry	B

Crash Landing

Physics	B
Biology	A*
History	PENDING
French	A
Drama	A
Music	C

Yours sincerely,

George Obernackle
Deputy Headmaster in Charge of Upper School

'Hello?' Summer said, crushed by the lack of response as she charged from the attic to the ground floor waving a printout.

There was chaos by the open front door. It was raining heavily and a soggy chauffeur was struggling to fit Jay, Len and Erin's suitcases in the back of an S-Class Mercedes.

'I told you to send the guitar with the rest of the gear,' Len told Jay.

'It's the expensive one Theo bought me,' Jay explained. 'I don't trust roadies.'

Hank and June stood just inside the front door, looking miserable because their daddy was leaving. The toilet under the stairs flushed and Heather stepped out behind Summer.

'Finally got my results,' Summer gasped, keen for some attention.

Heather grabbed the printout and read through. 'Why do none of *my* kids get five As?' she shouted, as she planted a kiss on Summer's cheek. 'Are you happy?'

'Sure,' Summer said modestly.

'Bet you'd have got all A-stars if things were normal,' Jay said, as he came inside to see her results. 'What's *pending*?'

'The main history exam was the day of Nan's funeral, so they agreed to base my whole mark on my coursework,' Summer explained. 'Another A hopefully.'

Dylan was already in the back of the Mercedes and the chauffeur didn't look happy, seeing him get out and run splashing up the driveway, when he was trying to herd the rest of his passengers in.

'Certainly better than my *get sent to prison and do no exams at all* system,' Dylan said, as he hugged Summer.

'Why does Dylan get to see his dad fly away when we don't?' June moaned.

'Because there's not room for everyone in the car,' Heather shouted, loud enough to make June spring backwards. 'Stop whining and go give Daddy a hug.'

The chauffeur finally got his trunk closed as Len scooped up his two youngest kids. Jay hugged them too, then his Auntie Rachel, Summer, Patsy and Adam. He settled into the back seat of the Mercedes as a crash of lightning made his younger sister yelp and bolt inside.

'Proper British summer weather,' Len joked, his eyes blurred with tears as he shut the front passenger door and looked behind at Jay, Dylan and Erin in the back.

'All set?' he asked.

They wound the windows down and waved. June cried and

Crash Landing

Hank chased the Mercedes as far as the postbox at the end of the street.

The rain kept pounding and visibility on the M25 was horrible. Google Maps estimated the journey at an hour and ten, but an accident had shut two lanes, so the ride to Biggin Hill took almost twice that.

Len worried they were late as they pushed a luggage cart into the tiny airport's private aviation terminal. But everyone had faced the same traffic and the girl on the luggage desk explained that it wasn't a problem: all departing flights were being delayed by an hour or more, because the heavy rain meant reduced visibility and bigger safety margins between aircraft taxiing on the ground.

Dylan wasn't flying, but had a permit to go through customs and say goodbye to his dad. Jay laughed as Dylan's ankle bracelet set off the security scanner and Dylan struggled to explain that he couldn't take it off to a security officer who barely spoke English.

The terminal catered exclusively to private aircraft and the area beyond security was full of comfy leather sofas, with a free bar and a couple of upmarket food concessions. Dylan located his dad on a stool at an oyster bar, dressed in a loose linen suit ideal for a long flight and accompanied by the addiction counsellor, who US promoters had mandated accompany Jake Blade for the length of the rescheduled tour.

'Have you thought any more about school?' Jake asked.

'I've got an interview at an FE college,' Dylan said. 'Summer wants to do her A levels there too.'

'He's in love,' Jake explained to his hippyish counsellor. 'This is the first time I've seen him more than a metre away from Summer since he got released.'

Dylan thought about this for a second and realised that he'd only been staying at Heather's house for a couple of nights, but it already felt more like a proper home than his dad's sprawling Scottish mansion.

Across the terminal, Jay and Erin found Salman and Babatunde staring through glass at the airfield. Most of the planes were little business jets, with under a dozen seats, but amidst them was an Airbus A330, painted black with Terraplane written on the side and the band's logo on the tail.

'Check the engine under the wing,' Salman said.

It was hard to see with drips running down the window and rain pounding the tarmac, but Jay just made out the Jet logo, painted on the big plane's engine pod.

'Jet on a jet,' Babatunde said. 'I just put it on my Instagram, with the comment *Someday we'll have our own plane, but for now this will do.*'

Jay snapped a picture with his phone. The weather meant it wasn't the best shot, but he sent it in a message to Bailey, who was holidaying in France with her folks. *Like our ride?*

With private jets, people typically clear customs and walk straight out to their plane. But weather delays meant the sofas were getting busy and rumours swirled that certain flights wouldn't get to take off before the airport's night-time noise curfew.

The five members of Jet sat on two facing sofas, while

people who thought they were important drank free wine and wandered around speaking loudly into their phones. Just when it was starting to look like everyone would be spending the night in a hotel, the call went out.

'*All members of the Terraplane USA Tour party to present passports at Gate D for immediate departure.*'

There were as many passengers on the Terraplane flight as all the other delayed flights combined. The band mates grabbed their stuff and joined a scrum of roadies, publicists, engineers, backing singers and journalists at the gate. Jay looked for Dylan, but apparently he'd already left because he had to be home before curfew.

The rain was unrelenting and Jay held his flight bag over his head as they dashed a hundred metres, following a red line painted on the concrete. By the time they'd climbed steps up to the plane, they were all dripping.

'Welcome to the tour,' Harry Napier said, shaking hands and doing an impressive job of remembering everyone's name as they came aboard. 'Jay, Erin, Babatunde, Salman, Alfie.'

Len was next up the steps and the handshake was decidedly limp.

'You're in row thirty-three,' Napier said acidly. 'Enjoy.'

They'd entered the plane up by the cockpit. There were fifteen huge cream leather seats, which could recline into flat beds and had stewards serving champagne and caviar crostini.

'Nice,' Jay said, but he was less impressed as they moved past the galley and into the twin-aisled plane's main section.

While the front had been refitted for VIP luxury, the rest of the interior showed the plane's age, with shabby seats, several overhead bins sealed shut with hazard tape and warning notices and safety cards with the logo of previous owners, Botswana Airways.

There were fifteen rows of tatty-but-spacious business class seats, which were steadily being occupied by not-quite VIPs, such as music journalists and band members' offspring. Len was seething as Jay found their row, amidst a few rows of tatty economy style seating right at the back of the plane.

'That bastard Napier!' Len hissed, so tall that his head touched the ceiling. 'This is his way to get back at me.'

'It's not full,' Jay noted, as he let Erin through to a seat in the middle. 'We can spread out.'

'That's not the point,' Len said. 'Tours have a hierarchy. Headliners and their wives up front, then backing musicians and support bands, and winding up with roadies and technical staff at the back. This is a very public insult.'

Jay looked up towards the nose as a cowboy-hatted roadie sat in the row in front.

'Who did you piss off?' the roadie joked, as he threw a battered NATO backpack in the overhead.

'Napier,' Jay said weakly.

'Bad idea,' the roadie grinned.

'I can't even get my legs behind these seats,' Len said, as he tried to sit down. 'I'm gonna talk to the old sod.'

'Something wrong with your seat, Leonard?' Napier grinned, as the billionaire wallowed in his giant first-class armchair. 'It's *only* ten and a half hours. Though I might ask them to do a couple of circles over Chicago and make it a round eleven.'

The skinny woman sitting next to Napier was obviously in on the joke and laughed so hard that she slopped champagne on her tights.

'It's not safe,' Len roared. 'I'm six-foot six. I can't even get my feet on the floor without crippling myself.'

'Guess you'll have to fight one of the roadies for an exit row,' Napier teased, before putting on a posh accent. 'Now eff orf, I'm trying to eat my caviar.'

'Sir, the doors are closed and we're about to taxi,' a steward added firmly, as Napier guffawed. 'You need to get back in your seat.'

As Len stormed back down the plane, a titchy make-up artist in the penultimate row of business-class seats touched his arm.

'I don't mind switching,' she said. 'It's pretty empty back there and I can take a couple of seats and spread out.'

'You're very kind,' Len said, making a mental note to buy her a gift when they arrived.

But Len still seethed as he helped the woman grab her bag from the overhead and settled in to the much larger seat.

44. The End Of The Line

The A330 taxied from its stand. The big bird needed the full length of Biggin Hill's main runway, so it bypassed smaller planes and stood poised at the runway's western end.

'I'm sorry for this short delay,' the co-pilot announced. 'Unfortunately we're waiting for a backlog of smaller aircraft to take off further up the runway and three others coming in to land. The tower has given me a slot to depart in approximately twenty minutes. In accordance with Civil Aviation Authority regulations, I must ask all passengers to remain seated with their seat belts fastened . . .'

'Always when you need a piss,' Babatunde complained, as he clamped his knees together.

The back of the plane was less than half full. Jay and Erin had four central seats between them, while Alfie, Babatunde and Salman had moved from their allocated places and each bagged a pair of seats by a window. There seemed to be plenty of staff up front pampering Terraplane and their management,

323

but there was nobody down in the cheap seats and Babatunde followed a lead when a giant hairball of a roadie staggered down the aisle and into one of the toilets.

'Going for it,' Babatunde said, as he flipped his seat belt and made a dash.

An elderly stewardess sighted the roadie and came wobbling down the aisle.

'Sir, get back in your seat. We could take off at any moment.'

'The pilot just said twenty minutes,' the drunk roadie yelled from inside the bathroom. 'I'll piss my pants.'

While the stewardess argued with the roadie, Babatunde emerged unnoticed from a toilet on the opposite side of the plane. Just in front was a small galley area, and little cabinets filled with drinks and snacks.

Babatunde scooped handfuls of chocolate bars and miniature brandy bottles, stuffing them in the front pockets of his hoodie and tossing them to his band mates as he sat back down.

'Remy Martin,' the roadie sitting in front of Jay said, after deftly plucking the bottle out of midair and unscrewing the little cap. 'Don't mind if I do.'

Jay wasn't paying attention because he'd forgotten to put his phone in airplane mode. He had a message from Summer, who'd assumed that they'd taken off on time and would read the message when they landed.

Hope your flight was good. Just checked online and

Lavender Lady is No1 in the charts. Huge congrats. Call us
when you can. X

'We did it, ladies,' Jay shouted, as he shot out of his seat.
'Jet are number one.'

Babatunde wasn't surprised because Len had let the five-to-
one sales figure slip when he was drunk a few nights earlier,
but Alfie, Erin and Salman had no idea and started yelling.

A couple of roadies reached around and started shaking the
band mates' hands. Babatunde remembered seeing champagne
chilling in the galley and once again hopped out of his seat.
He sprinted, grabbed two full-sized bottles and was back in his
seat in less than half a minute.

'Champagne!' he shouted, handing a bottle over to Erin
and leaning across the aisle to kiss her on the cheek.

Jay shouted up the plane to try and get Len's attention, but
even though the engines were only idling, Len still didn't hear.
Alfie decided that this news was sufficiently exciting to be
worth incurring the wrath of a steward, grabbed the other
bottle from Babatunde and went sprinting up towards Len.

'Boss, we're number one!' Alfie shouted.

Len had put on headphones and only realised what was
happening when Alfie was right in the aisle next to him.

'Pardon me?' Len said, lifting up one ear cup.

'Number one,' Alfie shouted, twisting the wire and easing
out the champagne cork.

The bottle had gotten a good shaking and Alfie was
surprised by the spout of fizz shooting into the air. As Len

flinched to avoid getting his trousers soaked, the cork ricocheted off the bottom of an overhead rack and hit a woman sitting across the aisle in the face.

'Sorry,' Alfie gasped, as he realised that flying off to America and having a number one hit had over-stimulated his thirteen-year-old mind.

The young woman who'd been hit with the cork screamed and put a hand over her eye. In the same instant, the seat belt lights flashed and a bing-bong sound pealed.

The co-pilot came over the PA: 'Slight change of plan, ladies and gentlemen. Unfortunately, one of the small jets queuing at the mid-point of the runway has suffered a mechanical issue and is unable to take off. The good news is that this has cleared us for immediate departure. I repeat, immediate departure. Flight crew, take positions.'

Terraplane's manager Harry Napier had spent years sorting problems on tours. He'd heard the screaming woman and was storming down the plane as the co-pilot began his take-off announcement.

'What the heck is this behaviour on my aeroplane?' Napier shouted, as he charged a terrified Alfie.

Alfie started backing towards his seat, just as the pilot throttled up the engines to line up at the bottom of the runway.

'Napier,' Len roared, as he tried to stand up. 'He's just a kid.'

Alfie looked like he was going to crap his pants as he scrambled down the aisle of the accelerating plane. Len had a struggle getting his bulk out of his seat. His foot was in the aisle as the plane sent Napier stumbling forwards. The trip wasn't deliberate, but Napier assumed that it was.

'You oversized prick!' Napier shouted, keeping his squat frame upright by grabbing a seat back, then swinging a punch that was absorbed by the ample layer of fat over Len's chest.

Len had wanted to thump Napier for years and shouted, 'He's just a kid,' again as his huge fist crushed Harry Napier's nose.

A dental plate flew through the cabin as Napier sprawled backwards down the aisle. Meanwhile in the front galley, an anxious steward was on the intercom, telling the pilot that a fight had broken out.

A co-pilot always announces V1 – the point at which a plane would overshoot a runway if take-off was aborted – to his captain. There had been no announcement, so the pilot immediately threw both engines into reverse and opened the wing flaps to maximise deceleration.

At the back of the plane, Jay's neck snapped forward and his forehead slammed the folded tray table as the lap belt cut painfully into his stomach. Bags slammed around in the overhead lockers and he saw Erin's anxious expression as her iPhone slipped off her lap and slid under the seats in front.

Salman had a view out of the window. Though it was nearly dark he could just make out the back of the wing through the plumes of spray and rubber smoke being thrown up by the plane's screaming tyres. They'd slowed significantly when he heard a bang, followed by a strip of metal smashing into the fuselage right next to his head.

'What was that?' Salman gasped.

The plane lurched violently left and began tilting sideways. There was a jolt as the plane's front wheels came off the runway. Still spinning, the right engine under the wing hit sodden grass, sucking in chunks of turf and pelting them against the side of the plane.

Out on the airfield, the airport emergency siren had gone up and a pair of fire engines were scrambling towards the runway. The crew in the lead vehicle watched as the friction caused by the engine pod digging into soft ground caused the wing to buckle and tear away from the fuselage.

Planes store most of their fuel inside the wings, so an airport fire crew's worst nightmare is a plane fuelled for a long flight sustaining wing damage. Everyone gasped as the plane stopped and the stewardess who'd yelled at the roadie sprinted down the aisle and started opening the rear doors.

'All passengers move to your nearest exit and evacuate immediate using the emergency slides,' the pilot shouted.

Salman was out of his seat, but a flash of orange made him look back out of the window. The portion of the wing directly above the engine had started to burn.

'The front exit and left wing exit are not safe,' a crew member announced. 'Please use right wing and rear exits only.'

As the stewardess opened one rear door, Babatunde and a sound technician managed the other. There was a sharp bang and whiff of smoke as bright orange slides inflated, over a metre and a half wide.

'You must remove high-heeled shoes,' the stewardess shouted. 'Do not pick up your luggage.'

'Ladies first,' Babatunde said, letting the sound technician go down the slide and plough into several inches of muddy water.

As Babatunde slid down one rear exit, Jay was first out on the opposite side and felt intense heat from an increasingly large fire around the engine pod.

'Keep moving to the end of the runway,' a firefighter was shouting, as her colleagues moved around the side of the plane with hoses.

Erin instinctively paused to grab her phone and got shoved in the back by Salman. 'Move, you idiot,' he shouted, giving her a massive shove.

There was a queue building for the rear slides, and enough smoke in the cabin to sting their eyes.

'Go, go,' the steward was shouting. 'Quickly, quickly.'

Lightning flashed as Erin and Salman made it out of the plane. Heat from the fire burst one of the huge tyres. The crowd backed up the plane's aisle was starting to panic and the stewardess was screaming for people to stop pushing.

'Move to the assembly point,' the firefighter shouted to Jay on the ground.

The make-up artist who'd given Len her seat had twisted her ankle at the bottom of the slide. Salman and Erin grabbed her under the arms and walked as fast as they could. Foam had started blasting out of a cannon on top of a fire engine, but there was a much larger bang as one of the fuel tanks exploded.

Flaming jet fuel spewed high into the air and ripped a riveted section of fuselage like it was the lid of a sardine can. Alfie had been thrown violently when the pilot slammed on the brakes and was still dazed as he came down the slide in the tattooed grasp of a roadie. Burning fuel had now reached the rear slide on one side and two choking passengers jumped down into flames.

Now blinded by smoke, the elderly stewardess made her own escape into the arms of a firefighter. There had been people lined up behind, but the smoke was crippling and just one person jumped down after her.

'They're just inside,' she told the fire crews. 'You have to pull them out. The smoke is too thick.'

Jay and Babatunde had run a couple of hundred metres and were soaked with rain. As they looked back, they saw that the fire had spread across the wing on the far side and now burned fiercely in the centre of the cabin. Fire engines aimed thick jets of foam, while the two rear doors billowed smoke like dragon's nostrils.

'Safest form of travel, my ass,' Babatunde shouted furiously.

'Nobody up front could have got out,' Jay said desperately, then managed a relieved smile as Salman and Erin emerged through the rain, with the make-up lady draped around their backs.

'I saw Alfie come out,' Salman shouted. 'Big guy rescued him.'

'What about Len?' Jay asked.

'He was standing, so he must have gone flying when the

pilot put the brakes on,' Babatunde said. He was stronger than Erin, so he took over her role helping the make-up lady.

'Uncle Len's way too big to carry,' Erin said anxiously, as she tipped her head back, hoping the rain would clear her burning eyes.

There were people jogging or limping down the runway. Ground staff in waterproofs were shouting, 'Follow the blue line to the terminal.'

Jay flicked dripping hair away from his eyes, trying not to breathe too hard because he'd pulled a muscle when the seat belt dug into his chest. Then came a blinding flash and bang. He stumbled sideways as radiated heat hit his body, then dived to the floor as a smouldering, fist-sized chunk of aluminium skimmed past.

It smashed into a grass verge less than three metres away, turning puddled water into steam.

45. Top Of The Hour

'This is 24/7 News, I'm Grace Longford. Our headlines at eleven p.m. . . .

'More than fifty passengers and three crew are feared dead after a wide-bodied Airbus plane burst into flames at Biggin Hill airport, south of London.

'The privately chartered jet was heading towards Chicago with the band Terraplane and a substantial tour entourage on board. We now go live to our correspondent Enrique Grimshaw, who was inside the terminal when the incident occurred. Enrique, what's the latest?'

Viewers at home saw a cut to a man standing on a road outside Biggin Hill's VIP terminal.

'That's right,' Enrique began. 'I was in the terminal with a documentary crew, waiting to fly out to film wildlife in the Amazon, when this incident occurred. The terminal was very busy because our flight and many others had been delayed, due to persistent thunderstorms and poor visibility over the airfield.

'Biggin Hill is a small airfield. There are no scheduled passenger flights from here, but it is frequently used by VIPs, including Her Majesty the Queen and government ministers. Shortly after nine thirty this evening the doomed aircraft began its take-off. It was an Airbus A330 wide-body jet. This is significantly larger than most of the planes that take off from Biggin Hill, so myself and many others inside the terminal were very aware of this large jet lumbering along the runway.

'Quite early in the take-off run, the plane began to brake. People who were aboard the plane say the abort was called because several passengers were fighting and out of their seats. The plane had almost come to a noisy, but relatively orderly, stop when it dramatically changed course and veered off the runway.

'Several other pilots were waiting to take off in smaller aircraft close to the incident. I spoke to one pilot who said that as the jet broke, she witnessed a large piece of the wing flap breaking away from the aircraft.

'The pilot explained that on large aircraft these wing flaps are deployed on the ground to create drag and slow an aircraft down. If a flap breaks away on one side, the difference in drag between the two sides can be enough to make the plane veer off course unless the pilot makes a rapid course correction. There was an extraordinary din as the plane swerved on to a muddy grass verge, while still travelling at around forty kilometres per hour.'

'What about the plane itself?' Grace asked. 'The studio has

received several tweets and messages suggesting that this particular aircraft has a somewhat chequered history.'

Enrique nodded. 'The A330 is a very successful aircraft design, with over one and a half thousand built and an excellent safety record. However, the aircraft in this incident is one of the first A330s built and is now well over twenty years old. All aircraft have a unique identification number and there is a lot of information on the internet about this one. Its first owner was a German airline, then it spent over a decade in service for Botswana Airways.

'Since that airline went bankrupt, the aircraft has had a number of different owners and two quite serious accidents. Interestingly, just six months ago, the aircraft suffered major damage to the left wing after a landing in bad weather and spent four months undergoing repairs in Bangladesh.

'Given my pilot witness's description of a major component breaking away from that wing during the aborted take-off, I'm sure that repair is going to be very closely scrutinised by air crash investigators.'

'And what is the latest on the casualty situation?' the studio newsreader asked.

'An A330 can take over three hundred passengers. But as I understand it, this plane had been reconfigured for VIP travel, with mostly first- and business-class seating and a total capacity of one hundred and ninety passengers. The airport press office has confirmed that when the plane took off, there were a hundred and twenty-four passengers and nine crew members aboard.

'They also confirmed that a total of seventy-eight people made it off the plane, around half of whom have been taken to hospital, mostly suffering from smoke inhalation and other minor injuries. However, nine people, including two crew members who used an exit rope to leave by a sliding cockpit window, suffered broken bones, burns or other serious injuries.

'That leaves fifty-five passengers or crew unaccounted for. Tragically, two firefighters with breathing apparatus had boarded the plane to try and rescue passengers who'd passed out, and another firefighter who was on the ground close to the rear of the plane suffered serious injuries.

'My understanding is that cabin crew chose not to deploy exits at the front of the plane because of the proximity of the fire, and that most of those who survived were seated towards the rear of the plane.'

'Thank you,' Grace said, as the director cut back to the studio. 'We're taking you away from Enrique, because we've just received a press release from Sue Willoughby, who is the publicist for the band Jet. Jet were one of the bands in the popular talent show *Rock War* and they were travelling with Terraplane as one of the support bands for the US tour.

'The statement from Jet reads: *It is with relief that we can announce that the five members of Jet all emerged relatively unscathed from tonight's horrific incident. Alfie Jopling is in hospital receiving treatment for a minor concussion. Sadly, our manager, Leonard 'Big Len' Crouch was caught in the final explosion moments after leaving via the over-wing exit. He has been transported to a specialist burns unit for emergency treatment. We ask all our fans to pray for Len's speedy recovery, and for all the other people lost or injured.*

'Enrique,' Grace continued. 'It's interesting that we've received a press release from one of the two bands on the plane, but nothing about Terraplane from their media representatives.'

The director cut back to Enrique, who nodded solemnly.

'In circumstances like this, we're always wary of giving false information and causing unnecessary grief to family members. But I spoke to many of the uninjured passengers as they came back to the terminal. They confirmed that the members of Terraplane were in first class, at the front of the plane, furthest from the functioning exits.

'Nobody I spoke to had seen any sign of the five members of Terraplane, or their manager, either here at the airport or amongst those taken to the hospital. So while I'm reluctant to make a definitive statement until we have an official casualty list, I think any fans of Terraplane who are watching should brace themselves for the worst possible news about their idols.'

Five Months Later

46. Snow In New York City

Sixteen-year-old Noah from Belfast shot an impressive personal best score of 586 in the eighteen-metre sixty-arrows category, adding a gold medal to the silver he won in the thirty-metre thirty-six-arrow. Noah must now be rated as one of the favourites for next summer's indoor world championships, and a leading British medal hope for the 2020 Paralympics.
Archery Today, 24 December

Terraplane would never stand on their fourteen-million-dollar hydraulic stage. But Heinz de Mol had built it just once, for a New Year's Day charity gig inside New York's colossal Met Life Stadium. Two dozen of the biggest names in rock, grunge and indie had agreed to play in an epic, seven-hour tribute gig.

There was snow on New York's streets and a chill blast whipped over the eighty-five-thousand-strong crowd. Jay had met a bunch of lifelong idols backstage, and since Jet's four-song set was sandwiched between rock gods, he feared that a lot of the crowd would use it as a toilet break.

'So we finally found a plane that actually made it across the pond,' Erin told the crowd blackly, as she led the band on stage.

The five regular members of Jet were joined by Summer and Michelle as backing singers and a one-off appearance by Theo, who Americans knew as a host of *Rock War*, rather than a former contestant.

The crowd roared as the Jet logo on a jet engine picture appeared on a single huge screen behind the stage. When Jay sent the picture to Bailey on the night of the crash, he thought very little of it. But the rain-smeared image of the black plane, taken an hour before its demise, had been posted on the band's website and wound up being reproduced in hundreds of newspapers around the world. When it came to choosing artwork for Jet's first album, a subtly photoshopped version of the now-iconic image was a unanimous choice.

'Three Thirty' by Jet had peaked at four in the US album charts, got to number three in the UK and remained in the top twenty in both countries two months after release. But the band played it safe for the memorial concert, opening with their familiar foot-stomper 'Strip', with Theo belting out the vocal, just like the version used on the TV show.

They followed up with a track off the album called 'Budget Homes', losing the audience slightly before winning it back with 'Lavender Lady', which had now topped the charts in five countries and been Jet's first sizeable hit in a dozen more. They'd also just been offered a seven-figure sum to allow the song to be used in an advertisement for a mobile phone company.

Pretty much every act had chosen to wind up their set with a Terraplane song. Several big acts had asked to play the band's biggest hit, but being pals with Jake Blade's only surviving relative conveyed certain advantages.

'I'd like to introduce a very special guest for our final track,' Salman said. 'He got a bit banged up in the summer, but his picking fingers work just fine. He played on the original version of this track. I give you, Big Len Crouch!'

Len waved as he limped on stage. Over a quarter of his body had been burned and the lower part of his face was covered with white gauze to protect recently grafted skin. Hardcore Terraplane fans knew Len's place in the band's history, but the bulk of the audience didn't go crazy until Len placed the opening chords of 'Grace'.

'Give me graaaaaaaaaaace!' Salman sang, as eighty-five thousand people rose to their feet, cheering and clapping.

Terraplane's original version lasted seven minutes, but Jet stretched it out to ten, much to the chagrin of a stage manager with a tight schedule and a lot of talent to keep happy. As 'Grace' finished, an overhead wire cam swung across the stadium, showing the faces of crying fans.

The next band on stage looked furious as Jet took bows and ran off, because anything they played after 'Grace' would be an anticlimax. The gig was being shown live on TV and streamed around the world, so Jay and Salman were stopped by a camera team and the comedian and chat show host Dan Trombone stuck a microphone in their faces.

'You are so young and so talented,' the comedian told them. 'You have absolutely no idea how much I hate you.'

'Cheers,' Salman laughed, piling on his London accent, because he knew the Yanks loved it.

'So you're sixteen years old and you just blew the socks off an eighty-five-thousand-strong crowd and millions watching live on ANT. How are you planning to top this?'

'Ma says I need to focus more on my schoolwork,' Jay joked. 'I'll amount to nothing if I get a D in geography.'

'My mum is keen for me to become a doctor,' Salman added. 'Or failing that a pharmacist.'

'The pharmacists earn big money,' Dan said, as he roared with laughter. 'But I hear you're heading off to do some acting?'

'Teeny bit,' Jay said, holding his fingers a few millimetres apart. 'While we're out here, we're recording some extra music for *Tenured*. And we're gonna be extras on the show. Like, sitting in the classroom on campus or whatever.'

'I wanted to say a line, but you have to be in the actors' union,' Salman added.

'Then we're shooting a promo video for our next single in Mexico,' Jay said.

'And I hear you're up for a Grammy in February?' Don said.

'Best non-classical song adapted for visual media category,' Jay said.

'I think that's like the most important Grammy,' Salman

joked. 'Way bigger than best artist, or best album.'

'Great talking to you guys,' Don said, as he tapped his earpiece. 'Now my director is telling me that the next act is ready to play, so let's cut right back to the stage.'

47. Loadsa Money

THE BABY BILLIONAIRE

Every January sees the publication of CA$H Magazine's list of Europe's wealthiest people. Following the sudden death of Terraplane front man Jake Blade, Britain has its youngest ever billionaire in his only offspring, seventeen-year-old Dylan Wilton.

Despite lifelong struggles with addiction, Jake Blade accumulated more than $300 million from his career with Terraplane, and a whopping $160 million insurance payout from backers of his US tour.

As Blade's only child, Dylan Wilton's inheritance also includes a 40% share in Rock War and Super Chef producer Venus TV, worth an estimated $340m. A 50% stake in Wilton Music, which owns the Terraplane back catalogue and currently has chart-toppers Half Term

Haircut and Jet on its label, is worth at least another $90m.

Other assets inherited by Wilton include a vast collection of classic vehicles and aircraft worth at least $175m. Adding significant property holdings in Edinburgh, film industry interests and a contemporary art collection which includes more than a hundred valuable works by Wilton's mother, brings the teenager's inheritance to around $1.6 billion.

Even though most of Blade's assets were held in trusts, Europe's youngest billionaire still faces an estimated $350 million inheritance tax bill, so for the purposes of our charts, we have conservatively estimated Dylan Wilton's net total wealth at $1.25 billion. (All figures in US$.)

CA$H Magazine, Jan 2018 issue

'I don't care if he is a billionaire,' Heather told the journalist on the doorstep as she put out the recycling. 'He still takes his turn stacking the dishwasher and folding the laundry like the rest of the family.'

The press loved CA$H Magazine's Baby Billionaire story, and Heather's quote gave them perfect headlines: Baby Billionaire Still Folds Laundry, 17YO Moneybags Does Dishes. One website noted that Dylan could earn £50,000 per day in interest if he put his fortune into a savings account and did nothing for the rest of his life.

Dylan had been a reluctant member of the Pandas of Doom and squirmed every minute he'd spent on stage. Now there were journalists and photographers outside the house every morning as he left for college. Same dumb questions, over and over:

'*Is it true you're selling Venus TV to Karen Trim?*'

'*Did you and Summer get engaged?*'

'*Have you made an offer on any of the mansions you viewed over the weekend?*'

Dylan rarely answered, but he was as grumpy as any other teenager when he left for college at 8:15 in the morning and lashed out when asked about the house.

'Yes, I'm buying a bigger house where we can all live behind a big gate and not have you turds taking photos through the curtains and asking me idiotic questions every day.'

Baby Billionaire loses cool over £12 million mansion . . .

Sue, the publicist, hoped that the interest in Dylan's wealth would die down. But the media remained fascinated by the idea of a teenaged billionaire, living in a regular north London street with his girlfriend, a member of an increasingly successful rock band, plus Len, Heather and her sprawling family.

Although Dylan hated the limelight, Sue persuaded him to do an exclusive interview for the Chi Rock YouTube channel. She hoped that speculation about Dylan's life and future would die down if he answered a list of pre-selected questions with the celebrity vlogger.

Summer also agreed to be interviewed and they met in an upscale art gallery close to St Pancras International station. The exclusive was a huge coup for Lulu Chi. In return, Sue had insisted on an approved list of questions, and full editorial control over the online video and an accompanying newspaper feature.

Summer and Dylan sat on a boxy leather sofa. To emphasise their ordinariness, Sue had them both wear trainers and polo shirts, as if they'd just spent the day at college. Lulu faced them in an office chair. She had turquoise hair, lace-up leather bodice and neon knee socks coming out of her battered army boots.

'So so so!' Lulu squealed to her camera. 'I just arrive from Paris on Eurostar and I am super, super, SUPER excited to have this exclusive Chi Rock interview with Dylan Wilton and Summer Smith. Hi, guys. Everyone is talking about you and it's so fantastic to have this opportunity!'

'Our pleasure,' Dylan said warmly.

'Great to finally meet you,' Summer added, as she flicked hair off her face.

Lulu was bouncing in her chair. 'I wanna start by asking about when you two first met,' she began. 'Was it like, who cares? Or was there an instant spark?'

Dylan laughed. 'I guess we met on the first day of *Rock War* boot camp. I think everyone was annoyed because the Pandas arrived in my dad's helicopter and they made everyone else wait outside. My first memory of Summer is that she got sunburn, and the skin on her shoulders was peeling.'

'Eww,' Summer said, whacking Dylan fondly. 'Trust you to remember that. I'm not sure exactly when I first noticed Dylan. There were actually a lot of cute guys by the pool that first night. I mainly remember that Theo and Adam Richardson were so ripped.'

Lulu cracked a toothy smile, while Sue stood behind the camera giving the couple a thumbs-up, because their chemistry was perfect.

'So I guess it was much later when I fell for Dylan,' Summer said. 'As *Rock War* went on, I got a sense that he was a good guy. And it was while he was in on the run that we got really close.'

'Now there's a rumour doing the rounds that you two got engaged just before Christmas. No secrets allowed! You *have* to tell Lulu!'

Dylan laughed and Summer covered her face.

'We did,' Dylan admitted. 'It wasn't a huge thing and there wasn't a ring, or a party or any of that. I was like, *So we're gonna get married some day and Summer said yeah*, and I said, *I guess that means we're engaged.*'

'We might have been a little tipsy,' Summer suggested.

Dylan shook his head. 'You might have been. I don't touch alcohol.'

'We're not idiots,' Summer said. 'We love each other, but we're sixteen and seventeen. Things will change. We're not about to run off to Vegas and get married.'

'Five years' time,' Dylan suggested. 'After university, or something like that.'

'And what about your career, Summer?' Lulu asked. 'You've talked on social media about recording an album, with Dylan producing.'

'We will,' Summer said, nodding. 'But after last year, with my nan and Dylan's dad dying . . .'

'It's nice going to college and hanging out, being normal teenagers for a bit,' Dylan agreed. 'Last year, I was in deep trouble. Banged up with other inmates threatening to kill me. When I got out, I had maybe the happiest few days of my life. Then suddenly, *bam* and my dad is dead. Then we're at the hospital every night not knowing if Len is going to live or die . . .'

'We're working on songs, and we will record an album,' Summer said. 'But there's no fixed schedule. We'll probably wait a year. Maybe even two.'

'And meantime, your friends' band Jet just getting so big now,' Lulu squealed, as she bounced and clapped her hands. 'They're totally one of my favourite bands now.'

'It's been an amazing few months for Jet,' Dylan agreed. 'All five members are great friends of ours and they're on my record label, so I'm really happy for them.'

'Do you think inheriting your father's money has affected you?' Lulu asked.

'I still feel like me. But I go to my local college in Barnet, and there are kids in my GCSE classes whose parents clean offices or work in supermarkets. It's strange to think that I have more money than they'll earn in their whole lives.'

'Is there a guilty feeling?' Lulu asked.

'I guess, a bit,' Dylan said. 'Babies starving in the world and stuff.'

'College people joke around, but mostly they're cool

about it,' Summer noted.

'But is there anything really extravagant that you want. Like a Ferrari?'

Dylan laughed. 'I have twenty-six Ferraris in a giant garage under my dad's house in Scotland.'

'You really should start driving lessons,' Summer teased.

Dylan smiled. 'If there's one thing I've learned in the past year, it's that possessions don't matter. My dad had houses, money, cars. But when I remember him, he was always alone with some project: restoring a car, working on a movie soundtrack. And he'd go off to his room and do drugs and hardly ever speak to anyone. I don't think he was a happy person, from when my mum left until he died.'

'And the drug situation. Are there feelings of addiction now?'

'I don't smoke or drink,' Dylan said. 'I use the gym at college three times a week.'

'We started running together for a while,' Summer said. 'But after the billionaire story broke, we got sick of being followed.'

Dylan nodded. 'Skid in a dog turd and it winds up on the front page of a tabloid.'

'And is your mother, the famous artist, part of your life now, Dylan?' Lulu asked.

Sue stepped in front of the camera waving frantically. 'That is *not* on the agreed list of questions.'

'I don't mind,' Dylan said, though his expression suggested that he did. 'The only contact I've had from my mother since

Dad died was a letter she sent to the executors of my dad's estate, claiming that a bunch of sculptures and paintings in the house actually belong to her and asking to have them back.'

Summer put her arm around Dylan's back. 'You have other people in your life,' she said soothingly.

'I feel like I've stumbled into the family I've always wanted,' Dylan explained. 'Heather and Len took Summer in after her nan died, and they're officially her guardians until she turns eighteen. Now they're going through the same process for me. But there's a lot of us in the house. Len isn't fully recovered, so he's home all the time, and Heather's oldest son is due out of young offenders' in a couple of months. I'm buying a bigger place, so we can all get some privacy.'

'And to cut down the queues for the bathroom in the morning,' Summer added, smiling.

'So I guess that's actually the answer to your earlier question, the fancy thing that I want is a good place to live with my new family and to have some privacy.'

'And Hank wants you to buy him a dirt bike when we move,' Summer added.

'And you've made a charity?' Lulu said. 'The Eileen Smith Foundation.'

'Sure,' Dylan said modestly. 'I've put in an initial five million pounds, plus some of the money raised at the Terraplane memorial gig. The charity is named after Summer's nan, and we're going to give grants to kids who work as carers. So they can have holidays, or exam tutoring after they've missed lessons.'

'Or even just really simple stuff,' Summer added. 'Like money for a taxi to a doctor's appointment, or a birthday cake. I basically had to count every penny from when I was eleven and my nan got sick. I used to take toilet rolls from school to save money, and one of the school dinner ladies used to give me a plate to take home and microwave for my nan.

'And the bit that *really* ticks me off is that adult carers get attendance allowance, but you get nothing extra if you're under eighteen. And you're scared to ask for help, because they might do an assessment and take you into care.'

'The Foundation sounds really amazing,' Lulu said. 'You'll put smiles on faces, for sure!'

'I hope so,' Dylan agreed.

'And it was announced last week that you and Harry Napier's widow sold your stakes in Venus TV to Karen Trim. Was that a tough decision?'

'I need cash to pay a very big inheritance tax bill,' Dylan explained. 'Karen Trim has a ton of experience in reality TV. *Rock War* is being shown in fifteen countries now with more on the way. I hear they've got a great host lined up for *Rock War France*.'

'Me, me, me,' Lulu sang as she shook her skinny fists in the air. 'I start filming in three weeks, it's mega exciting!'

'Karen Trim has plans for *Pop War* and *Country War* spin-offs,' Dylan explained. 'We're also auctioning off the big house in Scotland to pay the tax.'

Summer laughed. 'Dylan is the only talent show contestant

in history who got voted off, but ended up owning the entire show.'

'So my next question is directed at both of you,' Lulu said, sounding more serious. 'Two years ago you were average everyday kids. One at boarding school, one living in a small flat. What do you think you've learned from everything that has happened?'

'Snorting cocaine is a very bad idea,' Dylan joked.

'It's totally changed my life and I've made some special friends,' Summer said. 'But even in sixty years' time, when me and Dylan are babysitting our grandkids, I reckon I'll still think about my nan every day.'

'Actually, I do have a non-flippant answer to that question,' Dylan added. 'People who go on shows like *Rock War* want to be famous. They think they'll be happy if they're admired and envied, with designer clothes and pretty girls all over them. But there's nothing in that.

'I know I've inherited a ton of money, but I'd rather eat Heather's shepherd's pie than dine at a restaurant with three Michelin stars. I'd rather sit in Tristan and Alfie's cabin after college, writing a song with Jay and Babatunde, than play in front of ten thousand screaming fans. And I'd rather watch a movie at home with Summer's freezing-cold feet on my lap than attend some glitzy movie premiere. Because the most important thing *Rock War* taught me is that the only thing that really makes you happy is the time you spend with the people you love.'

NO.1 BESTSELLING AUTHOR OF *CHERUB*

ROBERT MUCHAMORE

ROCK WAR

MEET JAY. SUMMER. AND DYLAN.

JAY plays guitar, writes songs for his band and dreams of being a rock star. But seven siblings and a rubbish drummer are standing in his way.

SUMMER has a one-in-a-million voice, but caring for her nan and struggling for money make singing the last thing on her mind.

DYLAN'S got talent, but effort's not his thing ...

These kids are about to enter the biggest battle of their lives. And they've got everything to play for.

ROCKWAR.COM

JAY, SUMMER, DYLAN and their bands are headed for boot camp at Rock War manor. It's going to be six weeks of mates, music and non-stop partying as they prepare for stardom.

But the rock-star life of music festivals and glitzy premieres isn't all it's cracked up to be. Can the bands hold it together long enough to make it through the last stage of the competition, or will there be meltdown?

THEY'VE GOT EVERYTHING TO PLAY FOR.

ROCKWAR.COM

CHERUB

THE RECRUIT

Robert Muchamore

A terrorist doesn't let strangers in her flat because they might be undercover police or intelligence agents, but her children bring their mates home and they run all over the place. The terrorist doesn't know that one of these kids has bugged every room in her house, made copies of all her computer files and stolen her address book. The kid works for CHERUB.

CHERUB agents are aged between ten and seventeen. They live in the real world, slipping under adult radar and getting information that sends criminals and terrorists to jail.

WWW.CHERUBCAMPUS.COM

Hodder
Children's
Books